MEN aRE
FROGS

Books by Saranna DeWylde

Men Are Frogs

Fairy Godmothers, Inc.

The 10 Days Series

How to Lose a Demon in 10 Days

How to Marry an Angel in 10 Days

How to Seduce a Warlock in 10 Days

MEN ARE
FROGS

Saranna DeWylde

ZEBRA BOOKS
Kensington Publishing Corp.
www.kensingtonbooks.com

First Zebra Trade Printing: August 2021
ISBN-13: 978-1-4201-5315-6
ISBN-10: 1-4201-5315-3

ISBN-13: 978-1-4201-5318-7 (ebook)
ISBN-10: 1-978-4201-5318-8 (ebook)

10 9 8 7 6 5 4 3 2 1

Printed in the United States of America

Dedicated to Jenn LeBlanc and Amanda Gordon
You both know why
Love you!

PROLOGUE

Petunia "Petty" Blossom was currently fluttering around the boardroom of Fairy Godmothers, Inc., making quite the sparkly mess. Glittery fairy dust followed in her wake as she zipped from one project to the next like an overcaffeinated bumblebee with too many luscious blooms to choose from.

Of course, it was Gwen's fault for bringing them so many of her decadent espresso brownies.

Oh, bless that child. Petty made herself a mental note to shake some fairy dust into her coffee. She needed to get things moving so Gwen and Roderick would be a done deal before Roderick's previous MIA fairy godmother could thwart her lovely plans.

"Petunia!" Bluebonnet's voice startled her, and Petty dropped out of the air and landed firmly on her rounded bottom.

She rubbed her rump. "I don't know why they call it extra padding. I don't feel padded at all."

"Never mind that, sister. I see that look in your eye. What are you up to?"

Petunia widened her eyes and blinked slowly. "Whatever do you mean?"

Bluebonnet squinted at her. "I've known you for too long. You're wearing your meddling face."

"Of course I am. That's what we do." Except Petunia and her sisters had all agreed they'd be leaving Roderick and Gwen alone to find their way when they were ready. Petty just didn't think she could risk Roderick's FG messing up their plans. His FG hadn't seen the whole thread. Actually, she hadn't seen much of anything since she'd fallen off her broom, and with magic stores low, it had taken her several years to heal.

Jonquil popped her head in the door. "Did I hear the sounds of meddling in the morning? I brought coffee from Bernadette's!"

"Oh!" Bluebonnet clapped. "Bernadette's cappuccino always pairs well with meddling."

Petty spread her wings and used them to lift herself off the floor. She also zapped herself in the bottom with her wand because she wasn't about to deal with a bruise.

"We have a fresh batch of espresso brownies from Grammy's Goodies. Gwen made them," Petunia said. "Also, I need you each to eat at least one or extra hijinks may ensue. You know what it's like when I'm on the caffeine."

Bluebonnet and Jonquil were quick to come to her aid and each grabbed several brownies from the pretty red box.

"Is that why you're such a firecracker this morning?" Bluebonnet asked.

"Mmm." Petty nodded after taking a sip of the coffee.

"Oh, wait. Then perhaps you *shouldn't* be drinking the magic-bean juice?" Jonquil dared to ask.

Petty growled at her and clutched the coffee close to her chest.

Jonquil held up her hands in surrender. "Calm yourself. I swear, you're acting like Grammy on a full moon."

"Sorry." Petty slouched. "It's just we have so much to accomplish." She glanced skyward, then over both shoulders. "Not that I'm complaining. It's a blessing to be so busy. Ever After is flourishing, as are our charges, and our wedding planning business. But it is a lot of balls to keep in the air."

Bluebonnet snorted her coffee and spewed it out of her nose like a geyser. "Balls!"

The three of them cackled, and with a wave of Bluebonnet's wand, she cleaned up the mess as if it had never happened.

"You're worse than me, I swear." Petunia took the opportunity to swipe the last brownie, which her sisters had so lovingly left for her.

"Can this be right?" Bluebonnet nodded to the seven different columns on the far wall, where each column had been allocated for a different wedding. Then she turned her head to the opposite wall, which had been plastered with their ideas for the spring carnival.

"We have a lot of work ahead of us," Jonquil said. "Don't get me wrong, I'm thrilled that after Ransom and Lucky's debacle we've gotten so many bookings. The magic wells in town are full, and we're able to begin exporting. I just don't know how we can keep up this pace."

Bluebonnet squealed so loudly that Petty's spectacles cracked.

Petty sniffed and wiggled her nose, trying to get the glasses to move without touching them with her fingers.

"Sorry," Bluebonnet apologized. "I'm so excited. Zuri will be here tomorrow."

Jonquil zapped Petty's spectacles, mending them instantly before she said, "I'm afraid she's going to be a project as well. More so than any help to us."

"She's a modern woman." Petty gave up and adjusted her glasses with her fingers. "She can do both."

"Hmm. But should she have to?" Bluebonnet asked.

The three of them turned to look at the growing wall of projects laid out before them. The sisters then looked at one another and said, "Yes!"

"I have been noodling on this," Jonquil said. "First, we shall start her testing the wedding favors and services from the local vendors. That way she gets to meet everyone, she knows what we have to offer clients, and I think it especially important we get her set up with one of those wish favors."

Petty clapped gleefully. "Oh, you're brilliant. Just brilliant."

"But there's more," Jonquil teased in a singsong voice.

"For an additional twenty-nine ninety-five?" Bluebonnet asked.

"For free." She tapped her wand on the long table. "Listen. We put her on the Petrovsky-Markhoff wedding. It's important."

Petunia narrowed her eyes. "Are we sure that's what we should do? I mean, the last wedding she worked on, the bride took her dress off in front of everyone and lit it on fire. *Fire,* Jonquil."

"Hmm. Quite." Jonquil nodded. "Don't tell me that you'd have done any less if you'd discovered your groom had been having an affair with the wedding planner. Actually, that's really rather mild in comparison."

"Oh yes!" Bluebonnet agreed. "The bride was quite reasonable. After all, it's not like she turned a prince into a frog. *Forever.*"

Petunia rolled her eyes and flopped back in her chair. "Oh my gods. Will you two give it a rest? I have apologized profusely to Charming. And really, he hasn't yet apologized to us, Bon-Bon. I mean, he's sorry. I made him sorry." Petty narrowed her eyes at the memory. "But the actual apology, being sorry for his actions because they were wrong, he hasn't owned that."

Jonquil shrugged. "His problem, I suppose. Maybe that's why none of the kisses have worked to free him from his green hell?"

"Hmm," Petty mused.

"Hmm," Bon-Bon agreed.

"When you have time, dears, you should really look at their threads. They're all tangled up like a cat in a basket of knitting," Jonquil advised.

"I should start brewing headache powder now, shouldn't I?" Petty asked.

Bluebonnet waved her off. "Oh, hush. You know this is your favorite part."

Petty grinned. "It really is."

"Seven weddings. I can't believe it. I didn't think this crazy scheme of yours was going to work." Jonquil shook her head.

A knock sounded on the door before Gwen Borders stuck her head inside. She was new to Ever After, and their godchild Lucky's best friend. Who Petty definitely wanted to marry Roderick, Ransom's best friend. It was too perfect.

"My loves! How did you like the espresso brownies?" Gwen asked.

"We loved them. Petty ate most of them, but she needed the power boost," Jonquil said.

"Where are the little monsters this morning?" Petunia asked, looking for Gwen's children, Brittany and Steven.

"Grammy and Red took them out to the farm so they could help put in the garden."

Everyone in the room knew that Brittany and Steven wouldn't be putting in the garden, it would be more like getting covered in mud and playing with worms. Just as little children ought to do.

"Did we tell you we're hiring an assistant?" Bluebonnet asked her.

"You told me you were interviewing." Gwen pulled out another red box from behind her back and dropped it casually on the table. "You must keep your strength up."

"You're the best. Just the best," Jonquil said.

This time, the box contained lemon bars with a candied ginger topping.

"So have you decided on someone?" Gwen prompted.

"Mmm," Petty said around a mouth full of lemon bar. "She's coming for the interview tomorrow. We're counting on you to help her get settled in."

"Absolutely."

Petty enjoyed how Gwen didn't question how they knew

they were going to hire her before the interview. Gwen accepted magic was real fairly easily and had integrated into their little world without a bit of trouble.

"Oh! I've heard from Lucky. She and Ransom are going to try to make it back for the spring carnival, but they're still enjoying their honeymoon."

Petty waved her hand. "Those two will be on their honeymoon for the rest of their lives."

Bluebonnet and Jonquil sighed in unison.

"Isn't it great?" Jonquil asked.

Gwen, who was recently divorced, smiled and said, "It really is."

Petty looked at her sisters knowingly. Gwen had earned their help, not only by being Lucky's best friend but also by not being jaded. By not hating love even though her own story hadn't turned out the way she'd planned.

Fine, Jonquil mouthed.

Gwen picked up on the undercurrent. "What was that?"

"What was what, dear?" Petty asked her.

"You know very well what. Behave yourself, or I won't bring you any more treats."

Jonquil clutched her chest. "The betrayal. It burns. I can't believe she'd threaten us with such torture."

Gwen laughed. "You're all awful. I have to get back to work and get the kitchen clean before the monsters get home and mess it up again. They want to try their hands at soufflé."

Petty waved her wand and snapped it at Gwen. "There. It's clean. Go home and take a nice long bath."

Bluebonnet popped up out of her chair. "I almost forgot. I made this cherry masque for you." She pulled a small jar out of her apron pocket and handed it to Gwen.

"Thanks! It's kind of nice having fairy godmothers. Happy meddling!" she said on her way out the door.

Bluebonnet's grin turned sly. "Don't you just know that

the mushroom cottages are going to have a plumbing problem today?"

"Roderick is going to have to play rescue. Delightful." Jonquil nodded along.

"Ha!" Petty pointed her wand at each of her sisters. "I knew you couldn't leave them alone any more than I could."

Bluebonnet swatted her hand away. "Don't point that thing at me."

Petty pocketed her wand. "Sorry. But really."

Bon-Bon shrugged. "I can't help it."

Jonquil grinned at them. "We're awful. Absolutely wretched. If we didn't use our powers for good, we'd be wicked witches."

"Evil queens." Petty giggled.

"Damn," Jonquil swore. "I almost forgot. Those lemon bars were too delicious, and they made me forget. Our own evil queen, Ravenna, is going to be a problem."

"On purpose?" Bluebonnet wrinkled her nose. "I mean, she's always a problem, but is she going to try to thwart us, because we already lived that story, and I'm not about to tolerate any of her nonsense again. If she's not careful, why . . . I'll . . ."

"You'll what? Make her more miserable than she already is? She's not ready for love. It would be particularly unkind to give her what she's always wanted before she's ready for it," Petty said.

Bluebonnet crossed her arms over her chest. "I am feeling unkind. She thwarts us at every turn."

"Love is a gift, not a punishment, Bon-Bon."

Bluebonnet harrumphed. "I know. She just irks me."

"It seems she'll be at the center of the tangle." Jonquil gestured to the wall. "Of all of our threads."

"This calls for more fortification," Petty declared.

"Loose the dogs of war!" Bluebonnet cried, shaking her fist.

"Um, no. I was going to suggest we eat the rest of the lemon bars," Petty said.

"I seem to recall someone telling me I simply needed more sugar," Jonquil offered soothingly. "And I did, and it all worked out just lovely for Ransom and Lucky."

"I suppose. Perhaps an ice cream soda to wash it down?" Bluebonnet replied softly.

"That's the spirit," Jonquil said.

"Wait, so what about the Petrovsky-Markhoff wedding is so important for our new assistant?" Petty brought them back to the subject at hand.

"Closure, as far as the threads of fate seem to be concerned."

Bluebonnet shook her head. "That doesn't bode well. Weddings are about beginnings, not endings."

"We'll all find out soon enough," Jonquil promised.

This definitely called for ice cream sodas all around. Perhaps the kind that could only be had at the pub.

"I say we take a break with a more adult kind of fortification at Pick 'n' Axe," Petty suggested.

"Why, Petty, it's not even noon." Bluebonnet pretended to be scandalized.

"It's brunch somewhere, dearies!" Jonquil said. "They have those delightful shakes. The ones with the mango ice cream and the rum."

"Sugar is always the answer." Petunia nodded. "If it can't be fixed with a brownie, try an ice cream soda. If that doesn't work, well, we go to the sugarcane spirits."

Bon-Bon giggled. "That's what I'm going to call it from now on. We're consulting the spirits."

Jonquil cackled. "Let's go consult the spirits."

Petty linked arms with her sisters. "I wonder if they'll have any answers for us."

As they headed out the door to make the short walk to Pick 'n' Axe, Petty saw a geyser of water shooting out from one of the mushroom-capped cottages beyond the square.

"Right on time," Bluebonnet said. "Roderick should be running to her rescue in five, four, three, two . . ."

Petty squinted through her spectacles, and they enhanced her view just enough so that she could see the door to Roderick's cottage as it opened and he sprinted to Gwen's.

She grinned. "A decent round of meddling before brunch."

"Quite." Jonquil said, obviously pleased with their efforts.

Even if the shrieking from mushroom cottage number two said rather the opposite.

Chapter 1

The bride had lit her dress on fire.

When Zuri Davis, wedding planner extraordinaire, had realized the man who had been wooing her for the past three months was also the groom in her client's wedding, it had come as a complete and utterly devastating surprise.

The groom, one celebrated surgeon Alec Marsh, hadn't been present for any of the usual things. He'd had medical conferences, emergency surgeries, and it had been just the perfect storm that kept them from crossing paths until the day of the wedding.

When the bride, Jenn, realized that her Alec was Zuri's Xander, she hadn't turned on Zuri. No. She'd taken a single moment to compose herself, directed her maid of honor to unzip her dress, and she'd stepped out of that Vera Wang original and stood there in her silk slip while she lit her wedding dress on fire with an altar candle.

No one had made a move to stop her.

Not even Alec.

Zuri had thought that, surely, Jenn would turn her fury on her. But she hadn't. Instead, she'd thanked her for showing her who the man she was about to marry really was and invited Zuri to join her on her honeymoon cruise.

Zuri, for her part, should've said yes.

Oh, the sheer power of that woman. Zuri had to say she admired her for so many reasons.

Mostly because she knew right at this moment, Jenn Gordon was not sitting surrounded by the ashes of a life that had gone supernova.

She was living it up in the Caribbean with her friends, sun, sea, and cabana boys with drinks with little umbrellas in pineapples. Jenn Gordon was getting massages, facials, and pampering herself while she nursed her broken heart.

And Zuri, well, she was trying to scrape all the ashes of her life into a dustpan and put them back together like some sort of snowman reject from hell. No one wanted to trust their wedding to a wedding planner who'd "stolen the groom."

Even though that's not what happened.

Even though Jenn didn't blame her.

She looked up at her twin sister, Zeva, who was helping her pack her things away in storage.

"Why do I still even want to be a wedding planner after this?" In fact, Zuri wasn't sure if she did. It was all she'd ever wanted since she'd realized giving people Happily Ever Afters was an actual job that came wrapped in a wedding planner bow. She'd never thought about doing anything else.

Only now, she was sitting in an almost empty condo, about to say goodbye to everything she'd ever known. All the accomplishments she'd worked so hard for, like this condo. She couldn't believe her whole life had been burned to the ground by a man.

A man she never would've gotten involved with if she'd known he was with someone else.

No, not just a man.

But love.

Love had helped her build this beautiful life, and love had taken a giant, steaming shit on her life, and she was struggling not to swirl down the bowl with it.

Zeva finished taping up a box and turned to look at her sister. "You want to be a wedding planner because love is still magic."

"But is it?" Zuri was doubtful. "I mean . . ."

"Of course it is. What happened with Jenn and Alec, you know that's not what love looks like. What happened between you and him, that's not love, either. Deep down, you believe."

Zuri sighed and slumped. "Why do you have to be right?"

"Because I'm the oldest." Zeva sank down and put an arm around her shoulders. "Listen, this interview is going to be great. Fairy Godmothers, Inc., already knows what happened. You were honest in your email application. They still want to interview you. This is good."

"Or maybe they just want to look at me. You know, see the pariah for themselves." She'd already had several wedding podcasters try to book time with her for a wedding consultation, only to try to interview her about the wedding that wasn't.

"I don't think they're like that. Not at all. They've had their own struggles, what with the 'Billionaire Fake Wedding Turned Real.' Come on."

"I think the fact their godchildren were willing to get fake married for them speaks to how much their godchildren love them. They're probably really great people." Zuri nodded slowly, driving the point home to herself.

"See? And they want you." Her sister squeezed her.

"I suppose, but I don't know how I feel about moving to a small town in Missouri named Ever After. It's definitely not Chicago." She looked out the window at her stunning view of Lake Michigan and the blue sky.

"I think it's fantastic that it's not Chicago. Which is just what you need. So is renting out this place to pay your bills so you get to keep it no matter what happens."

"I know you're right; it's just scary. What if I go on this interview and they don't hire me?"

Zeva rolled her eyes. "Obviously, you'll live with me. But I have a feeling about Fairy Godmothers, Inc. I think this is going to be just what you need."

Zuri wished she had the same confidence that Zeva did,

but she had to do something, and this was the only path available at the moment.

"I still can't quite believe that Jenn lit her wedding dress on fire," Zuri whispered. "In the church."

"What a woman," Zeva whispered with awe.

"Indeed. Alec didn't deserve her." Zuri crossed her hands over her chest. She didn't want to admit it, but she missed him. Or, at least, she missed the guy she'd thought he was. The one who wanted to hear all her wedding stories, the one who told her that he believed in Happily Ever After, too.

"Or you," Zeva reminded her gently.

"Wasn't there a rom-com where this happened, but the ending was much better?" Zuri flopped back into the mess of packing boxes, tissue paper, and bubble wrap.

"Yes, but we're not at the end part of the story. This is your beginning."

Zuri raised up on her elbows to look at her sister. "Are you sure?"

"More sure than I am you're going to be able to survive in Ever After with just two suitcases and a train case." Zeva glanced over to where Zuri had stacked her luggage.

"I'll have my briefcase with my laptop, too." Zuri grinned.

"You know what I mean."

"I do. Which is why I think I'm putting off finishing packing. All we have left are the dishes. When that's done, this part of my life is officially over."

"Honey, you haven't left the house in two weeks. I'd say it's been officially over. This is just cleaning up what's left. It's all going to be okay. I promise."

"You're going to come visit me, right?"

"As soon as I can. Have you looked up this place online? It's ridiculous in the best way." Zeva snatched Zuri's laptop and pulled up the Ever After website. "Those three actually look like what I'd want my fairy godmothers to look like. I mean, aside from the fact they're white. Otherwise, all they're missing are wings."

When she turned the laptop around, on the screen was an image of three kindly old ladies. One wore pink, one wore blue, and the other yellow. They each wore their hair up in buns on top of their heads. One of them wore tiny spectacles on the end of her nose. The three of them had round, rosy cheeks and happy crinkles around warm eyes.

Zuri's gaze was drawn to something in the background she hadn't noticed before. There was more than one castle. One of them—the one she remembered—was white, with blue-tiled roofing, and waving blue banners, and whitewashed walls. It was every inch a fairy-tale castle.

The other one, the new one, was black as night. It rose up out of the forest like jagged obsidian.

"Look at the dark castle!" Zuri whispered. "That's perfect. I hope they do weddings there, too. Not every girl wants to be a princess."

Zeva turned the laptop back around to study the image. "Oh, wow. How did I miss this the first time around? Can you imagine getting married there at midnight with red rose petals and moonlight? I wonder who lives there."

"Me too. How exciting."

"Oh, look. The proprietor of the princess castle's name is Phillip Charming. Are they serious? I need a picture of this guy." She clicked on the trackpad before rolling her eyes. "Of course this is Phillip Charming. He's a Ken doll."

Zuri looked at his picture, and something unfamiliar twisted in her gut like dancing snakes.

First, he was beautiful. She hadn't expected otherwise. His hair was an impossible shade of golden blond, like wheat fields but with streaks of sunlight. A strong jaw, ridiculously long lashes, and eyes that were the kind of green that had to have been photoshopped. Or contacts.

"Zuri! The castle offers long-term rentals for people moving to Ever After for work!"

"No." She could see where her sister was going before she got there. The answer was *absolutely not.* "I don't even have the job, yet."

"Yet. You know how sometimes I just know things? You will get the job. You're going to move to Ever After. And Phillip Charming is in your future."

"Maybe as my landlord."

"Maybe." Zeva was smug.

"Maybe you should be the one interviewing to work with FGI."

"Maybe I just should. Imagine me, Zeva Davis, fairy godmother extraordinaire."

"I can see it," Zuri agreed easily.

She really could. Zeva had a kind and nurturing nature, but she also had a spine of steel. She liked to help people and was good at helping them, even if they didn't want it.

Actually, that was one of the many places where Zeva excelled.

But where did Zuri excel? Where did she fit? She'd thought it was wedding planning, but now she wasn't so sure.

As a wedding planner, she'd really thought she was changing the world, one Happily Ever After at a time. Maybe that had been naïve.

"Stop it."

"Stop what?" Zuri asked, blinking innocently.

"You know what. I can feel it when you start with that self-doubt. This is just a tiny setback." Zeva held up her hand. "I know, it doesn't feel tiny right now. But in the grand scheme of things? You're going to look back on this one day and everything that's happened is going to be a bump in the road that you're going to laugh about with your children."

Zeva was right about most things, but Zuri wasn't sure about this. "I was always so sure about who I was, what my strengths were. I thought I had an eye for love. Now, I'm not so sure."

"Zuri—"

"I'm not even sure I believe in love anymore."

Zeva snorted. "Of course you do. Unless you don't love me?"

Zuri got up and slid her hands into her jean pockets. "Of course I love you, wombmate. That's not what I mean. I mean romantic love. It's all crap."

"Look, you can't hold all men responsible for Alec's actions."

"I'm not, but . . . You know? That's not it at all. It's that none of them are actually Prince Charming."

"You should clarify that, because none of us are fairy-tale princesses, either. We're just human. We are all flawed."

For some reason, those words made her heart break just a little more.

"Oh, honey." Zeva got up and pulled Zuri into a tight hug and held her there. "Listen. And I mean actually listen. It's not about finding someone who is perfect, it's about finding who is perfect for you. You and Alec, your angels played well together, but your demons didn't. Also, he was a lying shitbag of the lowest order."

"Prince Shitbag of the Shitlords of the Round Table?" Zuri sniffed.

"Exactly. Your person will not be a shitbag. He'll have angels and demons just like all of us, only his will fit with yours."

"I want to believe you." Zuri's heart wanted to believe more than anything, but it was still hurting and afraid. She found comfort in Zeva's arms. In her warmth. In her strength. In her absolute surety. Zuri inhaled deeply, holding in her scent of coconut oil and the vanilla she dabbed behind her ears. Just like their mama.

Zeva laughed. "So what's stopping you?"

"It's just I've kissed so many frogs."

Zeva pulled away, and her eyes searched Zuri's. "Maybe they're all frogs because you keep hoping that you're the magic that will turn them into a prince. It doesn't work that way. People aren't projects. You have to take them as they are."

"What about all that rot about the magic of love?"

Zeva laughed. "It's not rot. Love makes you better. It makes you want to be your best you, but you have to work on yourself because you want to. Not to be worthy. You're already worthy."

"That doesn't make any sense."

"You'll see," Zeva said knowingly.

"I hate it when you do that." Zuri picked up a box and carried it downstairs to the pickup truck they'd borrowed to move the last of her boxes into storage.

"And I hate it when you do that," Zeva said from behind her with another box.

"What?"

"Walk away from me before I'm done with my pep talk." She grinned.

A strange wave of homesickness washed over Zuri. "What was I thinking? I can't go to Ever After. What am I going to do without you?"

"Everything? It's all going to work out. You'll see."

"How do you know?"

"The same way I've always known. I just do."

They went back inside and carried down the rest of the boxes until all that was left to do was finish packing her dishes.

"This is it," Zeva said. "The last thing before you start your new adventure."

A new adventure. Zuri liked that. She wished she could have the same wide-eyed hope about it that Zeva did.

"What are you going to do while I'm having my new adventure?" Zuri asked.

"Oh, cry. Miss you. Clean out my closets. That'll be an

adventure, too." Zeva wrapped another dish and packed it carefully in the box.

"You haven't said much about work. Everything okay?"

Zeva was a social worker who worked at St. Marigold's Orphanage. She talked about the kids a lot, but she'd been quiet all day, and Zuri had the feeling it was for a reason.

"Not really. I'm feeling a little burned out. Too many kids who need me, and not enough of me—or the resources—to go around."

"They're lucky to have you, Zeva." She put a hand on her sister's shoulder as she grabbed another box.

"Not lucky enough." Zeva's mouth set into a grim line. "But I'm going to fix that. I don't know how, but I will find a way."

"I know you will." If anyone could help all the children at St. Marigold's Orphanage, it was Zeva. "Maybe we could get some of the businesses in Ever After to sponsor them."

"Look at you. You're already carving out your own space in Ever After and you're not even there yet."

"Nope, you're not going to deflect back to me. Come on. Tell me. Let me be the shoulder for you that you are for me."

Zeva taped up the last box. "It's nothing new. The same struggle. It's kind of like rushing water against a rock. It wears it away over time. I'm not giving up, but I think I do need to try and get my brain outside my current box."

Zuri had an idea. "If I get this job in Ever After—"

"You will."

"Let's not put the Happily Ever After before the apple."

Zeva arched a brow. "So you admit you're at the beginning of your story?"

"Never mind that. We're talking about you and the kids. What if we got Fairy Godmothers, Inc., to sponsor a trip for them to Ever After? It would be great for FGI and great for the kids. If it doesn't do anything else, maybe it'll help those kids believe in magic."

"Hmm. And here I thought you didn't believe in magic anymore, either. Just goes to show you."

"I already said you were right."

"I know you said it, but that doesn't mean you're ready to believe it."

"We're not talking about me are we?"

Zeva laughed, and it was a textured, rich sound that came from deep in her belly. "Fine. You let me know. After you have the job. Although, I think just in case, we should have celebratory mimosas and brunch."

"Brunch is my favorite meal of the day." Zuri nodded. "That place over on Madison? You know the one."

"Of course I know the one." Zeva grinned. "I may or may not have made you an appointment to get your hair done and a facial at the spa, too."

"You should— No, I was going to say you shouldn't have, but I was just bemoaning the fact that I said no to going with Jenn on her cruise and getting facials and whatnot. So I won't even fight you. I'll gladly accept."

"Good. I wanted more sister time before you go."

They turned to look at each other. "Terrible Twin Trouble!" they said in unison, and laughed.

Zuri was still nervous, but arm in arm with the best weapon in her arsenal, she started to believe that she was about to launch herself on a new and exciting adventure.

Ever After was in for it, she decided. Hurricane Zuri was about to make landfall, but instead of being a disaster, she was determined to make it every inch a fairy tale.

Chapter 2

Phillip Charming absolutely hated the mermaid fountain. He hated it more than most anything.

Except being a fucking frog.

He spent his days perched on the stone bust of the mermaid in the giant fountain that marked the halfway point between the town and his castle.

Phillip wasn't sure when it started, or even why he went to the fountain. When the sun rose, he would hippity-hop his fat green behind all the way to the mermaid. No matter what he'd decided to do during his hours as a man, when it was frog time, it was fountain time.

He'd built himself a rather lovely pond in his private quarters. It had a sunroof he could open with a smack of his back legs, or hands, depending on the time of day. It was filled with fat lily pads, tasty little frog treats, and even other frogs so his daytime frog self wouldn't be lonely.

But did he sit in it?

No.

He tra-la-la'd all the way to the stupid fountain that he hated.

When dusk fell, if he hadn't prepared by coming to the fountain by dawn in his human form, he'd have to run through the woods back to the castle stark naked.

It was quite undignified.

It wasn't completely awful, though. He'd made some frog

friends. He wasn't sure if any of them were cursed as he'd been cursed, or if they were natural frogs.

Although, what could really be called natural in a place like Ever After? Nothing, really. Fairy-tale castles, fairy godmothers, dwarves named after beers, birds and mice that liked to sew . . . nope. It was all screwed up.

Phillip was pretty sure he'd learned his lesson after the first week he'd been a frog, but that hadn't mattered.

He'd kissed everyone in Ever After, trying to break the curse.

Every single creature with lips.

Even his best friend. The one they called the Beast.

He, too, had been a prince once upon a time. His castle had long since been lost to the mist and the Beast, or Hunter, as Phillip liked to call him, since that was his name, lived in the dungeons of Castle Charming.

The sun began to fall below the horizon, and he was grateful when the green mist enveloped him and the world around him grew much smaller, and dryer.

He stretched his limbs as he stepped from the fountain, naked, and . . . and . . . his mouth tasted like he'd licked a caterpillar. He stuck his tongue out and ran it along his teeth and realized with dawning horror that he still had dragonfly wings in his teeth.

"Don't yark!" Hunter's voice called from behind some rustling underbrush. "You know it's worse if you have to taste it again."

Phillip was sure he wasn't going to have a choice. A skein of mead was thrust into his hands, and he drank it gratefully, washing away the bits of wing and whatever else might've been left over from his day's adventure.

"Thanks." He licked his lips and was immediately sorry. He took another long pull of the sweet, crisp honey mead.

Hunter tossed him his clothes. "Hurry up. Pub trivia starts in twenty minutes."

"I know, I know. I can't get this out of my mouth. It's awful."

"It's like you haven't done this before." Hunter tossed him his bag, which had a toothbrush and toothpaste.

"Honestly, I forgot it was trivia night." Phillip shrugged.

"I know." Hunter nodded to his rumpled clothes.

"Whatever. They let you in. And you don't wear pants."

Hunter bared his teeth. "Listen, pal. I'd wear pants if I could get them on over my haunches, but I can't. So loincloth it is."

"It's not like you could button them with those claws anyway." Phillip couldn't resist the tiny poke at his pantsless friend.

"It ain't about the button, brother." Hunter winked at him.

"So, serious question."

"No."

"Oh, come on."

"No. I know what you're going to ask, and I'm not discussing it with you."

"Surely you must've wondered."

"Just like half the women in Ever After," Beast growled.

"Come on. Tell me. Do you know?"

"I've already passed the part of my curse where it's permanent. This is just me. Forever. So, no, I don't wonder if the curse was broken if *my* beast will go back to human size, too."

Phillip cackled. "Man, sucks to be you. No chance of being a prince again and no castle with a big library. The hits just keep coming."

Hunter narrowed his eyes, and Phillip had to keep from cackling harder. He looked like a very concerned bear/werewolf hybrid with Groucho Marx eyebrows pasted on his forehead.

"Laugh it up, Phillip. But aren't you concerned that when your spell is broken your manhood might be reduced to froghood? Works both ways."

Phillip's smile froze in place. He hadn't actually thought of that.

"Petty would be that . . . well, petty!" Phillip cried.

"Wouldn't she just?" Hunter teased.

Phillip finished dressing. "Do I smell like pond water?"

Hunter sniffed the air. "No, but there's some cologne in your bag."

Phillip rummaged around in the bag some more and pulled out several bottles. "What is this?" He held one up. "Piranha Pride?" He removed the cap and sniffed. "This smells like a turtle tank."

He found another bottle. Premium Panther. What in the ever-loving hell? He sniffed it. It actually wasn't awful. He sprayed a bit on himself.

"Better?"

"Yeah, that one's okay." Hunter wiggled his massive snout. "Oh, shit. That's me." He laughed and took the Premium Panther from Phillip and sprayed under his arms and a little on his chest.

Phillip brushed his teeth and put the grooming products back in the bag. "This is all actually crap, you know."

Hunter looked up at him. "What is?"

Phillip gestured to their surroundings. "This."

"Ever After?"

"No, our curses. This is complete trash."

"You'll not get any argument from me there."

"Aren't you mad?" Phillip demanded.

"About what? I crossed a witch. It's just how the story goes."

"No. You didn't do anything wrong."

"Let's not be hasty. I know what I did was wrong."

"Fine, putting one old lady out in the snow was pretty shitty. But does it deserve three hundred years of this? No. Even if you spent her life span as a beast as recompense, that would be fair. But this?"

Hunter shrugged impossibly large, furry shoulders. "No

one loved me. I stayed a beast and learned to love myself. It's not the worst thing that could've happened to me. I could've lived my life as I was. A spoiled prince who never learned how to care for others. I don't really mind it. I like me. But I understand why you don't like you."

"Hold on, I never said I didn't like myself."

"You're a frog. You don't want to be a frog. Ergo, you don't like yourself. You can't say you don't like a part of yourself and say you do like yourself."

"Can't I?"

"I mean, you're a prince, I guess you can do anything you want." Hunter smirked.

"Except not be green."

"Have you tried apologizing to Petty?"

"I have apologized until my green face turned blue."

"Did you mean it?" Hunter asked.

"I . . ." He'd been about to answer with of course he'd meant it, but Phillip stopped to consider. "I don't think I did, at first. I was just angry."

"As one would be, being turned into a frog. It happens. I'm sure she understood that."

"She did, and she did have every right to be angry. When she was younger, Petunia Blossom was smoking hot. So was Bluebonnet."

"Sometimes, I do wonder why they like to toddle about like old grannies when they could choose to look any way they please," Hunter mused.

"Oh, I know the answer to that. Women of a certain age go unnoticed. They're constantly and completely underestimated. It helps them get away with so much more."

"Is Petty still mad at you?"

"She says she's not. She's even tried to get most everyone in town to kiss me. They're doing that spring carnival thing, and Petty has promised me a kissing booth so all the tourists will come kiss me and maybe break my curse."

"Or give you mono. But I imagine if she's trying to help you break the curse, then she's not mad at you anymore."

"I think I'm ready for trivia. That is not of a personal nature."

Hunter laughed, and his roar startled the birds from the nearby trees so that they took flight, screeching their displeasure. "I actually might have an idea."

"Oh, really?"

"You've tried everything with the godmothers. Kissed literally everyone. What about Ravenna Blackheart?"

"I kissed her, too."

Hunter growled. "No, I know that. But have you asked her if her magic might bring you a cure?"

"Did you just growl when I mentioned kissing Ravenna?" He elbowed his friend knowingly.

"No." His thick eyebrows raised to the top of his head. But then he growled again.

"You did."

"Shut. Up. We're not talking about me. We're talking about you. Ravenna. Dark magic."

"There's always a price for dark magic. I don't know that I'd be willing to pay it and Ravenna's price. You know she'll have one."

"She would, but isn't almost anything worth being rid of fly wings in your teeth every night?"

"They were dragonfly wings," he corrected.

"Or worth knowing your chef isn't going to cook you for dinner?"

"Hey, I've forbidden frog legs in the castle!"

"You know good and well that you can forbid all you like, but . . ."

"No one would do that! They all know I'm a frog!" He'd been so sure, but now that he thought about it, what if Hunter was right?

"And what if you have a disgruntled employee who gets a taste for the green?"

Phillip was horrified. He'd never thought of that. "That's actually diabolical."

"I know. It's why I thought of it, of course." Hunter shrugged

"Maybe you would be a good fit with Ravenna after all."

"I shouldn't think so, but I think she's especially beautiful when she's plotting something evil. The worse she is, the better I like her. I'm a sick, sick beast." Hunter shook his head.

Phillip decided to cut his friend a little slack. "She is gorgeous. There's no denying that. Terrifying, but gorgeous."

"I like that she's terrifying."

"Probably because that means she wouldn't be afraid of you."

Hunter shrugged again. "I've dated. I mean, most of the people here know I'm just a prince who was a dick. I'm not like a werewolf or anything."

With a puff of pink fairy dust, Petunia Blossom appeared with fluttering pink wings and her wand at the ready.

"Did you say something disparaging about Grammy? If you did, I'm gonna have to take matters into my own hands," Petty swore.

"I . . . sorry," Hunter said. "I forgot about Grammy's little affliction."

"Indeed." Petty popped him on the snout with her wand, and a bit of fairy dust went up his nose, causing him to sneeze with all the force of a tornado and send him sprawling back into the underbrush.

He wiggled his snout. "What the hell?"

"Sorry. My dust gets a little antsy when I'm riled. You okay?" Petty asked him.

Hunter scrambled to his feet. "I suppose. I can't very well snarl at a fairy godmother, can I?"

"I mean, you can. But I wouldn't recommend it." She grinned. But then she zapped them a box full of chocolate chip cookies. "Here, darlings."

Phillip looked at Petty floating there, her round little pink-cheeked goodness just flitting through the air, and was overcome with the urge to really apologize for what he'd done.

He'd said he was sorry in a million different ways, but he'd never just apologized without any expectation of something in return. While he desperately wanted to end this curse, he realized he didn't know if Petty had actually forgiven him.

He wanted that.

He wanted to know that Bluebonnet had also forgiven him.

"Petty," he began.

"Don't worry! I know there are a lot of new wedding bookings coming in, and that's so great for our magical stores, but I haven't forgotten about the carnival or the frog-kissing booth. I promise."

"That's not what I was going to ask you about," Phillip said.

"Oh?" Her wings fluttered, and she landed, both feet on the ground. She wiggled her nose and pushed up her spectacles. "What is it?"

"I wanted to say I'm sorry."

"For what, dear?" She cocked her head to the side.

It was so hard to reconcile this version of her with the woman he'd been infatuated with. Except, he could still see glimpses of her in the sparkle in her eyes.

"For what happened."

Hunter motioned for him to go on.

"For being a side-winding piece of shit and kissing you and Bluebonnet both. It was wrong."

"You've already apologized. I've forgiven you long ago." Petty waved her wand, as if to say that was all old business and had been forgotten.

"Yes, but all those other times I apologized, I was sorry.

But only because I was being punished. I thought apologizing would get me something. I haven't apologized just because I mean it. I'm sorry, Petunia. To you and to Bluebonnet."

Petty's cheeks grew even pinker. She reached out a hand to cup his cheek. "Oh, Phillip. Me too. You have to know that if I could undo this curse, I would. In a second. It was so wrong of me. I used my powers against you for personal gain, and that's not what they're for. Can *you* forgive *me*?"

Phillip wanted to say he didn't forgive her. That she was right, what she'd done was wrong, too. Especially to leave him like this for three hundred years. But one look at her, and knowing how much it cost her to say it, he did forgive her.

"I do." He took her hand.

"Well, isn't this just lovely. Okay, can we please get to the pub? Or to Ravenna's. Either is fine, but let's get moving," Hunter grumbled.

"You should know, I've petitioned Fairy Godmother Academy for help to break the curse. I should've done it long ago. But I'm hoping they can . . ." She shook her head. "Wait, what? Ravenna? Why would you two be going to Ravenna's?" Petty cast a shrewd, assessing glance at Phillip.

He felt like his governess had just caught him with both hands in the cookie jar.

"Uh, Hunter has a crush."

Petty didn't take her eyes off him for a second.

"That very well may be, but let me tell you both, Ravenna is not for you. Either one of you."

"Stop meddling with us, Pets. Go see to your charges. You know, the ones for whom you are supposed to meddle," Phillip said.

"Promise me you won't go to Ravenna with this," she demanded. "Dark magic and love are never a good mix. They're anathema."

Hunter coughed.

Phillip shuffled his feet.

"Guys, I'm serious. This will end badly for everyone involved. Do *not* fuck with fate."

Hunter made a rumbling sound that might've been a cough. "Listen, if something is fate, you can't get away from it no matter what you do. So how is it fucking with fate if we see Ravenna?"

Petty sighed the longest, most harried sigh Phillip had ever heard issue forth from another living being. "Listen, Berries for Brains, if fate has to move things around to put you where she wants you, you will definitely not enjoy the ride."

Hunter snorted. "I'd say it's already about as bad as it can get."

Petty rolled her eyes skyward. "Deliver me from dumbasses." Then she turned her eyes on Phillip. "Promise me that you won't go to Ravenna for a cure."

Phillip didn't want to promise, but he also didn't want to make Petty angry. He'd already been on the losing side of that once before.

He crossed his fingers behind his back. "I promise."

"Good." She pulled out her wand. "I have to get going. I'm in the middle of hiring an assistant, booking another wedding, and finishing up the last touches for the Taylor wedding tomorrow."

"The Taylor wedding is fine, Petty. It's all fine. My staff have everything under control. Even the champagne fountain and the cheeseball sculpture."

"Cheeseball sculpture? I didn't agree to this. That wasn't in the plan." Petty looked panicked.

"It's the groom's idea. He wanted to surprise the bride with a cheeseball sculpture in her likeness."

"Oh dear Lord," Petty gasped.

"Don't worry. It's fine. My chef handled it. It couldn't look any better if a Renaissance master carved it out of marble," Phillip reassured her.

"I really must go. I'll see you soon. Remember your promise." Petty disappeared.

Phillip locked gazes with Hunter.

"So are you keeping your promise?" Hunter said casually.

"Hell no. I had my fingers crossed. She hasn't been able to fix this and neither has any standard cure. There's no reason not to give Ravenna a bite at the apple."

"Phrasing, my dude. Remember where we are," Hunter said.

"Oh, right. Yeah." Phillip grinned.

"Not one word to Ravenna about my . . ." Hunter seemed to struggle for the right words.

"Feelings?"

Hunter growled.

"I got your back."

"Can we go to trivia now? I preordered my burger, and the bun's probably soggy and the crisp lettuce leaf is probably wilted."

"Saints preserve us from soggy buns, my friend." He clapped Hunter on the back, and headed toward the town square with a strange, almost sour hope in his heart.

Chapter 3

Zuri Davis fell in love with Ever After as soon as her driver passed the city limits.

It was even better in person than it had been on the website.

The downtown area was the most wonderful and ridiculous thing she'd ever laid eyes on. The coffee shop was shaped like a French press, and it looked like there were places to sit on the roof and enjoy the view under the umbrella of what would've been the plunger on a real French press. The dress shop was what really got her. Cinderella and Fella. It was an A-line building but painted to look like a ball gown.

Fat, happy flowers with orange, yellow, and lavender blooms framed the town square and the pink stone walkways.

An evergreen forest rose up against the backdrop of the tiny town, and just like in the pictures, two castles loomed like mountains over it all.

No, the website didn't do it justice.

The car rolled to a stop, and her driver pointed across the square. "There's what you're looking for. Fairy Godmothers, Inc."

Zuri looked to where he pointed and saw a short, squat building where the facade had been crafted to look like two wings and the letter *i* in the sign was shaped like a magic wand. A thrill shot through her at the prospect of working there.

She was sure the people who lived in Ever After were probably inured to the kitsch that was somehow more magical than gimmicky, but Zuri was entranced.

If she couldn't plan beautiful weddings here, well, there was just no hope for her.

"If you don't mind, most of the residents walk in the square. The pink stone is delicate, you see," the driver said.

"Oh! Of course." She moved to get out.

"I'll have your things waiting for you at the Charming B and B. It's that castle over yonder," the driver pointed out. "By the way, I'm Hansel. You give me a call if you need a ride up there after the godmothers have run you ragged." He winked at her.

Zuri found herself smiling. Maybe it was foolish, but he immediately set her at ease. His manner was warm and genuine.

"Do you live here, Hansel?" she asked.

"I do. I own the lumberyard and I do most of the woodworking. Sometimes the guys from the Pick 'n' Axe help out. We all do what we can. We take care of one another. It's a good place to live."

Just then, she spied what looked like cottages, but they were shaped like fat, red-capped mushrooms.

"Who lives there?"

"Those are guest cottages. They're all occupied at the moment. And, after I'm done with you, there are some things in one of them that need fixing."

"A Hansel of all trades, huh?"

He grinned. "That's me! Good luck with the interview, but I'm sure you don't need it."

She paused only a moment before thanking him and exiting the car. In Chicago, she wouldn't have left anything with a driver and trusted that her belongings would get to where they needed to go. But something about this place washed away her good sense.

She clutched her leather messenger bag close. Inside was basically her whole life. Her laptop, her cell phone, her wallet, and her portfolio that chronicled every single wedding she'd organized.

Zuri remembered each couple fondly, from the first to the last.

Well, next to the last.

And for the last, she remembered the bride fondly.

She noticed as she walked toward the building, many of the townspeople stopped what they were doing to look at her, but after a moment's glance, they all had a friendly wave or a greeting.

Zuri would swear that even the woodland animals were part of the greeting committee. She saw foxes, squirrels, rabbits, and deer all lurking at the edges of the forested area. Squirrels that were in the square proper crept closer to her than she would've expected.

When she stared back at them for too long, they would go back to whatever task they'd been doing. Like eating flower blossoms.

Of course, that had to be her imagination.

When she stepped through the front door of Fairy Godmothers, Inc., she was promptly assaulted by a burst of glitter to the face.

"Bridge too far, you think?" a kindly voice asked on a whisper.

"Oh, definitely, Bluebonnet."

"My dear, are you okay?" another kindly voice asked.

She spluttered and spat out glitter and coughed as she tried to catch her breath.

"Let's get her a glass of water."

"Or maybe we should help her sit down. I don't think the poor thing can see."

Zuri allowed herself to be led to a plush couch, and she accepted a glass of water. Gentle hands dabbed at her face, and she finally opened her eyes.

She was surrounded by the godmothers themselves.

They were all three wearing the same capped sleeve dress with a sweetheart neckline but all in different colors. Pink, yellow, and blue. But each of them had accessorized with a crisp, white apron tied at their ample waists and pockets stuffed with this and that.

"You must be Zuri," the one in the pink said. "I'm Petunia, this is Bluebonnet, and the grumpy one is Jonquil."

"I am not grumpy." She tugged on her apron. "Maybe I am, just a wee smidge."

"Are you all right, dear?" Bluebonnet asked.

"I think so." Except the glitter had gotten in her mouth. "I . . ."

"You need a rinse. Jonquil, will you show her the restroom so she can freshen up?" Petunia asked.

"She wouldn't need to freshen up if you hadn't hit her with fairy dust."

Oh no. It was going to be in her hair. She'd just had her hair done.

There wasn't a curse word strong enough to encompass how she felt about that, but she allowed Jonquil to lead her to the restroom, and she was shown a closet that had been stuffed with single-use toiletries.

"Don't worry, we recycle." Jonquil winked at her. "I'll just leave you to it."

Zuri selected a mouthwash and rinsed her mouth three times. She didn't see any glitter in her teeth, but she could still taste it. For some reason, it tasted like peach cobbler.

In fact, she realized the whole shop smelled of peach cobbler, and her stomach rumbled loudly. So loudly, it startled her.

"The poor dear is hungry," she heard a whisper from outside the door.

"Let's get Gwen to bring over some treats," another voice said.

"You know very well Gwen is upset with us."

A tittering of what might've been giggles greeted her next.

Zuri had to admit, despite the glitter bomb to the face, she already adored the godmothers. She could be happy working here.

Except for the damn glitter in her hair.

Although, on closer inspection, it wasn't that bad. There was a sparkle here, a sparkle there. Almost as if each individual sparkle had been artfully placed.

Too bad it wouldn't last. Perhaps working for a place called Fairy Godmothers, Inc., warranted a little sparkle.

Zuri met her own eyes in the mirror, and while she didn't completely recognize herself, she didn't dislike what she saw.

New adventure, she mouthed to herself.

Her stomach rumbled again, almost as if it were answering her.

She'd been too nervous to eat breakfast, and she was definitely paying for it now.

Zuri squared her shoulders, lifted her chin, and dusted some glitter off her shoulders and went back out to meet with, hopefully, her new employers.

The women gathered around her and led her back to the couch, making a general fuss.

"I'm okay. I promise," she reassured them.

"But are you?" Bluebonnet asked.

There was something about her, just the way there'd been something about Hansel. Zuri found herself wanting to spill her guts all over the place, much like the glitter bomb. She wanted to tell Bluebonnet everything. Her hopes, her fears, and she just had the sense that somehow, Bluebonnet could make it all better.

Only, she knew well enough that no one could make it all better. Zuri had to give herself time and the space to heal.

Suddenly, Bluebonnet took her hand. "You can tell us."

For a moment, Zuri panicked. She didn't know how she could be so wrong. They wanted the nitty-gritty details on the wedding that wasn't. Except as soon as she had the thought, it rang false.

Petunia took her other hand. "Go on, dear. Unburden yourself."

"We're your godmothers now," Jonquil reassured her.

This was insane, but somehow just what she needed. Only, she didn't know where to start.

Petunia seemed to understand. She nodded knowingly. "Dearie, you'll soon find that while my name is Petunia, people in Ever After call me Petty. It's not just a nickname. A man once tried to court Bluebonnet and me at the same time. His perfidy did not go unpunished."

"We've all been there," Bluebonnet reassured her.

"It's like Lizzo says. Why are men great until they gotta be great?" Jonquil added.

This made Zuri snort-cackle. Her imagination was pleased to present her with images of the three older ladies bopping around their kitchen, shaking it out to current music and singing along. She'd bet her last dollar that whatever she imagined wasn't as great as the real thing.

Suddenly, it took the wind out of her sails. She deflated.

If even in this magical place, with these magical women, and they still got done dirty by a man . . . nowhere was safe.

Was she really doing anyone any favors by being a wedding planner? Wouldn't it be better if she got out of the love business completely?

Bluebonnet squeezed her hand as if she knew the exact direction of Zuri's thoughts. "Come now."

Zuri found herself talking. Her mouth moving when she hadn't given it permission to do so, but that wasn't really anything new. "I don't know why I still want to be a wedding planner."

Well, now she'd done it. She'd shat in her own cornflakes and just cost herself the one job with the one company that was even willing to interview her.

Petunia took Zuri's bag from her and with gentle hands, pulled out Zuri's portfolio. She opened it to a page in the middle. "Because I bet you can tell me whose wedding this is. What the meal was, and the song that was played. I bet you sent them an anniversary card this year. And I bet that their wedding wouldn't have been what it was without you."

"The Mellenchamp wedding. The flowers she wanted were crocuses. They had a vegan menu. Their song was 'Take My Breath Away,' and this year was their fifth anniversary," she recited.

Zuri remembered how beautiful the bride looked, how radiant. How when she walked down the aisle to meet the groom, he had tears in his eyes. They were a wonderful, happy couple who had just had their first child. They were perhaps the best example of the work she'd done.

"See? Look at the groom's face in this picture. He would never treat her the way Alec treated you and Jenn. She would never do that to him. They're still so in love. You got to be part of that, Zuri. How beautiful is that?" Petunia said.

Even Jonquil, the supposed grumpy one, was nodding along. "Beautiful."

"We know your little heart is broken, and your faith is wavering," Bluebonnet said.

"How could it not?" Petunia asked kindly.

Zuri swallowed. "I don't understand why you wanted to interview me if you know all this."

"I told you, we're your godmothers now," Bluebonnet replied.

Zuri laughed. "You know who I think deserves a fairy godmother? It's Jenn. The former bride."

"Why is that?" Jonquil asked.

"Because she deserves good things to happen to her. If you three were actually fairy godmothers, I'd ask you to give her wishes, or whatever."

"Do tell us more," Petunia urged, with something bright sparkling in her eyes.

"I think she already got quite the gift," Bluebonnet said. "You saved her from marrying someone who didn't deserve her."

"I still feel guilty," Zuri confessed.

"Why? You didn't do anything wrong. You didn't know," Jonquil insisted.

"That's the patriarchy keeping you down," Petunia said. "It's this expectation that women are responsible for men's actions. Especially when men betray their partners."

This was absolutely not what she expected when she'd walked through the door.

Of course, she hadn't expected to get hit in the face with a glitter bomb, either, but here she was.

"If he wants to act like an alley cat—" Petunia began.

"No! No!" Bluebonnet said, grabbing Petunia's arm. "Remember what we talked about?"

Petunia sank bank down. "Oh, fine."

"Who else would you give wishes to?" Jonquil asked.

"How many do I get?" she asked.

Petunia raised a brow, but then said, "I don't know. Go nuts."

"St. Marigold's Orphanage. Every single child there," she said without hesitation. "And of course, my sister. But I think her wishes would be pretty close to mine."

"Indeed, I think they would," Bluebonnet said. "She works at the orphanage, right?"

Zuri nodded. "After seeing Ever After, it would be wonderful if they could come. Even if you don't hire me, I would love to connect you with Zeva and see if you can't work something out."

"Of course we're going to hire you. As if we weren't." Jonquil rolled her eyes.

"Even after I said I don't know why I still want to be a wedding planner?"

"I just said—" Jonquil began.

"What she means to say is yes. We have a lot of work, and while we're glad to have it, there's only so much time in a day," Bluebonnet said.

"Quite," Jonquil agreed.

"You'll start off as our assistant. Then you don't have to call yourself a wedding planner. You're a wedding administrator," Petunia offered.

Bluebonnet clapped. "Or office manager. Really, whatever title you'd like."

"Assistant to fairy godmothers? That sounds pretty great," Zuri admitted.

"Of course, you'll have paid time off, vacation, but for the love of fey, please don't take it in the spring or summer. We're pleased to include lodging at the B and B. The castle has been totally remodeled. You'll have a suite, of course, and Phillip can go over the kitchen access and so forth when you get to the castle tonight."

"Tonight?" Zuri asked.

"We'd like you to start right away," Jonquil said.

"As in now," Bluebonnet added.

The door to the shop opened, and in stepped a woman carrying a large red box. "Godmothers, I brought you cupcakes. Even though you don't deserve them."

Bluebonnet tittered. "Yes, we do."

"Oh, hello." The woman flashed her a warm smile. "I'm Gwen."

"Zuri Davis. Newly minted assistant to the godmothers."

"This is perfect!" Petunia said. "Gwen, do you have time to take Zuri around to gather favor samples?"

"The first job we'd like for you to tackle is testing these wedding favors," Jonquil said.

Bluebonnet handed her a coin. "This is a wish coin. There's a mermaid fountain on the path to the B and B. Make a wish and toss it in."

"And report back?" Zuri was doubtful.

The godmothers all nodded eagerly.

"Okay, what else?" Zuri tucked the coin into her messenger bag.

"Here's a list," Petunia handed the small pink square of paper to Zuri. "But first, cupcakes."

"Definitely cupcakes," Gwen said. "I baked them fresh this morning. Red velvet. Cream cheese frosting."

"Those are my favorite!" Zuri said.

"Well, maybe I baked them for you instead of the godmothers," Gwen said. "I knew someone needed cupcakes."

"We were actually about to call you for some cookies," Jonquil said.

"I'll have Brittany bring them over."

"You two run along now," Bluebonnet said as she shooed them toward the door.

"What about the cupcakes?" Zuri said as her stomach growled again.

"It's on the list. You'll need to go try the lunch at Pick 'n' Axe. Take a cupcake with you, of course," Bluebonnet said. "Or two."

Zuri decided not to be shy. She grabbed a cupcake and shoved it in her mouth.

As soon as it touched her tongue, flavor exploded. The cake itself really did have a texture like velvet. It was the best thing she'd ever eaten.

"Well," she said, after she'd finished, "I can say for sure we're going to be great friends."

Gwen laughed. "I'd like that."

"Yes, yes. Do all your getting-to-know-yous. But can you do it while you gather samples? We have much to accomplish today."

"Like fixing the plumbing in my cottage?" Gwen demanded.

The godmothers looked at one another and blinked.

"We don't know what you mean." Petty began shuffling papers.

"I hope you don't buy that innocent act. They're up to something," Gwen said.

"She's new here, Gwen. Don't go telling stories," Bluebonnet said.

Something passed between them, but Zuri wasn't sure exactly what.

"Oh, I see. Well, you're in for one hell of a ride." Then she turned back to the godmothers. "But I mean it. Stop it."

The godmothers were suddenly very, very busy. But that didn't stop Gwen from fixing each of them, in turn, with a hard look.

"Uh-huh. Well, we better get going. We'll stop at Bernadette's for some coffees to wash down those cupcakes."

"It's on the list!" Bluebonnet chirped.

Zuri handed the list to Gwen, and the other woman smiled. "It looks like most of today is eating."

Zuri followed Gwen out the door, and the other woman laughed again. "They want you to taste-test the sunflower seeds they'll throw instead of rice? To make sure the birds will like it? Oh no."

Zuri arched a brow. "I . . . really?"

"How are you to know if the birds will like it?"

"I suppose we could try feeding it to them in the park and see if they like it?"

"I don't know if you're ready for the Ever After wildlife just yet."

"They all seem pretty tame," Zuri said.

"Some of them are, for sure." Gwen shook her head.

"Earlier, when you told the godmothers to fix your plumbing, what did you mean?" Zuri studied her. "I mean, if you don't want to talk about it, that's okay, too. Just tell me to mind my business."

"Oh. That. Well, once you've been here long enough, you'll know about all their plans for everyone. I'm sure they'll get you in on their well-intentioned meddling, too. So I'm sure you know about the fake wedding."

Zuri nodded. "It was part of what made me want to work for FGI."

"Really? Why?"

"I figured if their godchildren loved them enough to get married to help them, they must be really wonderful people."

Gwen's expression softened. "Yeah. They really are, and they have the best intentions. So, the bride, Lucky? She's my best friend. The groom, Ransom . . . well, he has a best friend, too, if you see where this is going."

"They're trying to matchmake?"

"I've heard they're really good at it, but Roderick is so not my type. Plus, I just got divorced, and I don't need another complication."

"I am in touch with that. One hundred percent."

"What are you going to wish for with your wish coin, if you don't mind me asking?"

"It's not real anyway. I don't know. A million dollars." She shrugged. It was dumb anyway.

"Did they ask you what you would wish for, if you had the opportunity, before they gave it to you?"

"They did."

"Then wish for that."

"Wishes. True love. Fairy tales. I just don't have it in me to believe right now."

"I know exactly what you mean," Gwen said.

Zuri had the feeling that she did. "Can I tell you a not-so-secret secret?"

Gwen gave her a conspiratorial smile. "Anything. I'll be the vault."

"I'm a wedding planner, and I don't believe . . ." She was about to say she didn't believe in love, but that wasn't true. It wasn't even true that she didn't believe in romantic love, because Petunia had reminded her of the Mellenchamp wedding, and it was most definitely the best incarnation of romantic love. "I don't believe love is for everyone. I don't believe it's for me."

"We should start a club. Ever After Lonely Hearts Club."

"We could have our meetings up at that big, dark castle."

"Oh, the woman who owns that? Her name's Ravenna Blackheart."

"Ever After Blackhearts. If we name the club after her, she has to invite us for tea and some fancy little sandwiches, right? Or at least a tour," Zuri teased.

Gwen fixed her with a serious look as she lay the list back on the counter. "Actually, I'm sure she'd absolutely love it."

"When I first saw this town on the website, I was telling my sister that if they don't have weddings there, they should. Not every girl dreams of being a princess."

"Some of us are Evil Queens," Gwen agreed. "I am dying to see the inside, myself."

Zuri picked up the list. "'Candied apple from Snow's Market'? I don't know if I'm up for that."

"What? Give me that." Gwen took the list back. "Oh. Huh. I don't know if I'd put that in my mouth, either. But definitely Pick 'n' Axe. Let's go there first and get some protein in you. The godmothers survive on sugar, but a good stew for lunch and maybe some axe throwing will perk you right up."

Axe throwing? "No darts?"

"Trust me. You'll enjoy the axes."

Yes, Zuri decided, she was most definitely on a new adventure.

Chapter 4

Zuri realized what the godmothers had done in having her collect and sample the various favors and treats from the shops around Ever After.

She now had a firm inventory from each vendor of what they had available, an idea of the other things they could do, and she'd met everyone she needed to meet in one day without the pressure of an introduction just for the sake of an introduction.

It was genius, really.

To top it off, she'd gotten to throw axes and drink the most delicious honey mead she'd ever had. Not that she'd ever tasted honey mead. She was a champagne sort of woman.

The mead had been *after* the axe throwing, of course.

She was sure that was going to be a new favorite hobby.

Zuri couldn't wait to text Zeva and tell her everything.

She had one more favor left to sample, and to be honest, she was very glad it was nothing else to eat. She'd eaten far too many sweets. Although, if she were to be presented with more, Zuri had no doubt she'd stuff them in her face. They were too good to resist.

That was something that had surprised Zuri. Chicago had many fine restaurants, and there was always somewhere new to try, a new favorite, and she'd thought she'd be giving up fine cuisine to move to a small town.

Not that small towns couldn't have good food, but she'd expected the food to be more comfort food instead of fine dining.

Ever After had everything.

She pulled the wish coin out of her messenger bag and inspected it.

It didn't seem like anything special. Nothing out of the ordinary. Just a gold-plated bit of metal on her palm. She rubbed her thumb over the smooth surface and found she liked how it felt.

The only fountain to throw it in was the mermaid fountain on the way to the B and B.

She looked up at the sky and saw that the day was almost gone.

Even though the little town was quaint and cute, she didn't want to be gallivanting through some little path in the woods at night. Even if it was as well-lit as everyone had repeatedly promised her.

A fat red cardinal flew past her to land on a low-hanging branch. He chirped and cocked his head from side to side, watching her. He seemed to say, *Move it along.*

Or maybe that's just what she needed to hear.

Zuri had saved the wish for last because she'd told herself it was easier since it was on the way to the B and B, but the truth was, she didn't know what she'd wish for. Not that it actually mattered.

Wishes, fairy godmothers, and Happily Ever Afters weren't real. So what did it matter what she wished for?

The coin had absorbed the heat from her palm and was warm to the touch. The surface she'd previously thought was smooth suddenly had edges, and she opened her palm to investigate.

For Yourself was etched onto the coin.

How had she missed that?

The bird chirped at her again.

"I'm coming. But only if you come with me," she said to the little bird. As if he could hear and understand her.

To her great delight, he hopped from branch to branch as she made her way into the forest and followed the stone path. She saw that it was indeed well-lit, as the small white lights lining the walkway began to flicker to life.

Zuri wondered what it must've been like to grow up in Ever After. No wonder people here seemed to believe in magic.

She made her way to the grand fountain with the mermaid and saw a gigantic frog sitting on the mermaid's bosom.

A sound began low in the frog's throat, and Zuri could hear a great bass buildup to what she was sure was going to be the loudest and most terrifying sound she'd ever heard from a frog. His throat expanded, and the sound burst from him.

"My guy. That was rough."

The frog seemed to regard her momentarily before launching himself into the water and splashing her.

"It's already happened with glitter. Why not fountain water?" At least it wasn't pond scum, she consoled herself.

She sat on the edge of the fountain and studied the coin again. Then she looked up for her little bird friend to find that he, too, had abandoned her.

A wish.

What would she actually wish for if wishes came true?

Zuri didn't know the answer.

She wanted to wish for her sister to have her heart's desire, but the coin seemed to tell her that the wish had to be for herself.

Zuri remembered what her mother used to tell her. When faced with a tough decision, after weighing the pros and cons, if she still couldn't come to a solution, she gave herself one second to choose. The first thing that came to her mind was the path she should take.

So Zuri held the coin close to her heart.

"Tell me what to do, Mama. What should I wish for?"

She tossed the coin into the fountain and the words came to her.

"My heart's desire," she whispered.

"And just what is that?" A deep voice startled her from the other side of the fountain.

"Jesus H.— Didn't your mother ever teach you not to sneak up on people?"

A man came around from the other side. He was tall, blond, and . . . oh dear Lord, it was the Ken doll B and B owner. His eyes really were that green in real life. The same color as that damned frog.

"Sorry, I would've introduced myself, but you seemed kind of busy making a wish."

"Oh, you too, with the wish stuff, huh? Well, I tested it. I made a wish." She looked around. "I don't see anything manifesting itself here other than you."

He flashed her a grin. "Maybe it's me. You never know."

"It's definitely *not* a man." Even as pretty as that one was. "No offense."

He laughed. "Blessings come in unexpected places. Perhaps, if your heart's desire is to be warm and cozy by a fire with a hot chocolate, then I am the answer to your wish."

She arched a brow at him. "Okay, that's not a pickup line I've ever heard before."

"That's because it's not one."

"Why not?" She didn't want to be insulted, she didn't want to care whether he thought she was pretty, but an invitation to be cozy by a fire was usually a pass. Wasn't it?

He laughed again. "Because you were pretty clear that you're not interested in being pursued."

"A gentleman who is still a gentleman after being told no. I think we can be friends. I'm Zuri."

"Ah, yes, my expected guest. I'm Phillip Charming." He bowed. "Ever at your service."

His words caused a strange stab of desire deep in her core.

"Oh. The B and B owner," she said out loud, because apparently she needed reminding. "I imagine that the hot chocolate and the fire are just a couple of the many amenities of a fairy-tale castle."

"Indeed."

"Sorry if I was . . ." She wasn't quite sure the word she was looking for.

He held up his hands. "Not at all. You're alone with a strange man in a forest. You should always, always stay on the path and trust your instincts. You never know who is going to be a wolf on the inside, am I right?"

"Exactly that. Too many of them look like princes but end up being frogs."

"Hey, what's wrong with frogs?" He looked gravely insulted.

"Nothing, really. There was a big granddaddy of a frog here earlier who seemed okay. A little indigestion, maybe. Not really the kind for kissing, either."

"He might be." Phillip arched a brow. "No?"

"Seriously?"

"Seriously. It's a local legend that he's actually a prince under a curse and only true love's kiss can break it. You should give it a try. Everyone in town has done it. It's a rite of passage."

Zuri sighed. "I suppose it couldn't be any worse than the last frog I kissed. Although, if I was smart, I'd tell myself that I shouldn't be kissing frogs and expecting princes. Sometimes, a frog is just a frog."

"Wanna talk about it?"

"No." Zuri crossed her arms over her chest. "Maybe."

"It's overwhelming to tell new people your story. How about you let me ask questions, and you answer the ones you feel like talking about."

"And what, three passes?" She wasn't sure if she wanted to play this game.

"As many passes as you want."

She studied Phillip for a long moment. He seemed sincere, but she didn't know why he was willing to walk her drama llama.

"A person I cared about betrayed me. He lied about who he was."

"That sucks, and I can see why it would sour you on people. And poor, innocent frogs." He sat down on the edge of the fountain.

"Not only did he break my heart, but he also trifled with my money. That's really what's unforgivable." She made a moue with her lips and was a little upset all over again. She would get past the heartbreak, but Zuri didn't know if she'd let go of the fact he'd played fast and loose with her livelihood.

Phillip grinned. "Oh? How did he do that? Leave you a bad review?"

"He was the groom in a wedding I was planning. No one wants their wedding planned by a groom-stealing hussy. I'm really surprised that Fairy Godmothers, Inc., hired me."

"Ouch. Although, since they did hire you, I imagine it was much more complicated than it sounds. Petty, Jonquil, and Bluebonnet fix things. They know what they're doing." He looked around and gave her a conspiratorial wink. "Mostly."

"You think I need fixing?" Her sister kept telling her she wasn't broken, but she had her doubts.

"Not you, but your situation. That's kind of what they do."

"Believe me, I know that they're capable of things. You can't walk around with a nickname like Petty and not be a force to be reckoned with."

He nodded. "That is most definitely correct. Having been on the wrong side of that woman, it's not something I'd recommend to anyone."

"You? What did you do, cut her off in the checkout line in Snow's Market?"

She was actually dying to know what he'd done to make the adorable old dear angry. It was either something incredibly banal or something awful. There wouldn't be any kind of in-between.

He appraised her for a long moment. "I'll tell you, but not until after you've been here a while."

"Wow, that sounds ominous." Okay, good to know that her instincts were still determined to lead her astray. It had to be something awful, and here she was, getting all soft in the head over him.

"It's just . . . you won't believe me."

"Try me." She'd rather find out now so she had a solid excuse with which to remind herself to keep her distance.

"I will," he promised. "But later."

Zuri decided that sounded like bullshit, but she didn't want to be pressured about her situation, so she wasn't going to pressure him. It wasn't like the answer mattered. Zuri wasn't looking to get to know anyone intimately.

Liar, liar pants on fire, a voice in the back of her head screeched at her. She definitely wanted to get to know Phillip Charming in the most intimate of ways.

Her heart said no, but her body said all the yes.

Her brain, well, it tried to mediate and focus on breathing and heartbeat, and things that didn't involve all the dirty scenarios her imagination was happy to conjure.

Logically, she could pursue a physical relationship with Phillip Charming. Wouldn't that just be the big, fat flower in her Easter hat? When she was younger, many of her friends had advised the best way to get over a person was to get underneath another one.

She coughed and shook her head, trying to clear out those thoughts and get herself right.

"Later, huh?" Zuri couldn't keep the skepticism out of her voice.

"You'll understand. I promise."

"Makes no difference to me." She shrugged. "You don't owe me anything."

"If we're going to be friends, you should be able to trust me. I should be able to trust you."

"Who said anything about being friends?" She felt like she was once again back in comfortable meaningless-banter territory. "Maybe we're not going to be friends."

"That would be a shame, because only my friends get hot cocoa by the fire."

"If you throw in as many marshmallows as I can fit in my mug, then I'll accept your offer of friendship."

"You drive a hard bargain, Zuri."

Her name on his tongue was better than cake.

His mention of something hard caused her gaze to travel down the length of his body, unwittingly.

Nope, she wasn't going to look at . . .

Oh dear God. She coughed and looked away. "Do I? I suppose I should mention I need a lot of snacks, too. You can't plan weddings without a lot of sugar."

"Oh, love. You've come to exactly the right place. The Blossom sisters are famous for their ice cream sodas. My kitchen isn't too shabby, either. I have a chef on duty at all hours."

"Must be nice."

"It is. So, have you decided if you're going to walk with me to the castle?"

"I suppose. The headline will read 'Wedding Planner Disappears: Lured by Hot Chocolate.'"

"I promise you're safe with me."

"Do you keep your promises?"

"Good question." He offered her his arm. "As a fairy-tale prince, I am bound to do so."

"Mm-hm. I imagine with a last name like Charming . . ."

"It is a bit of a family tradition, yes."

She accepted his offer and put her hand on the inside of his arm. Correction. Make that well-sculpted arm. His muscles were carved from stone.

A nervous giggle welled in the back of her throat and she swallowed it. She despised giggling, not as a general rule, but just when it came to men. She was a full-grown, powerful woman.

She would not giggle just because his muscles were delicious.

Or because he smelled like fuckboy cologne. (Which to her great chagrin, she loved.)

Or because he was too pretty to actually exist.

Or even because he was all those things and he was taking her for hot chocolate with as many marshmallows as she could cram in her cup.

No. Giggling. Allowed.

So of course her entire body decided to betray her.

She tripped over a tree root like an absolute moron, and when he reached out his other hand to steady her, his hand warm and delicious on her skin, she giggled.

"Hold fast," he said, then coughed. "I mean, are you okay? The path is usually very well maintained, but I'm not sure where that came from." Phillip glared at the tree, as if it were the tree's fault.

"I'm okay. We're the ones in the way. The tree is just living its best life." Hopefully, he'd forgotten about her giggle.

But she hadn't forgotten about his hold-fast comment. How antiquated. Strange. Yet, she found it oddly charming.

"I suppose we are," he agreed, albeit reluctantly. "Watch this forest, though. It's easy to get turned around. There's a reason it's called the Enchanted Forest."

"No, it's not. Really?" She looked up at the dark sky and

the branches that arched over them. "It is kind of magical. I mean, if you're the sort to believe in that kind of thing."

"I am." He nodded. "And if you stay here long enough, you will be, too."

He led her down the path without further incident, and when they stepped from the forest and onto castle grounds, Zuri was stunned.

It was . . . a fairy tale. Exactly as it had looked in the picture, with white spires and a blue-shingled roof. So many towers and arches and . . .

"This is insane. Who would build a castle in the backwoods of Missouri?"

"My ancestors. They had the castle brought over from the old country when they settled here."

"I can't believe I get to stay here."

"You'll be tired of it soon enough. Drafty hallways, a long walk to work . . . It's not all it's cracked up to be."

"I do believe there was the promise of fires and cocoa?"

"If that's all it takes to make you happy, you'll be delirious. At least, for a little while. I've allocated a whole wing for weddings, guests, and activities. However, you're going to be on the other side of the castle. That way it feels like you at least get a break from work. You don't want the guests to have easy access to you in your off time."

That was so thoughtful, not that Zuri would've complained either way.

He led her inside the castle, and it was all she could do not to ooh and aah out loud. She pulled out her phone to snap a few pictures to send to Zeva and saw she had a text. Zuri dismissed the notification; she'd look at it later.

They got on an old elevator that was very Gatsby in its old-world charm and style, and he pulled the lever over to four. It took the ancient thing quite some time to haul them up to the appropriate floor, but Zuri found it retro and charming.

When they emerged, she followed him down an impossibly long hallway to a gilded white door. He opened it for her, and when she stepped inside, she realized her accommodations were bigger than her apartment in Chicago.

"This was recently renovated. It was formerly the Queen's Suite."

She looked around and couldn't for the life of her keep her mouth closed. Her jaw dropped farther at each and every new thing that was revealed. From the huge stone balcony, with the wall of windows, to the very modern kitchen, the river-stone fireplace with a roaring fire, and the marble stairs that led up to a loft that was all bed, covered in emerald satin with heavy velvet curtains, and a small hallway that led to what could only be described as a wet room. A Roman stone bath that looked like it could hold twenty people, to the one-hundred-showerhead glass enclosure . . . everything about the place screamed over-the-top luxury.

The front room bore rich Persian carpets and satin and velvet pillows on plush, brightly colored furniture.

"This is for me?" It couldn't possibly be. It was too much.

"The godmothers wanted you to have a kind of retreat. There's also a guest room, if you'd like to have your sister visit."

"Ever After is still like every other small town. Everyone knows everything about you."

A knock sounded on the door.

"Ah, that will be our hot chocolate." He opened the door, and a man in a uniform brought in a tray with a silver teapot and two mugs, as well as an array of toppings. "That will be all, thank you."

The man left as silently as he'd come, and while her head was still swimming, Phillip pointed to a screen on the front of the refrigerator.

"Anything you'd like stocked in your kitchen you can type in on this screen, and someone will take care of it. You can even specify a time, but we prefer to get it all done on Wednesdays. It gives staff time to rest after our wedding guests leave on Mondays. You can also use this screen to order food from the kitchen if you'd rather not bother with cooking. You can also make special requests, but you must give them time to acquire the ingredients if it's something different from what we normally have on hand."

"This. Is. Ridiculous."

"Not at all. We want you to be comfortable and able to focus on your job. You can't do that if you're eating microwave dinners," he said.

"I'm never leaving. I need you to know that. Even if FGI fires me. You will never get me out of this room . . . no, house. Whatever. It's mine forever."

He barked out a laugh. "Stay forever, said the cursed prince to the princess."

She snorted. "You're so weird."

But she found she liked that he was weird, because it was honest. That was what she liked best about him, how genuine he was. How real. Even though he was obviously stupid rich.

They drank their hot chocolate, and he was true to his word. He gave her as many marshmallows as her soup bowl of a cup would allow.

The first sip of the chocolate on her tongue caused her to moan. "This is the best thing I've ever tasted."

"It's Mayan drinking chocolate."

"And you let me put marshmallows in it. For shame."

"I like marshmallows in mine." He grinned, and he had bits of chocolate at the edges of his mouth.

Oh, but Phillip Charming was dangerous.

He was handsome, and silly, and . . .

And if she hadn't just had her heart broken, she'd have taken him to bed. Right then, right there.

She still wanted to.

It wasn't just the sexual gratification she wanted. Zuri

wanted to feel the other things he seemed to offer, too. An honest connection, whether it was love or not, she wanted to be touched by someone who saw her for who she was. Who let her see him for the same.

There was just something about him. Maybe it was his warmth, his openness, she didn't know. Zuri found herself spilling her whole sordid tale about Alec/Xander, the wedding from hell, and the way her life had imploded. He didn't judge her, and even better, she could tell that he didn't pity her either.

"His loss is Ever After's gain. And yours too, I think. You know you're well rid of that douchebag, right?"

Her lips bloomed into a grin. "Yeah, I am. The bride and I both are."

Silence stretched out between them, but it wasn't awkward or uncomfortable, even though it was weighted with expectation. Something changed in that moment. She looked up from her chocolate, and their eyes met. He held her gaze, and the unique green of his eyes darkened. Her heart beat faster, and she inhaled a shaky breath.

If he made a pass at her now, she knew she wouldn't say no.

She was torn between wanting him to grab her, kiss her hard, and bang her like a screen door in a hurricane, and hoping against hope that he'd take pity on her and let her be. That he'd remember she was vulnerable and be worthy of her trust.

Not that he wasn't worthy of her trust if he acted on this thing they both obviously wanted, but . . . she just wanted him to be better. She wanted him to be more than Alec Marsh. She needed to feel like she meant more, too.

Why did her feelings have to be so complicated? It wasn't practical. Not in the least.

Phillip put his cup down on the counter and took her hand. "It's been a pleasure, Zuri Davis. I'm happy you're in Ever After."

Then he did something devastating.

He brought her hand to his lips and pressed the most chaste of kisses on her knuckles and left.

She flopped down in front of the roaring fire and held her hand close to her heart.

Oh, she was in so much trouble.

Her sister had been right.

Speaking of Zeva, she grabbed the phone to text her and remembered the earlier text she'd received.

Zuri opened it, expecting a text from her sister, but instead, it was from Xan—Alec.

Can we talk?

Her first instinct was to say hell no they couldn't talk. Or ask him what he thought they had to talk about.

Then Zuri remembered her wish. She'd asked for her heart's desire.

Double-checking the time stamp on the text, she realized he'd texted her right after she'd made her wish.

Was hearing from Alec her heart's desire?

Had her wish come true?

Chapter 5

Zuri Davis was the most beautiful woman he'd ever seen. She was smart, and obviously had a huge, loving heart all wrapped up in an hourglass shape that he couldn't stop thinking about getting his hands on.

Could he be so lucky that she'd be the one to break his curse?

He'd wanted to kiss her earlier. That moment when their eyes had met and their gazes locked, it had seemed like that moment had stretched into eternity, but was still somehow over way too soon.

He kept remembering how she'd said she didn't want a relationship, but the fact that she'd tossed the coin just as he'd regained human form wasn't lost on him.

At one time, Phillip wouldn't have doubted he was the answer to someone's wish. He'd been arrogant and really had thought he was a gift.

Now, he wasn't so sure.

Phillip had promised her the truth, and he'd give it to her. After she learned about magic. He was sure that if she decided to stay in Ever After, the godmothers would tell her.

Which meant he'd also have to tell her what he'd done to make Petty angry enough to turn him into a frog.

He should probably also introduce her to Hunter. At some point. If she met him before he could warn her about his . . . condition . . . well, it could be traumatic for both of them.

After all, she was bound to find her way down into his abode one way or another.

Speaking of the man, the myth, the Beast . . . he could hear Hunter's claws on the marble steps.

Just in time, too.

Phillip noticed his friend's cloak was a brighter red than he'd ever seen it, and his facial fur was neatly groomed.

He'd taken extra grooming steps to go visit the Evil Queen.

"Not. One. Word." Hunter eyed him.

"I just noticed you put in some effort." Phillip didn't know if he'd have taken it that far, but he wasn't going to give Hunter too much grief over it. A little, to be sure. But no more than necessary to keep the bonds of their friendship solid.

Hunter needed a little teasing now and then.

"It's not easy to groom facial fur with these claws, brother."

"I imagine not."

While, at first, Phillip had been excited about the possibility of Ravenna being able to help him with this curse, that excitement had faded. He didn't want to get his hopes up for no reason. So really, this visit to the dark castle was more for Hunter than himself.

He knew his friend had a major thing for the dark queen.

Not that he blamed him. Ravenna was beautiful, and slightly terrifying.

"Did you get her a gift?" Hunter asked. "We have to take her a tribute."

What did one take to a woman such as Ravenna? He had zero idea.

"Chocolate? The hearts of her enemies? Ah, the hearts of her enemies dipped in chocolate?" Hunter asked hopefully.

"Those are all great suggestions, and a good thing, too. Because I forgot we needed to take her a tribute."

"Damn it, man!" Hunter swore. Then he perked. "Cheese. We could take her cheese."

"How did we get from the hearts of her enemies to cheese?"

"I . . . it's just what we're doing. Cheese. Who doesn't love cheese?" Hunter declared.

"What if she's lactose intolerant?" Phillip couldn't resist needling his friend.

Hunter perked, his ears folding forward on his head. "Do you think she is?"

"No." Phillip laughed. "Listen, it's going to be fine. We'll take her a bottle of champagne. A night-blooming carnivorous flower and some absinthe truffles."

"That's good. Yeah. Good." Hunter nodded. "I . . . I shouldn't be doing this, should I? This is dumb."

"It's not any dumber than asking her to break a curse. Which, incidentally, she knows I've been cursed for the last three hundred years and hasn't done anything about it."

"Well, you haven't asked, have you?" Hunter prompted.

"You're right. I keep forgetting she's not like everyone else. She doesn't help unless she's asked."

"We were both her. Once upon a time, my friend."

Phillip realized he was right. Even now, sometimes, he warred with himself over doing the right thing. For a long time, he'd been angry that people just expected him to do things without a please, and sometimes without a thank you. But that wasn't why people did good things. Or at least, it wasn't supposed to be.

The point of being good was doing good when no one was looking.

He certainly understood wanting a cookie once in a while.

Or all the time, actually.

"So, are you going to get that Medusa plant from the greenhouse to take to your girlfriend, or what?"

Although, Hunter didn't actually have to go anywhere. The castle was enchanted to respond to their needs, and the Medusa plant, truffles, and a bottle of champagne appeared secured for their travel through the woods in a basket.

"You've got the red cloak and the basket," Phillip pointed out.

"Shut. Up," Hunter grumbled, but picked up the basket carefully.

They set out on the newly designed path into the deep, dark part of the Enchanted Woods.

"Lots of stories start this way. This could be good," Hunter said.

When the forest got darker, older, more overgrown, and the animals they spotted in the foliage got darker, too, they looked at each other and shook their heads.

"I did not just see a rabbit with vampire teeth. I didn't," Phillip said, and shook his head, while he tried to not get too clear a picture of the rest of the wildlife that followed them up the trail.

"I'm comforted by the fact my teeth are bigger, but it makes me imagine what else is out in these woods. It wasn't like this before her castle came back."

"It's fine, though."

They nodded together.

"Honestly, she's probably watching us through some security system crystal ball and laughing at us for being little bitches."

Hunter's brows furrowed, and he straightened, squaring his shoulders. "It's not creepy at all." But his head swiveled to the left when something moved in the underbrush, and he bared his teeth ready to fight.

"Coming to the castle?" A voice surprised them.

Phillip looked around and saw a giant flying fox hanging upside down from a nearby tree.

"Yes, we'd like to visit with Ravenna. We come bearing gifts," Phillip said, and Hunter held up the basket.

"Oh, presents!" The flying fox did a flip and landed on her feet. "Anything in there for me? Maybe a tasty strawberry or two?"

"We didn't know to expect you. Next time, we'll bring you some strawberries. If that's okay?" Phillip asked.

"I like that you think there will be a next time." She laughed and jumped up onto a higher branch. "I'll let her know you're coming."

The giant flying fox spread her wings wide and drifted across the canopy of trees.

"Security bats. I like it," Hunter agreed.

"Of course Ravenna has security bats. At least they weren't flying monkeys."

"I wouldn't want to know what that looks like. Can you imagine how much crap there would be everywhere with flying monkeys?"

"I don't want to." Yet, Phillip couldn't stop himself from imagining it. He shuddered. Awful. Just awful.

Suddenly, small mushrooms lining the new path flickered to life, and Phillip could see the path winding all the way up to the dark castle.

"That's nice. See, people have misjudged Ravenna. Just like everyone misjudged us," Hunter said.

Phillip didn't trust it, but he wasn't going to say so to his friend. He knew Hunter was at that part of infatuation where Ravenna could probably step on his tail or use it as a back scrubby and he'd be grateful.

He, personally, hated that part.

They followed the path the rest of the way up to the castle, and when they emerged from the dark forest, the black castle was alight with brightly burning torches and a fountain of fire. Phillip wondered if they hadn't accidentally wandered into hell.

A homey hell, with happy flying foxes and giant vampire bunny rabbits, but hell nonetheless.

The giant arched doors opened, and the mistress of the castle herself stood there waiting to greet them. She was regal in her bearing, dripping with onyx jewelry and black pearls on a shimmery, yet still black, baroque-style dress. He had to admit, Ravenna knew how to make an entrance.

"Esmerelda informed me we're having guests," she said, arching a perfect black brow. "Do come in."

Phillip hadn't thought that his friend could square his shoulders wider, or stand up taller, but he did. He was like a full-grown grizzly standing on its back legs.

A full-grown grizzly with an addiction to beard oil.

Phillip bit his cheek to keep from snickering and followed his friend toward the stairs.

When Hunter approached Ravenna, he bent at the waist and offered his massive paw for her hand.

Ravenna studied him for a long moment before giving him her hand.

Instead of brushing his snout over the back of her hand, which would've been awful all around, he pressed it to his forehead.

"It's a pleasure to see you, Ravenna."

"Is it?" She curled her lips in a smirk and looked to Phillip, obviously waiting for his greeting.

"Majesty," was all he could offer. He noticed that the place smelled like incense and cinnamon. Unexpected.

"Hmm. So proper. So polite. You must want something, and you must want it badly to have made the trek in the dark to my humble home."

"I would've come just to visit if I knew I'd be received," Hunter interjected.

"Really? Would you like to come for tea, then? Come sit in my parlor with my spiders and eggplant sandwiches and blood orange tea," Ravenna teased.

"I would like that. I'll bring my mother's spell book and share a reading or two, if you'd like."

Ravenna laughed. "Oh dear. How could I say no to that?"

"I'd rather you didn't."

Hunter's blunt honesty was endearing, even to Ravenna,

Phillip could see. He didn't want his friend to get his feelings dumped in the shredder, and Phillip was pleased to see that it didn't seem like Ravenna had any dark intentions toward his friend.

"I think you might've lost your mind, Hunter. But come for tea and we shall see. Now, tell me what you really came for."

"Perhaps in the parlor?" Esmerelda suggested.

"Oh, I suppose."

Esmerelda led them inside the castle, and Phillip realized it was the perfect mirror of his own home.

"I hope you don't mind, I may have borrowed some ideas for upgrades. Like the elevator," Ravenna said to him.

"Not at all. This is beautiful. It's like the Wonderland version of my castle."

Ravenna laughed again. "I'll admit, it's nice to have visitors."

Phillip suddenly saw her in a whole new light. He hadn't made an effort to be her friend. To get to know her. Not many in Ever After had. She was the Evil Queen, after all. So why would she have offered to help him with his affliction?

Why would she say yes, even now?

"What made you rebuild your castle? I thought you were content living above the bank?" he asked.

"Like a dragon hoarding my gold, you mean?"

"I'll be honest. I would," Phillip confessed.

"Ah, yes, but you're a man, and you can do all the things I've done and all you get is turned into a frog. Me? I'm a pariah."

"Listen, the change back with dragonfly wings still in my teeth every day for the last three hundred years hasn't exactly been a picnic." Then he shook his head. He'd been eating out of doors. That was, by definition, a picnic. "At least not one I'd choose to attend."

Ravenna wrinkled her nose. "Eww. That's horrible."

"So, the castle?" Hunter asked.

"There was finally enough magic back in the world that I could. I wasn't going to take from the town wells that keep us safe from outsiders, so I waited." She narrowed her eyes. "But don't let that confuse anyone. The town wells kept *me* safe from outsiders, too. It wasn't selfless or anything." She lifted her chin.

"Of course not," Phillip agreed easily.

Hunter said nothing but continued to stare.

"Why is he staring at me?" Ravenna demanded, obviously confused.

"You're gorgeous?" Phillip shrugged. He thought it would be obvious.

"I want to be terrifying. I want to be the destroyer from the deep. The end of all things. The darkness at the end!"

"Bitch Goddess of Doom," Esmerelda supplied.

Ravenna nodded. "Gorgeous." She rolled her eyes. "Bah."

"Oh, you're terrifying, too," Phillip reassured her, while Hunter continued to stare. Phillip kicked him. "Tell her she's terrifying."

"Terrifying," Hunter repeated. "A hurricane. A volcano. An asteroid meaning certain doom."

"Majesty, he does say the sweetest things," Esmerelda replied.

"Oh, off with you both." Ravenna waved them both away. "So, would either of you care for a drink?"

"Bourbon, if you have it."

"Of course I have it. Or would you rather have a shot of pálinka? It's a Hungarian plum spirit that will knock you on your ass."

"Yes, we'll have that," Hunter agreed for both of them.

Phillip was glad to have something to steady him because he was having not only second thoughts about asking

Ravenna for her help, but also thirds and fourths. Fifths, if they stood there long enough.

He downed the spirit with a practiced hand, and it burned all the way to his gut, but left a surprisingly welcome and sweet warmth in its path.

"So tell me," Ravenna said after she'd downed her own shot. "Why have you come to see me?"

"Hunter wanted to tell you that you're beautiful, but I wanted to . . . we wanted to first give you this basket."

Hunter handed her the basket, and in such proximity to the Evil Queen, the Medusa plant awakened and stretched its bloom out toward her.

"Oh, what a darling!" Ravenna exclaimed.

Its leaves wiggled and shimmied like snakes, and Ravenna stroked them. The thing made a sound like it was purring.

"I do love her!" Ravenna looked at the remaining contents of the basket. "Absinthe truffles and champagne? Good choices. Expensive choices." She put the basket down and gave the plant an absent stroke. "My guess is you've come to ask for magic."

Phillip felt sheepish. Embarrassed. But he'd come this far. "I've tried everyone and everything. Except you."

"I really hope you don't expect me to kiss you again, because definitely not. Sorry. I know everyone in town gets a kick out of kissing the frog, but not a chance."

Phillip laughed, a strange sense of relief washing over him. "No, not at all. It's true love's kiss that'll break my curse, and we both know that's not a thing that happens. At least, not for people like me and you."

"Indeed." She popped a truffle in her mouth.

"But I never asked if maybe you have some kind of magic that can break the curse. A spell? A workaround? I don't know. I'm sick of being a frog, though."

"Aren't the godmothers going to do some kind of frog-kissing booth at this spring carnival? Wouldn't you rather wait for that? Do they know you're here?"

"No," Hunter answered. "In fact, they specifically told us not to ask you."

"But we agreed if they haven't been able to break this curse in all this time, I'm going to try every avenue, and they don't get to tell me not to."

"That's reasonable." Ravenna nodded. "But you know that dark magic has a price. It always has a price, and it's never something that, when push comes to shove, you find you can make yourself pay. All the stories around these parts end with defeating the dark magic. With breaking contracts. Can I trust you?"

"You absolutely can," Phillip promised. "You know what else happens in those stories? They meet their true loves. If I'd met my true love, this wouldn't actually be a problem. Can you help me?"

She narrowed her eyes.

"I suppose I should say, will you help me?"

"The first one was correct. These fairies with their curses and their blessings are a giant pain in the ass." She turned to the flying fox. "Esmerelda, fetch me my gazing ball."

Esmerelda flew off and returned a short time later with a crystal ball and set it on the table in front of her mistress.

"Let's see what our options are, shall we?"

Phillip was surprised it had been this easy. It made him wonder why he hadn't done it long ago.

She leaned over the ball and cupped it with her pale hands. The dark sphere began to swirl with a mist of greens, blues, and purple. It was like a storm in the palm of her hand.

"Mmm," she said. "I see."

The swirling continued, and there was lightning and thunder in the little glass ball.

"Show him," she said, and held out the ball to Phillip.

He took it, and suddenly, he could see a whole world inside the ball. He could see himself. He was dressed in a tux and walking down a red carpet toward . . . Grammy.

Grammy from the bakeshop stood in a tux with a bow tie, and her long white hair bound up in a bun. The godmothers were flittering here and there, and . . .

It was a wedding.

This was his answer? A wedding? This was as useless as that True Love's Kiss nonsense.

He pinched his fingers over the bridge of his nose. "I know that love is the answer. This isn't helpful."

"Look again," Hunter advised.

Phillip looked again and realized the bride wore lavender. When he tried to see any distinguishing marks, all he could see was her dress.

And Esmerelda flying next to them.

He almost dropped the ball.

"No, that's not . . ."

Ravenna just watched him, obviously waiting for him to come to the correct conclusion.

"That can't be right," Phillip tried again.

"Listen, pal. I don't make the rules. This is what the ball says. That's your answer. Take it or leave it."

"What? What does the ball say? I can't see anything," Hunter said.

"I . . . wow, so I really don't want to offend you, but . . . ," Phillip started. "I'm already a frog, please don't smite me."

"Whyever would you think I'd be offended? That implies I'd be game for this little stunt."

"Oh, yeah. You're right. I'm a total dick. Still. Maybe I deserve to stay a frog."

"Will someone please tell me what the hell is going on?" Hunter growled.

At Hunter's growl, Ravenna blushed and then coughed.

"Well, there might be a wedding in our future. At least that's what the ball says."

Hunter looked the way Phillip felt: like he'd been bashed in the face with a shovel.

"I don't know what to tell you, boys. We asked, it answered. I told you there was a price."

"Always a price," Esmerelda repeated.

"You two must be going. Great pâté, but I've got to motor if I want to get my beauty sleep. Off you go."

"Ravenna, you can't just drop that kind of a bomb and then . . ."

"Ah, but I can. Go on. There's the door."

They found themselves being shuffled out the door, and it slammed behind them.

"What the hell was that?" Hunter asked.

"Obviously not the answer we were looking for." He clapped his friend on the shoulder. "Except you did get an invite to tea on Thursday."

"If you're going to marry her, it would be pretty pointless, wouldn't it?"

"I'm not going to marry Ravenna. She doesn't want to marry me. The crystal ball is cracked."

"Phillip," Hunter began.

"I don't want to hear another word about it. Petty was right. We shouldn't have come. At least, not about my curse. Just think about Thursday."

But what if Ravenna was the only way he could be free?

Looking at his best friend, he knew that wasn't an option he could take.

Hunter had been alone for a long time. He deserved to be happy. Even if that meant Phillip had to give up his only chance at breaking the curse.

He could eat a few more dragonfly wings. After all, Hunter would do it for him.

Chapter 6

Cinderella and Fella was the local dress and tux shop run by one Rosebud Briar, who seemed to be an absolute goddess with a needle and thread.

The shop itself was full of what Zuri liked to call wedding magic.

A lot of dress shops had a certain scent that she wouldn't quite call musty, but they were unpleasant. Cinderella and Fella smelled like spring and flowers. Not like perfume, but actual blooms. Sometimes it was lilacs, sometimes it was jasmine. It was always relaxing.

Rosebud had the windows open, allowing a gentle breeze into the shop that brought with it the melodious sounds of songbirds.

Zuri was sitting at the planning table drinking a cappuccino and munching on a wedding cake cupcake for breakfast while perusing the various dress styles that Fairy Godmothers, Inc., wanted to show to each bride.

She had pictures of each bride, examples of their styles, and pictures of their wish lists, and it was easy to imagine the women in all these beautiful dresses.

Helping with the dress was one of Zuri's favorite parts of the job. Some brides didn't want the wedding planner's help, but for those who did, Zuri just loved it. So much went into choosing a dress.

It wasn't only about how the dress looked. It was about

the memories that would be interwoven in the stitches. It was about the past, the present, and the future. It was about how the bride felt in the dress and about fulfilling a dream.

Zuri sighed with happiness and took a sip of her coffee.

"Someone is happy this morning," Petty said as she compared two shades of pink ribbon against each other.

"Oh, yes! Do tell," Jonquil prompted.

"I just remembered how much I love my job. This is my favorite part. The dress!"

Rosebud smiled at her. "It's my favorite part, too."

"No, no, love. Maybe baby blue?" Bluebonnet said to Petty, and handed her another ribbon. "My favorite part is the cake."

"Cake is good, too." Petty nodded and put the ribbon samples down next to one another. "But surely you have some feedback about the favor samples?"

"It was a great way to meet everyone in town, that was for sure." Zuri took another bite of her cupcake.

"We're dying to know, what happened when you tried the wish coin?" Jonquil asked.

She looked around the table and saw only excited faces. Even Rosebud. It was as if they all expected the coin to work somehow. Zuri supposed it couldn't hurt to indulge them.

"I made my wish at the fountain on the way to the B and B," she began.

And everyone leaned in closer around the table.

It was silly. So silly. As if wish coins could actually make wishes come true. But she found their excitement to be infectious, and she grinned.

"Well, I made my wish and right after I did, two things happened."

"Two? Oh my!" Bluebonnet fanned herself as if Zuri had said something scandalous.

She found herself giggling, but then composed herself. "I got a text from my ex. He wants to talk. I don't know if I should respond or not. My sister would tell me to light my phone on fire and get a new one, with a new number."

Petty nodded. "I second this. Unless he was your wish?"

"I don't know what my wish was."

"What?" Jonquil asked. "How do you not know what you wished for?"

"Can I say? Or will it affect the potency of my wish?" Zuri asked.

"No, you can tell us." Bluebonnet nodded.

"I asked for my heart's desire."

Petty huffed.

Jonquil sighed.

Bluebonnet shook her head slowly.

Rosebud, however, nodded. "I see how that would be complicated. Sometimes, we don't always know our heart's desire. Or we do, but we're afraid to admit it."

"I second your sister. I think you should light your phone on fire. We could give it a Viking funeral tonight, if you like," Petty said.

"Hold on just a sec. I think maybe she should answer him," Jonquil said.

"Whyever would she do that? After what he did? He is not Happily Ever After material. You do know that, don't you, dear?" Bluebonnet asked.

"I . . . I suppose I do." She pressed her lips together.

"But?" Rosebud prompted gently.

"But . . . when I was a kid, I had these fashion plates. You'd take the plates and put them under the paper and then use a crayon to transfer the figure from the plates. You could mix and match to make all kinds of different outfits. Alec was like that. The plates were my dreams and he fit with all of them."

"I see," Rosebud said.

Zuri got the feeling that maybe she really did.

"What else happened?" Jonquil asked. "Did you see the frog?"

"I definitely saw the frog. He was ridiculous. I didn't know frogs could get that big outside of the Jurassic period," Zuri said.

The table laughed.

"And I met Phillip Charming," she said in a rush.

"Did you, now?" Jonquil asked. "How did that go?"

"Well, he's definitely not my heart's desire. And neither is Alec. The last thing I'd wish for is a man."

"Too true," Bluebonnet encouraged. "But do tell us about Phillip. Was he . . . princely?"

"Quite. He walked me to the B and B and got me set up in the most beautiful room I've ever seen in my life. I don't know if I could even call it a room. It was more like a penthouse suite. I think he called them the Queen's Chambers, or something."

"Oh, really?" Petty grinned. "I see."

"Then what happened?" Rosebud asked.

"We just talked. Had hot chocolate. No, correction. Mayan drinking chocolate. He was nice."

"And funny?" Petty prompted. "I always thought he was funny."

"Yes, he was funny. If I was looking to date someone, I would be interested." When grins erupted all around the table, she reiterated, "But I'm not."

"No one says you have to date, dear. You could just . . ." Petty looked at her pointedly. "You know."

Bluebonnet agreed with a hearty nod of her head.

"You're worse than my sister. I don't want that, either. My heart is tender and looking for something that doesn't hurt. But just because it doesn't hurt, that doesn't make it a good idea."

"Wise." Rosebud nodded.

"Did you kiss the frog?" Jonquil demanded.

"I did not. No way."

"You really should. We all have," Rosebud said.

"What if he did turn into a prince?" Petty replied.

"What if he did? Wouldn't we have to evict poor Phillip from the castle? Princes need castles. So, see, it's just a bad idea," Zuri protested.

Then she remembered she didn't believe in fairy tales, or princes, and she definitely didn't believe frogs could turn into princes.

"Just give it a shot. For us?" Petty asked. "Consider it the last favor to try. Because we are going to have a frog-kissing booth at the spring carnival."

"If I'd known that kissing frogs would be part of this gig, I wouldn't have applied." Zuri laughed.

"Just this one. This one time," Jonquil encouraged.

"If I say yes, can we talk about these weddings instead of my apocalypse of a love life?"

"Oh, we suppose," Petty said.

"Fine. I'll kiss the frog. Now, what do we think of these dresses for the Seymour wedding?" She held up the sketches next to the bride's picture.

"Very fine," Jonquil said with a nod. "We've had another booking, though, and we're going to need you to focus exclusively on it. I have the file back at the office. It's the Petrovsky-Markhoff wedding."

"Yes, dear. It's kind of a last-minute booking, and they're going to need your wonder wedding powers the most." Petty nodded.

Markhoff. Why did that name sound familiar? Zuri couldn't quite place it. The buzz of familiarity was gone as quickly as it had come because her brain wouldn't stop replaying the godmothers' advice about Alec.

"So you really think I should answer Alec's text?"

"Yes, dear. You should. You didn't really get any closure, did you? Just a wedding dress on fire, your life in ashes, and he walked away free and clear. You didn't get a chance to express your feelings. Or even, really, to feel them." Jonquil reached across the table and squeezed her hand. "You were thinking of the bride. Of your business. But you didn't think about you."

"You know what? I think you should take today and go rest. Tomorrow is going to be very busy. The Markhoff party will be here then, and it's going to be rather busy," Petty said. "We'll send the file over for you to look at tonight."

Everyone nodded.

"We can meet back here tomorrow morning with the Markhoffs," Rosebud said.

"You could stop at the fountain on your way back," Jonquil said.

"I am not kissing any more frogs."

"Just one more," Jonquil said with a grin.

"You guys are awful," Zuri said, shaking her head.

Petty nodded. "We're great with peer pressure. If that doesn't work, we'll pull the well-meaning little old lady card."

Zuri couldn't help but laugh. She hadn't been here very long, but she already adored the godmothers.

"Plus, you need to call your sister and tell her all about Ever After. We'd love to have her visit as soon as possible," Jonquil added.

"We would?" Bluebonnet looked at her sisters. "Oh, *yes*. Yes, we would."

"Are you three up to something?" Zuri studied each of their kindly faces in turn.

Rosebud handed her another cupcake. "They're always up to something. You might as well just get right with it. Have a snack for the road."

Suddenly, a chittering squirrel was in the open window, and he kicked one of the songbirds off the ledge.

"Oh no!" Rosebud cried, and ran to grab a broom. "Whatever you do, don't let the squirrels have any of Gwen's cupcakes. It turns them into rabid little ninjas."

The squirrel stomped his feet, like he thought he was going to square off with Rosebud. Then he looked at Zuri.

She'd swear the little beast narrowed his eyes like a laser sight on her cupcake.

Instead of doubting what her own eyes told her, she shoved the whole cupcake in her mouth at once.

The little squirrel's mouth fell open, and the songbirds he'd displaced began pecking at his head. Rosebud waved her broom like it was a sword, and the poor little thing ran away, chittering angrily.

"I don't know what she's been putting in these things, but I swear." Rosebud shook her head.

"Hmm. I just wonder," Petty said, smirking.

"Might be all that unresolved sexual tension." Bluebonnet nodded. "In some cultures, they believe that the chef's or baker's emotions are absorbed by the food they make and can be tasted by their patrons."

Zuri liked that idea. Not the unresolved sexual tension, because who needed that kind of complication? But the idea that her hands could fill something she made with her emotions. Like love, or hope. All the good things that families and friends shared around a table of food.

"Wouldn't that be wonderful if it were true? If people I love could taste the things I want for them? Or if guests at a wedding could taste the love in the cake?" Zuri sighed.

"Except for those little bastard squirrels harassing my birds. Little shits. I give them their own feeder. I give them water. I brush their tails if they get matted or tumble through a briar patch, and this is the thanks I get?"

The birds sang back at her, and she just nodded at them.

"What are you waiting for? Go on. I'm sure the squirrels won't bother you now that you've finished your cupcake," Petty said.

"I'm going. I'm going. Geez." Zuri gathered up her things. "But don't forget to send me the Markhoff file. I want to be prepared tomorrow."

"As if we'd forget," Bluebonnet said. "Go on."

Zuri headed out of the shop and followed the pink stone path toward the B and B. She wondered if she'd see Phillip again. She wouldn't mind another dose of drinking chocolate and conversation.

For a moment, she considered the godmothers' suggestion.

Her body screamed yes.

Her heart knew it was a bad idea.

Phillip was incredibly handsome, polite . . . and his hands. Dear God, his hands. She knew he was probably richer than Midas, but he had the hands of a workingman. They were broad, and calloused, and they looked strong. She couldn't help but imagine what they'd feel like on her body.

It was his smile, really. Not the big, toothy grin, but that sort of half smirk that just made her panties fall off all by themselves.

No, she really shouldn't be having these kinds of thoughts about her landlord.

Oh dear. That wasn't the thought to help her, either, because she suddenly had a lot of ideas about paying rent.

Which was stupid, because she didn't pay rent. It was part of her pay from FGI.

At least, she consoled herself, she was able to think about intimacies with another man after what happened with Alec. That was a plus.

Her thoughts took a more serious turn. Jonquil was right. She hadn't really allowed herself the time or the space to grieve Alec. Not just Alec, but her hopes and dreams. The future she'd let herself imagine with him. It was about letting go of more than just a relationship. It was about part and parcel of all that came with the relationship.

Zuri wandered up to the fountain and she saw the frog was in his usual place.

He looked at her.

She looked at him.

Then his long tongue flicked out like a whip, and he ate a butterfly.

"Ugh, no. I just can't."

The frog cocked his head to the opposite side, as if to answer her.

It occurred to her the animals in Ever After were unlike any she'd seen before. Perhaps because the town was so in tune with nature and people walked everywhere. They were used to each other.

She sat on the side of the fountain and pulled out her phone, looking at the text from Alec.

She texted back: *Why?*

Her phone rang immediately.

She debated not answering it. Zuri was sure her sister would tell her she could get all the closure she needed by herself.

Zuri swiped to answer the call, but she didn't speak.

"Zuri? Are you there?"

The sound of his voice was familiar and foreign at the same time. Once upon a time, she'd been ecstatic to hear his voice. Now, she didn't feel much of anything. She'd thought it would hurt, or would at least be bittersweet.

"Yeah, I'm here, Alec."

"Can we get together and talk tonight?"

"We're talking now."

"I have some things to say to you that I should say in person."

When she didn't answer, he spoke again. "I'm sure you have some things to say to me, and I owe you the opportunity to say them in person if you want to."

Did she want to?

"Tonight isn't good. I'm working."

"I'm leaving early tomorrow. One of my fraternity brothers is getting married. So I'll be gone for a few weeks."

A few weeks? That sounded like a lie. "It doesn't take a few weeks to get married, Alec. Try again."

"I understand why you don't trust me. It's going to be one of those destination weddings, and everyone is invited to come for the planning through to the wedding. Since I'm the best man, I have to be there. At least tell me the door is open. Just to talk."

She was probably the dumbest creature on two feet to give him the answer she did, but it was out of her mouth before she could stop herself. "Okay. But just to talk."

The frog made a distressed sound. She turned to look at him and found him not on the mermaid's bosom but sitting right next to her.

"Thank you, Zuri. You won't regret it."

"I already do," she said with a sigh. "We should probably hang up while we're both ahead."

"Can I just say that I miss—"

"No!" she interrupted him. "You don't get to say that."

"Okay, Zuri. We'll talk soon. Text or call anytime you want. Even if you just want to call me an asshole."

"Asshole," she mumbled.

"Do you feel better?"

She could hear the mirth in his voice, and it was contagious. Zuri almost laughed, too. "Don't make me laugh while I'm angry with you. You almost destroyed my career. You don't get to just make me laugh and it's all forgotten. It was selfish and shitty and . . . and . . ."

"You're right. I'm sorry."

"For what. Say it."

"Everything?"

"I want a detailed list."

"Can I work on it? I need to make sure I cover all my bases. Next time we talk, I'll tell you everything I'm sorry for."

Was this closure?

"I guess. Whatever. I have to go." She hung up before she could do anything else stupid.

Zuri looked down at the frog, and he looked back up at her.

His round face seemed to say, *Well, it can't get any worse, can it?*

But couldn't it? It could, she was sure.

"In for a penny, or a wish coin, am I right?" She held out her hands for him.

The frog hopped into the bowl of her hands, and she almost dropped him. He was a heavy boy.

She lifted him up to her lips and cringed as she puckered up and dropped a kiss on the top of his head. Zuri expected him to be slimy, but he wasn't slimy at all. His head was a little cool, but not clammy or damp, thank all the powers in the universe.

"I hope you're not that kind of frog that's going to get me stoned."

Zuri studied him, and he continued to meet her gaze. Zuri swore she could see human understanding in his eyes.

Only, that was crazy.

Just like kissing a frog and expecting him to turn into a prince.

"Sorry, buddy. I tried." She put him back down into the fountain, and he hopped into the water.

Zuri looked down at her phone and considered.

If this wasn't the universe trying to tell her something, she didn't know what was.

Frogs did not turn into princes. Whether they were green and amphibian or the two-legged kind.

Chapter 7

Phillip had held on to the small hope that Zuri would be the one to break his curse.

Now, that hope had turned to dust.

She'd kissed him, and nothing.

Not that he'd expected it, after all these years. Only, the pull he'd felt between them had sparked a ridiculous flame of hope. Hope he should've known better than to have.

Phillip still found himself intrigued by the enigmatic Zuri and wanted to know more about her. He enjoyed their conversation, and he wanted more.

He also wanted to explore the other feelings between them. He knew he wasn't the only one burning in that fire. He'd be more than happy to be her rebound man. Only, that thought left him cold. Phillip didn't want to be a rebound, if he was honest. He wanted to get to know Zuri; he wanted . . .

Well, what he wanted wasn't on the docket anytime soon.

A knock on his door jarred him from his thoughts. It was late for visitors, and as far as he knew, Hunter had gone out for the night.

He opened the door, surprised to see Petty standing there, looking as fresh and bright as she had the last time he'd seen her.

"I have a file for Zuri. Can you make sure she gets it?" Petty shoved the pink, glittery file folder at him.

"You know, you could give it to her yourself. She's just down the hall."

"Is she? Hmm." Petty grinned at him.

"Your matchmaking efforts have not gone unnoticed, woman, but you should know, it's for naught."

"For naught, eh? Why is that? Don't you think she's beautiful, smart, kind, and all-around wonderful?" Petty put her hand on her ample hip.

"I do, I do."

"That's what we matchmakers like to hear best," Petty teased.

"Unfortunately, she's not the one."

"Why?"

"I don't know *why*. If I knew why, I could fix it." Wasn't that obvious?

"I mean, how do you know?" Petty demanded.

"She kissed me today. At the fountain. Nothing." Phillip sighed. "And she's still talking to her ex."

"Ex, schmex." She waved her hand. "Whatever. Things aren't always what they seem, Phillip. Don't lose hope."

"Petty, I'll be honest. Right now, hope hurts a lot more than despair ever could."

She patted his cheek. "It'll all work out, if you just trust me."

He studied her and decided to confess what he'd done. "I might've done what I wasn't supposed to."

"Which time?"

"We went to Ravenna."

Petty snorted. "Of course you did. Well? What was her answer?"

"A wedding."

"Excuse me, what?" Petty wiggled her nose to adjust her glasses.

"A wedding. Her crystal ball showed me an image of a wedding with a bride in a lavender dress and Esmerelda flying over the bride's shoulder."

Petty gasped. "You can't be serious."

"I haven't decided what I'm going to do."

"Not that. Marrying Ravenna is not the answer. I do promise you that."

Phillip didn't want to marry Ravenna, and Ravenna didn't want to marry him, but he didn't want to be a frog, either. He had a choice to make, and no one could make it for him except himself. He knew Petty meant well.

"Anyway, will you see that your guest gets this?"

He took the folder. "Yeah."

Petty disappeared in a puff of pink glitter, and he sneezed.

"I wish she'd stop doing that," he mumbled.

He didn't mind the excuse to see Zuri again. It probably wasn't the brightest course of action, either, but all his choices at the moment sucked.

He ran a hand through his hair and walked down the long hallway to her door, where he knocked lightly.

She opened the door, and his mouth went dry. He forgot what he'd come for. Hell, he was pretty sure he'd forgotten his own name.

Zuri was wearing leggings and a soft, lavender, seemingly cashmere sweater that clung to her in all the right places. Her hair was pulled back under a kerchief, giving him a view of the tender line of her neck.

She smiled. "Hi."

What was he doing?

Why had he come?

He was holding something, and he held it up in front of himself dumbly.

She arched a brow. "That's very sparkly."

He looked at it, then he looked at her, then back to the file. His brain finally took pity on him and switched into gear. "Petty dropped this off for you. She asked me to deliver it personally."

"Did she? If she were here, why didn't she deliver it?" She

accepted the file. "Not that I'm complaining about a visit from my new friend."

"I sense the wheels of matchmaking are furiously turning," he said.

"Do they ever stop turning with those three?" She stepped to the side. "If you wanted to come in and we could have more drinking chocolate, I wouldn't mind it. I've had one hell of a day."

"Me too." He followed her inside and closed the door behind him. "You can go first. Tell me about your day."

"I kissed a frog," she blurted.

He nodded. "You're not alone. Everyone tries. I'm sure the frog, if he really is a prince, appreciates it." The words were cold on his tongue.

"Does he, though? I mean, he didn't seem to be in distress."

"Kisses from a beautiful woman don't seem to be the kind of thing to be distressed over." He flashed her a grin and went to the screen on the refrigerator. He typed in the unnecessary request for the drinking chocolate.

The castle knew what he wanted and would deliver, but now was not the time to clue Zuri into the realities of magic.

She snorted. "Oh, please. I thought we were past that."

"Past me thinking you're beautiful? Nope. We'll never get past that."

She gave him a shy smile. "I mean, if you insist, who am I to disagree?"

"That's the spirit. I ordered some drinking chocolate."

"You could build up the fire, too. If you were feeling inclined." She sat down on the couch and thumbed through the file Petty had sent her.

He was happy to start the fire and get it roaring nice and high, filling the room with soft light and just enough warmth to make it cozy.

"Everything in this town is crazy. Even the weddings.

These people want me to pull off a wedding, from beginning to vows, in three weeks."

"You can do it."

"How do you know?" She grinned.

He sat down on the couch next to her. "Because I know the godmothers. They wouldn't have hired you if you couldn't. Nor would they have asked it of you."

Phillip was reminded of Petty's words earlier. Telling him that things weren't as they seemed.

"Thanks for the vote of confidence. They sent me home early today to 'rest' so I'd be ready to start kicking butt on this tomorrow."

"So what was the bad part?"

"I feel weird talking about this with you."

"Why? Is it about your ex? It's fine." He shrugged. "I like you, Zuri. I want to be your friend. Friends tell each other things, right?"

There was a knock on the door, and Phillip got up to answer it, to get the drinking chocolate.

He brought it back over to the couch and gave Zuri her cup, before sitting down next to her. Just as she was about to speak, her phone buzzed with a request for a video chat.

"It's my sister."

"I'd love to meet her," he said.

"Really?" Zuri held up the phone and swiped to accept the request. "Hey, Zeva. Say hi to my company, Phillip Charming." She turned the phone to Phillip.

He was surprised to see Zuri's mirror image looking back at them.

"Hello, Prince Charming," Zeva said with a big grin.

Startled at the use of his real title, he said, "Hello yourself, Zuri's pretty sister."

Zeva laughed. "You're a smooth one, aren't you? Is that hot chocolate? I cannot wait to visit your castle."

"You're welcome whenever you'd like to come," he said.

"I didn't send you pics of my new place yet, but trust me when I say, you could stay with me and not see me for days," Zuri said. "So, come."

"I do have some vacation time coming, but I don't want to leave the kids."

"You have children? Bring them. Ever After is a great place for kids," Phillip said.

"There's a lot of them, and they aren't mine." Zeva cocked her head to the side. "Correction, they're kind of mine. I work for St. Marigold's Orphanage."

"Bring them, too. I'm sure we could find something for them to do. The godmothers would get a kick out of them." He looked at Zuri. "It would also give them something to do besides bother us."

"Bother you?" Zeva asked.

"Matchmaking," Zuri replied.

"Oh, the worst of the worst." Zeva snorted. "But if you're serious, I will have those kids out there in a heartbeat."

"We should probably wait until the wedding fury has died down just a bit. The castle is mostly booked, but we could work something out for the fall, maybe?" Phillip said.

"When are you coming?" Zuri asked. "I need my sister."

"Okay, okay. I'll be there soon for a long weekend. Anyway, I'll call you back later. Love you, wombmate!" Zeva hung up before Zuri could argue.

"I didn't know you're a twin."

"Zeva is amazing. I am so lucky to have her as a sister."

"She seems like it."

"It was kind of you to offer to help her with the kids."

"Not at all. I love kids. Mostly." He grinned again.

He found himself doing that a lot with Zuri, smiling.

"Do you want them?"

Her question stopped him short and he put his hot chocolate down. "I haven't really thought about it. It didn't seem like finding someone to love me was even an option, so I hadn't considered having children."

Zuri's wide dark eyes filled with some soft emotion and he immediately regretted his words.

"I didn't mean it like . . . that sounded pathetic."

"It's not pathetic. We all have our crosses to bear."

"There are bigger problems in the world than if someone gives me the time of day."

"Touch, relationships, and emotional validation are all part of the hierarchy of needs. Zeva has a PsyD, and she'll tell you the same. So it's not wrong to feel things associated with those needs not being met."

"It just feels petulant when you're telling me about these kids who don't have families to focus on my own little problems. I've got a family. I've got a roof. I've got food. My needs are met."

She put her chocolate on the table and turned to look at him, her hands resting on his. "Are they?"

He felt he could trust her. He could be honest with her. "No."

"Me either. Not for a long time."

The moment seemed frozen in time, the heat that flared between them growing to an ever bigger blaze.

He took her hands in his. "So what are you suggesting we do about it?"

"It's the tritest thing ever to trite. I hate even saying it, but I know it's what I need. I think it's what you need, too."

"Say it. Whatever it is. Unless it's a punch to the face."

"Contact. Connection." She seemed to be holding her breath, waiting for his reply.

"Come here," he said, realizing what she wanted.

She wanted to be held. She wanted to be told it was all going to be okay. She wanted to feel protected.

He knew that, because those were the things he wanted, too.

He wanted to feel like he mattered. Phillip hadn't had that in a long time.

She allowed him to pull her close, and she rested her head on his chest, her arms around his waist. She smelled so good. He couldn't quite place the scent, but it was soft, feminine, and what he imagined heaven smelled like.

He drew his hand up and down her back in a gentle, soothing motion.

Phillip was thinking about how nice it was when he heard her sniff.

"Zuri?"

"I haven't had this in a long time."

"Me either," he confessed.

She felt so good pressed against him, and not just because she was a three-alarm fire in that sweater.

"Jonquil told me I needed to grieve, and I didn't feel anything for so long. Not even when I heard his voice today. He called me. We talked. I felt nothing. Now, I'm here with this hot guy holding me, and I wanna cry about it." She sniffed again.

"It's okay. Didn't you just tell me to feel what I need to feel? Same goes, princess."

Staying green didn't seem like such a big deal if it meant he could have this when he was a man.

The logical part of his brain told him he needed to reverse that train right back into the station because he just met her. Just because they were both lonely wasn't an excuse to imagine whatever was happening between them had some kind of future.

He was cursed.

She was brokenhearted.

These were not the ingredients for happiness.

"Tell me something good. What made you decide to turn the castle into a B and B?"

"It was the godmothers' idea. Our little town was dying, and they decided we could be a premier wedding destination. We're lucky it worked."

"What did you do before that?"

What did he do before that? Besides feel sorry for himself? Not much, if he was honest. "Eh, well. I was still deciding on my path. Did you always want to be a wedding planner?"

"From the time I was a little girl. I designed weddings in my Barbie mansion, and I catered them, too. We drove my mama nuts with the cupcake wedding cake, and I made steaks for all the guests by slicing hot dogs as thin as I could get them. With my mama's razor, of course." She laughed. "Oh, she put up with so much."

"Are you close to your parents?"

"I was close with my mother. My father, not so much. He wasn't distant, or a bad father. He just worked a lot. He died in a plane crash when we were ten, and my mother passed a few years ago. So it's just Zeva and me. Are you close with your parents?"

"I was. Yes. They've passed, too. A long time ago." He missed them more than he could say.

"You're alone in the world?"

The way she said it made it sound so sad. It wasn't. He'd had his parents for a long time. If Ever After had been enchanted sooner, he'd still have them.

"No, I'm not alone in the world. I've got the godmothers, and the rest of the town. We're all very close, and no matter what happens, we take care of one another. I've also got my best friend, Hunter. He's kind of like a brother to me. More, even."

"I don't think I've met him yet. What does he do in Ever After? Everyone is so like their job. What's his?"

"A beast of all trades, you might say." He continued stroking her back gently. "He's not usually around in the daytime.

He's got a bit of a . . . skin condition. The people here are used to him, but he's not sure how all the tourists are going to feel, so he keeps to the dungeons."

"Dungeons? Of course the castle has dungeons. I'd love to meet him. I can promise, I'm not going to be a jerk about a skin condition."

"It's severe."

"Consider me warned. If he doesn't want to meet anyone new yet, I understand. When he does, I hope I'll get to meet him."

He wondered if he could trust her with that. She said she understood, but once she saw him . . .

"It occurs to me that we're in the same predicament, here. We don't know how to trust each other."

"I think we're doing great."

"I don't."

"Why's that?" She tilted her head up to look at him.

Her eyes were wide, and her pupils dilated. Her lips looked dewy and soft, and he knew she'd taste like the drinking chocolate.

"All I can think about is kissing you. That's not very trustworthy, is it?"

"Maybe I'm not trustworthy, either, because all I can think about is wishing you'd kiss me."

He bent his head, and just as their lips were about to brush, Phillip felt the familiar tightness in his skin that signified his transformation.

He looked out the windows to see the sky was streaked with fingers of lavender and gold. Dawn approached. Phillip hadn't realized how much time had passed. Or maybe it was his curse kicking things into high gear. It couldn't let him be happy. Not for a single moment.

"I can't. I want to, but I can't." He launched himself from the couch and scrambled toward the door. "Shit!"

"Phillip? What's wrong?"

"I—" A horrible sound like a ribbit welled up in his throat. He tried to choke it back, but his mouth opened and . . . the only word for it was *blorped*. He *blorped*, and it was like a *ribbit* mashed up with a burp from hell.

Oh God, it tasted garlicky, like dragonfly wings.

Zuri stepped back from him. "What the hell was that? Are you okay?"

He shook his head, and his cheeks billowed out, and he did the only thing he could.

He ran.

Phillip could've sworn he heard Zuri's say, "Figures. I find a man I want to kiss and I make him sick."

Chapter 8

Spread out in the boardroom at Fairy Godmothers, Inc., Zuri refused to think about the night previous.

What had she been thinking anyway, to decide it was a good idea to get mixed up with a man? Especially Phillip Charming?

Wait, hadn't she just told herself she wasn't going to think of it?

Yet, there it was, twirling around in her mind like a jump rope from hell, and she couldn't stop with her mental double Dutch.

She tried to center herself and think about the meeting with Anna Petrovsky and Jordan Markhoff. Zuri was irritated they expected FGI to be able to deliver a wedding in three weeks, but she supposed for what they were paying, most anything should be possible.

She cleared her throat and then took a sip of her coffee, hoping to clear away the slight scratch in the back of her throat.

One might even say she had a frog in her throat.

Zuri tried not to snort out loud. She needed a cookie.

Petty appeared, an answer to her prayer. "Almost forgot the chocolate chip breakfast cookies."

"Breakfast cookies? Isn't that any cookie you eat for breakfast?" Zuri asked.

"Yes, definitely. But these actually have more protein. Gwen was worried we weren't feeding you well. Too much sugar." Petty winked.

"Calories don't count in Ever After, am I right?" She bit into the cookie and immediately felt fortified.

Petty turned to look over her shoulder at her own hip and wiggled it. "I don't know about that, but I'm fine with what I'm packing."

Zuri couldn't help the full-bodied cackle that erupted from her. "You should be." She ate another bite. "While we wait for the Markhoff people, tell me why you and your sisters never got married."

A wistful look crossed Petty's face. "None of us ever met the one, I suppose."

"That's the saddest thing I've ever heard."

"Is it? Because you were just saying that—"

"Oh, hush." She sipped her coffee. "You're not allowed to use my own arguments against me yet."

Petty cackled. "At least you admit it."

"No, but really. Tell me. Wasn't there ever someone?"

"Don't worry about us, dearie. We've had our adventures. Some of us continue to have adventures." She shared a conspiratorial wink. "We have so much love to share with our charges, our families. With each other. It will happen when it's right."

"Hmm. Will it? Is that why you keep trying to push me together with Phillip? Or why you keep trying to set Gwen up?"

Petty pointed her finger and opened her mouth to speak but then closed it. She nodded knowingly.

"See what I did, there?" Zuri snickered.

Jonquil and Bluebonnet popped their heads in.

"Did I just see Petunia Blossom with nothing to say?" Jonquil trilled.

"She got me." Petty shrugged.

"Wonders never cease. You'll have to tell me how you did it." Bluebonnet suddenly perked. "After we speak with the wedding party! They're here!"

"Are you going to glitter-bomb them like you did me?" Zuri asked.

"I hadn't thought of it. We should, though." Petty scrambled to the door.

"No, you shouldn't!" Zuri called after her.

Of course, the godmothers did it anyway.

When the bride and groom walked in, they were covered in glitter. The bride was rubbing her hands over her face, and her features had screwed up in disdain.

"It got in my mouth." She kept swiping at her mouth, but then she paused. "Why does it taste like peach cobbler?"

"Edible glitter, my loves. Isn't it wonderful?" Bluebonnet beamed at them.

Zuri watched the godmothers work their magic on the couple and transform them into edible-glitter aficionados. The godmothers made a general fuss over the couple and got them settled in with champagne, chocolate-covered strawberries, and a plate of cookies, wedding cake cupcakes, and other treats.

"We're so pleased you've chosen FGI to plan your special day." Bluebonnet went on to introduce herself, her sisters, and Zuri.

Zuri took the opportunity to clear her throat again and take another sip of coffee. Bluebonnet refilled her cup.

"So tell me about your dream wedding," Zuri said.

The bride smiled softly and took Jordan's hand. "I want it to be a fairy tale, because that's what we have. I want our guests to experience our fairy tale, if that makes sense."

Zuri nodded. "It makes total sense that you want your loved ones to feel your Happily Ever After along with you. We can do that for you."

Zuri coughed again. "Excuse me. Sorry about that. I think a bit of cookie went down the wrong way." She took another drink. "Why don't you tell me your love story."

The happy couple looked at each other.

"You tell it," they said in unison, and then laughed.

"Okay," he said. "I'll tell it." Jordan kissed the back of her hand. "We met at an art show. As soon as I saw her, I knew she was the one." He looked up at Zuri. "As soon as that thought entered my head, I decided I'd been listening to too many of my sister's stories."

"And I thought he was handsome, but . . ." Anna laughed. "He was friends with a couple douchebags, so I mean, you know, you are who you hang with."

They laughed again.

"She lost her shoe. The heel broke, and she was so frustrated, she just took them both off and headed to the cab. I grabbed her shoes and followed her, and the cabbie said he wouldn't take her barefooted."

"Really? That's unusual," Zuri said.

"I know, right? But I think it was some kind of magic that he did, because I offered her a ride home, and instead of taking her home, we went for coffee and talked all night."

"That cherry pie was the worst thing I've ever tasted, but I didn't want the night to be over," Anna added.

"The coffee was basically motor oil poured over char, but I'll love that taste forever."

They looked over at each other, both wearing big smiles.

"And our first kiss tasted like plastic cherry pie and motor oil," Anna said.

They brushed their lips together in a light kiss that Zuri knew would've turned spicy had they been alone.

Zuri couldn't help but sigh. She also noticed the godmothers looking particularly pleased with themselves.

"We couldn't be happier for you," Petty said.

"It's funny how sometimes fate meddles in just the right way to get you to where you're supposed to be," Bluebonnet replied.

"I mean, what if that cabbie had been like every other driver out there and hadn't refused? You two might not have crossed paths again," Jonquil said.

"We would've found each other, eventually. I'm just glad it was sooner rather than later." Anna was still gazing into her love's eyes.

"More time with my best friend," Jordan said.

The godmothers sighed in unison.

Zuri sighed right along with them. This was just what she needed. She needed to see a true and honest love in the wild. Not in a book, not in a movie, but real people who'd decided they wanted to take this adventure together.

Just from looking at them, and the way they spoke, Zuri could almost swear that she could see a golden thread between them that bound their hearts together. Silly nonsense, she admitted to herself, but what better place for silly nonsense than a place like Ever After?

Zuri wanted to believe. She needed to believe.

Here was her proof, just when she needed it most.

Zuri was determined to give them their dream. No matter if it took a hundred long nights, she'd make it happen.

She squirmed in her chair as her legs started to itch. She would definitely not be wearing this brand of pantyhose ever again.

"Your story is beautiful, and I am so lucky to be part of it. We're going to make this happen for you. Your dream wedding in three weeks. It's a challenge, but I love a challenge. We have a fairy-tale package that includes the ceremony and the reception at the castle. Most brides choose to have the ceremony outdoors and when we tour the castle later today, I can show you the various spaces. We have the pumpkin-style

Cinderella carriage, and if you like, our dressmaker, Rose-bud, she can get you glass slippers."

Anna's face lit up. "Real glass slippers? Wouldn't they be . . . delicate?"

"Not at all. In fact, I have an idea for your special day. I was thinking, instead of walking down the aisle, you could re-enact the scene where the bride loses her slipper, and when your Prince Charming comes to the rescue, he gives you not only your slipper but also your ring. Then you could say your vows."

Petty clapped. "That is positively inspired!"

"I love it. I'd also like for our guests to be here for the spring carnival. Do you have the lodging space?" Anna asked hopefully.

"We definitely do," Jonquil said.

Zuri wasn't sure about that, but she decided that Jonquil probably knew better than Zuri did about their housing capacity.

"Oh, thank you! I knew you were the right choice to plan this wedding. We were thrilled to see you'd moved to Ever After."

Zuri blinked. "So you know about Chicago, and you still want me?"

She couldn't have been more stunned.

"It's because of Chicago we want you," Jordan said.

Anna nodded. "None of that was your fault. And the wedding, before the fire, was really beautiful. Or at least what we were able to stream. Jordan was supposed to be in that wedding, but we were in Bali. We want you to have your fairy tale, too."

Zuri tried not to jump to conclusions. She didn't want a pity plan, but the couple did seem genuinely in love, and she could tell they really wanted everything she had to offer.

That was when Zuri decided to trust.

Things in Ever After were good. She couldn't pretend like

Chicago hadn't happened. Or that Alec hadn't happened. She could only go forward and keep building on her foundations. Whether she liked it or not, Chicago and the Wedding That Wasn't were part of her past, part of the foundation of who she was. It was time to accept it and forge on.

"Let's not worry about mine. Let's just make sure you and your guests get the experience you've dreamed of," Zuri said.

"Speaking of," Jonquil jumped to her rescue. "Is the rest of the wedding party on the way? We'd like to get your measurements in with the dressmaker today, so after you choose your colors and your style, she can get started."

"Oh, yes! The best man should be here any minute," Jordan said. "The rest of the wedding party will be here this evening."

"Good, good," Jonquil said, and then turned to look at Zuri. "My dear, are you sure you're okay?"

Zuri was a little warm, but she'd chocked it up to all the caffeine she'd had that morning. "I'm fine."

Her phone buzzed, and she saw that it was Zeva.

"Will you excuse me a moment? I have to take this." She got up and headed just outside the door to the boardroom.

"Are you okay?" Zeva said with no preamble.

"Why is everyone asking me that? I'm fine." She cleared her throat again, and a spot in the middle of her back began to itch like the devil.

"You're not fine. I feel it. I'm coming." Zeva hung up before Zuri could say anything else.

When she went back into the conference room, everyone in the room stopped what they were doing and turned to look at her.

Anna's mouth fell open, and her jaw worked, but no sound emerged.

"What?" Zuri's cheek began to itch and when she reached up to brush away whatever errant bit of hair that had dared to be out of place, her fingers met a strange bump.

"Oh dear!" Petty gasped.

"Not good. Not good a'tall." Bluebonnet got up and walked toward her slowly.

"By the powers," Jonquil gasped. "Lord, child. Don't touch it."

Suddenly, her whole body itched. It was as if she were one giant, angry mosquito bite. She wanted to scratch her face off.

"What's happening?" Zuri asked, trying to remain calm. Then she realized it was going to get a lot worse before it got better because Zeva had felt it and it had activated that twin connection, which was almost magical.

"I think it's an allergic reaction," Petty said to Anna and Jordan. "I'm sure you're fine and there's nothing to worry about."

"I just hope she's okay," Jordan said. "The best man is a doctor. He's going to be here any second. Let's not panic."

"Can you breathe?" Anna asked. "If she can't breathe, I have an EpiPen!"

Zuri took a deep breath. "I can breathe. I'm just very itchy. I need to go to the restroom."

Bluebonnet held up her hands to caution her. "I don't know if that's a good idea. Being calm is good. The mirror will not engender the calm."

"Just tell me, or I'm going to freak out. I already want to rip off my face. It itches like hell."

"You look like you have some . . ." Jonquil nodded slowly as she obviously looked for the right word. "Hives."

"Chicken pox," Anna said helpfully.

Everyone kept staring at Zuri, and she coughed again. "What else? Just tell me."

"They're green," Bluebonnet whispered in an awed tone. "I haven't seen this since 1898."

"Green?" she shrieked. "*Green?*" They would have to be neon green to show up on her dark skin. "Are you fucking kidding me?"

"No, no. We're not losing our minds. We're breathing," Petty said.

"You breathe. You're not green!" Zuri yelled.

"You're not green, either," Petty reassured her. "You're having an allergic reaction. I'm not sure to what, though."

"Oh. Oh no." Jonquil shook her head. "You kissed the frog yesterday. Are you allergic to amphibians?"

"The poor dear. She must be!" Bluebonnet reached out to take her hand. "Yes, just like that case in 1898."

What the hell was she talking about—1898? That was not helping.

Zuri looked down at herself and watched as the itchy lesions erupted over her arms and her hands.

"She kissed a frog?" Anna interjected. "Why would anyone kiss a frog? Unless it was one of those you lick to get stoned, which, I mean, no one could blame her, right? After Chicago? I would, too. Are you stoned?'

"I'm not stoned!"

"It's a thing we do in Ever After." Jonquil waved it off. "It's a rite of passage. But I've never seen this happen to someone."

Zuri inhaled deeply with tears in her eyes. Of course she was allergic to the stupid frog.

Of. Fucking. Course.

"Can this get any worse?" she murmured out loud.

Almost as if she hadn't learned that lesson about asking if it could get any worse. The universe, invariably, always had an answer to that question that the questioner would definitely not enjoy or even remotely like.

The door to the front of the shop opened, and a familiar voice called out, "Anna? Jordan? I'm here."

"That's the best man! He's a doctor. He can help!" Jordan said. "Back here, man."

Zuri turned to face the owner of that voice and saw *him*.

The destroyer of her future.

The beast that chewed up her heart and spit it out.

Dr. Alexander—Alec, or Xander if he was being duplicitous—Marsh.

And of course instead of seeing her thriving, happy, and living her best life, he had to appear now, while she was down, out, and looked like Shrek.

Chapter 9

After Zuri had been carried to her room and tucked in with some Benadryl and cookies, Petty gathered her sisters in the kitchen of the castle.

And, incidentally, also booted Alec Marsh off to his own quarters. He wasn't helping matters at all. Petty knew it was a magical affliction, anyway. All the MDs in the world wouldn't be any help in that department.

The castle supplied some snacks of cucumber sandwiches and lemonade, as well as snacks of crispy capers.

Petty was munching furiously while trying to think of what to do for their poor, darling Zuri.

"We were making so much progress with her, too," Bluebonnet said with a sigh.

"I know! Did you see the way her whole manner softened and the stars in her eyes while she was listening to Anna and Jordan tell their story?" Jonquil sighed as well.

Then, the three of them gave another collective sigh.

"Did you know about this best man situation, Jonquil?" Bluebonnet accused. "Is that why you've been on the closure wagon for the last week?"

Jonquil looked sheepish. "I might've known."

"And might you have enchanted the cabbie not to take that fare?" Petty narrowed her eyes.

"Listen, you can't be mad at me for that one. It was on my magical to-do straight from FG Academy."

"Hmm," Petty said. "I suppose."

Bluebonnet squirmed in her chair and couldn't seem to get comfortable. "Well, I suppose it's a good thing you did. They really are the cutest couple."

"All except for the part where the groom is best friends with Dr. Jackass," Petty said. "I told her to answer his text, not to look at his dumb face."

"His face really is dumb. I hate it," Bluebonnet agreed. "Could we give *him* the frog pox? He deserves it."

"I seem to recall we weren't doing things of that nature anymore?" Petty asked, although she felt a surge of hope. She'd love to give him frog pox. In fact . . . "You know, if we're going to be bad fairies, we could give him carnivorous anal warts? He has it coming."

"Oh, yes! Like a colony of Venus flytraps but on his colon. I like it." Bluebonnet munched harder.

"Sisters. Sisters," Jonquil said. "Far be it from me to interrupt our little vengeance jag, but you know he's going to get what he deserves. Fate will teach him his lessons. That's not for us to do. We spread the love. Not the lessons. Remember?"

Petty crossed her arms. "Maybe I want to spread the lessons this time."

"Uh-huh. Lesson," Bluebonnet said in solidarity.

"Sisters." Jonquil looked at each of them in turn with a stern frown.

"Fine," Petty caved. "I know you're right."

"But fate isn't going to give him anal warts," Bluebonnet protested.

"She might," Jonquil said helpfully.

"If we help her," Petty said as she perked. Then she sagged in her chair. "No, I know you're right. He just made me so mad." Petty had to keep reminding herself that she'd learned her lesson about doing bad things to people.

"He makes us all mad, dearie." Jonquil patted her arm.

"Here, let's make ourselves feel better. We can look at Jenn's love thread."

"Jenn?" Bluebonnet cocked her head to the side.

"The bride who lit her dress on fire? Duh."

"Oh, right. Let's." Bluebonnet nodded.

The sisters all used their fairy godmother powers to peer at the threads of fate and love that were spread out before them.

Petty loved looking at the threads, it was one of her favorite things to do. They were so beautiful, and each thread represented the path of a soul. Her biggest problem had always been touching, but the threads were much like butterfly wings. No touching, at least not from this vantage point.

She could do things on the ground to move the threads, to balance them, to twine or unwind, but never with her actual fingers.

They found Jenn's thread.

"How lovely! See?" Jonquil said.

Petty did indeed see. Jenn Gordon, on her not-honeymoon, with her tribe of girlfriends, had met the man of her dreams. And most every other woman's, too. He was tall, dark, handsome, and . . . British. He was an actor in a popular franchise, and he just happened to be vacationing at the same time. It had been love at first sight.

Well, actually, it had been "cunning linguistics" at first sight in one of the hotel cabanas, but Petty could see it was true love.

She sighed. "Oh my. He really is quite handsome, isn't he? How do mortal men that beautiful exist?"

"They don't. He's got a fairy in the woodpile. By the looks of it, a dark fairy. That's why his cheekbones and jaw do that thing." Jonquil nodded.

"You know what else does that thing?" Bluebonnet snickered. "Oh, our Jenn is a lucky lady."

"Pish. He's the lucky one," Petty said.

"Too true," Jonquil agreed. "He's the luckiest to get dear Jenn. But . . . back to Zuri."

"I've been looking up frog pox in Mama's spell book, and it looks like the only cure for frog pox is to kiss the frog that infected her," Petty offered.

Bluebonnet clapped her hands together. "That's juicy! I love it."

"Hmm. Could be a problem, though, because we're going to have to tell Zuri about magic. She's not ready for that. Not mentally, and definitely not emotionally," Jonquil said.

"Oh, right. Because Phillip is going to have to tell her not only that he's a frog, poor dear, but also what he did to get cursed," Bluebonnet replied. "Damn."

"You know, maybe it's better that she finds out now. Then they can work on building trust." Petty tapped her wand on the table as she considered.

Then she peered at the threads of fate again.

"Hmm. This will never do. Things are a mess!" she cried.

"What's wrong, sister?" Bluebonnet asked.

"Stupid Prince Charming. I swear!" she muttered as she clenched her hands to keep from physically grabbing the threads and yanking on them. "Everything is tangled up."

"How do you know it's his fault?" Bluebonnet asked.

"Oh, because he went to Ravenna to ask if she could break his curse," Petty grumbled.

"Really?" Jonquil rolled her eyes. "Didn't you tell him precisely *not* to do that?"

"I did. But now, all the threads are a mess. Ravenna's thread is tangled with Hunter's, and I don't know if there will be any untangling." Petty closed her eyes and pinched the bridge of her nose.

"No, no. We can't have that. That does not end with a Happily Ever After!" Jonquil cried. "Not for anyone. Zeva goes with Hunter."

"Wait, she does?" Bluebonnet asked.

"Do keep up." Jonquil sighed. "After she goes to Fairy Godmother Academy."

"At least she's on the way. That will help." Bluebonnet nodded and then fidgeted with the hem of her dress.

"What did you do?" Petty asked when she noticed her sister fidgeting.

"I might have made things worse. Or I could've helped," she said hopefully.

"Bon-Bon." Petty eyed her.

"Fine. I told Hansel that he should meander up to the dark castle and see if Ravenna needs any help. With. You know. Anything."

Jonquil cackled. "Ravenna is going to lose her mind."

Bluebonnet lifted her chin. "I wasn't trying to matchmake, but they're both lonely. I thought maybe they could. I dunno. Have some fun together."

Petty patted her shoulder. "That's a lovely idea, Bon-Bon. I'm sure you were trying to help, and maybe this will be the thing that helps to untangle all these threads. Where are we with the Roderick and Gwen situation?"

"We're leaving it alone. For now. Gwen specifically asked us to," Jonquil said.

"When has that ever stopped us?" Bluebonnet demanded to know.

"Eh, well. We could give it a minute. Lucky asked me specifically if we could give it a rest. So. There's that," Petty said.

"Are they still enjoying their honeymoon? When will they be back? I miss them." Bluebonnet stuck out her lower lip.

"It's better that they're there than here, lovie," Jonquil consoled her. "They're enjoying each other thoroughly, I'm sure. We'll get a visit in about a month, I think."

"Does that mean what I think it means?" Bluebonnet asked happily.

"It might. We'll have to see. The threads aren't clear yet, but if there's a baby . . ." Jonquil trailed off.

"Then we'll just have to get Juniper her Happily Ever After!" Petty declared. "Always work to be done!"

"Have you heard back from Fairy Godmother Academy yet on Phillip's situation?" Bluebonnet asked.

"Not yet, I'm afraid," Petty said. "I suppose I can't blame him for going to Ravenna."

"We can't blame him, but we sorta can," Jonquil conceded.

Bluebonnet nodded. "Sorta. Yeah."

Petty tapped her wand on the table again. "Back to the matter at hand. One of us needs to go tell Phillip that he has to kiss Zuri."

They looked around at each other before Bluebonnet's and Jonquil's gaze both settled on Petty.

Petty huffed. "Oh, fine. I'll find him."

"Good on you, dear." Jonquil stuffed a little sandwich in her mouth. "We'll keep the kitchen company."

"Hmm, yes. That works." Bluebonnet nodded and poured herself another cup of coffee.

"Should you really be drinking all that caffeine? You're going to be buzzing around like a mosquito from hell, and just as annoying," Petty told her.

"No, Pets. That's you. I need this much magic-bean juice just to keep me stable."

"Oh, you're right." Petty laughed and tapped her wand again. "I suppose there's nothing to do but to do it." Then she put her hands on her hips. "No, I have a better idea."

"Oh Lord." Bluebonnet shook her head.

"It should be you, Bon-Bon."

Jonquil snorted. "Why? Other than the fact you don't want to be the one to tell him."

"I don't mind it, honestly. I'm the eldest, I always get stuck doing these sorts of things." Petty rolled her eyes. "He's apologized to me. A real apology, and he asked me to tell you, Bluebonnet, that he was sorry."

Bluebonnet raised a brow. "And you're just now getting to this?"

"Slipped my mind."

Bluebonnet's face wrinkled with displeasure. "We've beaten this to death. No need to rehash."

"But he hasn't apologized to you. He needs to. For his journey. Let him."

"Fine." She dropped her cup back on the table and looked longingly at the sandwiches. "But I'm really hungry."

"Chop, chop, Bon. Poor Zuri is suffering."

Bluebonnet narrowed her eyes and shoved a whole sandwich in her mouth. "Ugh. I'm going," she said around her prize.

After Bluebonnet walked out the door, Jonquil asked, "Is that really why you sent her, or are you just trying to hog the cookies?"

Petty was offended. "I'd never do that." Then she flashed a sheepish grin. "At least, not while one of our charges was suffering."

"I'm excited to meet Zeva in person. We haven't had any new FGs in so long. I wonder how she's going to take the news."

"Oh, you mean that her life as she knows it is about to feel completely obsolete? You know it's always rough. It wasn't for us because we were raised knowing we were going to the academy."

"It didn't hurt that we're full-blooded fairies, either," Jonquil said.

"I wish I knew *why* Zuri caught frog pox."

"That should not have happened. It makes me question everything. What if we're totally wrong?" Jonquil asked.

"About what? We're never wrong." Petty coughed. "I mean, at least not about matters of the heart."

"Well, we're the ones who told her to kiss the frog. I'll never forgive myself if there are lasting ill effects from this."

Petty patted her sister's shoulder. "It's going to be okay. I'm sure of it."

Jonquil raised a brow.

"Really. They're not kissing on their own. This must be the hand of fate moving them together," Petty said.

"I suppose you're right. Nothing but trouble comes from questioning fate."

"Yet, even after all these years you continue to do it." Petty shook her head.

"I can't help myself. You know I'm the cynical one. It's just how I'm wired," Jonquil replied.

"Do you think Bluebonnet is lonely?" Petty suddenly asked.

Jonquil leaned over the table and dipped her chin into the bowl of her hand. "I do."

"What are we going to do about it?" Petty asked.

"Don't we have enough to do?" Jonquil asked. "Plus, she'd kill us. She'd kill us, bring us back to life, just to kill us again."

"She seems obsessed with the idea of matching everyone up just to, pardon my language, fuck like bunnies. I can't help but wonder if that's a reflection of her own feelings."

"Don't you think we should trust her to make her own choices?" Jonquil said, but then she laughed. "No, I'm sorry. It's like I forgot what business we're in."

"She needs a vacation after wedding season. Do you think she'd like fall in Vermont? Some cute little B and B?"

"Where a suitably silver-foxed bachelor might be staying as well?" Jonquil asked.

"Oh, yes. Hmm, maybe we should each book a vacation. I do like a man with a good patina." Petty wiggled her brows.

"Maybe hottie actor guy's dad."

"That's the best idea you've had all year," Petty praised.

"I have a good one now and again." Jonquil sipped her coffee but was obviously satisfied with her contribution.

"I'd say the three of us have earned a vacation." Petty was already planning their trip.

"I know it's all going to work out, Pets, but . . ."

Petty smiled at her sister, knowing what she needed to hear. Jonquil frequently needed reassurance, and Petty figured it was her job to give it.

"Yes, Jonquil. It's all going to work out."

"Happily Ever After," Jonquil said.

"And you said you were the cynical one." Petty nudged her.

"I am. I just choose to believe my sister."

Petty's heart was full in a way that it hadn't been in a long time. "You know, I think turning Ever After into a wedding destination was the best thing we've ever done."

"I will say this only once, and never again. You can't hold it against me," Jonquil began. "But yes, you're right."

"Damn, and Bluebonnet wasn't here to hear you say it."

"Exactly the way I like it." Jonquil smirked. "You can't prove a thing."

"And they think I'm the dangerous one."

"Well, I'm not the one who cursed a prince to be a frog."

"Will you ever let that die?"

"No, probably not. Neither will anyone else," Jonquil added, ever helpful. "It's been three hundred years. That's a minute to hold a grudge."

Petty cackled, unable to help herself, and not unaware how much she sounded like a wicked witch instead of a fairy godmother.

It seemed others thought so, too, because an answering cackle from the doorway startled Petty so much that she fell off her chair, and she looked up to see the Evil Queen herself.

"Looks like I'm no longer alone at the dark-side table. Our cookies taste better, anyway."

Chapter 10

Phillip was just getting out of the shower when a gentle tap sounded on his door. He wrapped himself in a towel, but the castle seemed to have other ideas and dressed him appropriately.

Suddenly, he was wearing joggers and a T-shirt, and while it wasn't his usual attire, he'd take it.

He opened the door to find Bluebonnet standing there, her gentle face as serious as he'd ever seen it.

"What's wrong?"

"May I come in?" she asked.

"Oh, of course. Sorry." He held the door wide for her.

Her yellow dress was a bright, happy relief to the dark expression on her face. He especially liked how it bounced when she walked. She was always like a ray of sunshine wherever she went.

"Don't freak," she began.

It weirded him out how she looked like someone's grandmother, well, was in fact someone's grandmother, but spoke with modern slang.

"Just tell me, Bon-Bon."

"It's Zuri. She's taken ill."

"Why wasn't I informed? Where is she? What can I do?"

"Remember when I said not to freak? Sit down, Phillip."

It must be beyond serious if she wanted him to sit down.

So he led her over to the divan and motioned for her to sit first. He did have royal manners, after all.

She sat and then patted the seat next to her. "Come along, now."

He sat and waited for whatever bomb she was going to drop.

"She's caught the frog pox."

"Excuse me?"

"Frog. Pox. Phillip, she's allergic to frogs. Or at least magical ones."

"She's allergic to me?"

"Please pay attention. What did I say?" Bluebonnet admonished him. "Frogs. Not you. Just . . . when you're a frog."

"So what is frog pox? What can I do?"

"You'll have to kiss her, of course."

Phillip spluttered. "I can't do that. We're not ready for that."

"Well, you'd better get ready rather quickly, or she's going to turn into a frog, too. Remember how itchy you were?"

"Does she . . . does she have the green lesions?"

"Yes. The only cure is to kiss her. While you're you, anyway." Bluebonnet picked up a candle, sniffed it, and obviously found it lacking, because her nose wrinkled with disdain.

"Is that really the only way?" It was too soon.

"Why? Don't you want to kiss her?" Bluebonnet studied him.

"Of course I do. But I'll have to tell her why."

"A part of me says that you don't have to tell her, but you really should. You can't build anything together without honesty and trust."

"She's never going to trust me when she finds out what I did." Phillip knew that this wasn't about him, but he had a hard time letting go of the idea that he'd had a shot with Zuri.

Bluebonnet patted his leg in a motherly fashion. "Yes, she

will. It may take some time, as all trust does, but she will. That was so long ago. If Petty and I aren't mad about it any longer, she can't be."

"She was betrayed," he began.

"So she was. You're not Alec." She took his hand. "And you're not the same you that you were all those years ago, either."

"Speaking of that, Bluebonnet." He took a deep breath and searched for the words that would encompass all that he wanted to say.

Phillip was glad she didn't wave him off, or tell him it was fine. She gave him the space to speak the words that she deserved and that he needed to say.

"I have been sorry, but I haven't apologized. I'm sorry for what I did. It was wrong. I know it's no excuse, but I was raised to believe I could have anything I wanted. I wanted you both, and I didn't think about how that would feel to you or Petunia. I was selfish. I was cruel. You deserved better than that."

Bluebonnet squeezed the hand she still held, and she took a deep breath. "I see now why Petty said it had to be me who came to speak with you. I didn't think I needed your apology. I thought your punishment was enough, but that's all I really wanted: an apology that you meant."

"I do mean it. And not just because I'm sorry that I'm a frog." He gave her a half smile. Phillip wanted good things for all the fairy godmothers. Not just because of who they were to the town, but because over the years, he realized they'd become actual friends. That mattered to him.

"I forgive you. We all do. Even Jonquil, who was enraged on our behalf. She was mad about it longer than Petty or I was. Since we're confessing, I want you to know that I believe in you. I believe you learned the lessons that you needed. I believe that you will break the curse and that Zuri is your Happily Ever After. I need you to remember that HEA may not look the way you think it should. Trust your heart. It won't steer you wrong. Even if it breaks itself."

Phillip listened to what she had to say, and while he didn't like it, he knew she was right. "You're kind of good at this fairy godmother gig, Bon-Bon."

"Yeah, it's sort of what I do." She pulled out her wand and tapped it on her palm. "Okay, Prince Charming. Chop-chop. It's time to make with the kissing. You know that's how these things work."

Fear knotted itself in his gut. He feared Zuri's rejection. He couldn't blame her if she did reject him. He would, if he were in her place. How could he expect her to do something he wouldn't? Only there was something more dangerous in his guts than fear. It was that faint ember of hope that refused to be extinguished.

Regardless of what it meant for him, he had to help Zuri.

"Where is she?"

"Not too far. She's resting in her rooms. Are you ready?"

He got up and walked with purpose to Zuri's rooms, not bothering to see Bluebonnet out. She knew her way around the castle.

Phillip didn't bother knocking, either, so when he opened the door and strode up the stairs to Zuri's loft bedroom, he got the shock of his life when he saw a strange man sitting next to her bed.

"Who the hell are you?" The guy in the chair demanded.

Phillip was about to ask him the same, but one look at poor, beleaguered Zuri in her bed and he knew that was absolutely the wrong tack to take. "I'm her friend. Phillip Charming."

"Charming? Are you shitting me?"

Phillip arched a brow. "I'm the owner of the castle. Care to tell me who you are and why you're in my home?"

"Dr. Marsh. I'm here to help Zuri."

Zuri's eyes fluttered open, and she looked back and forth

between the two of them before shaking her head and pulling the covers up into a cocoon over her face.

Realization dawned. "Dr. Alec Marsh? Or should we call you Xander? Which do you prefer?"

"That doesn't matter now. I'm here to help her."

How was he supposed to kiss her with this guy hanging around? The balcony doors fluttered opened and closed, as if being rattled by a slight breeze. Phillip knew it was the castle suggesting he pitch the man out into the lake. He knew the castle would help. While the idea delighted him, he knew that wasn't the answer.

At least, not yet.

"And what exactly are you doing to help her?" Phillip asked.

Alec narrowed his eyes at him and opened his mouth to speak, but before he could say anything, the door opened and the Evil Queen stood there in all her dark glory, with the godmothers right behind her.

This Alec guy did not understand the level of shitstorm that was about to be unleashed in this room.

"All of you, out!" Alec demanded. "She needs rest."

Ravenna was particularly unfazed. She moved forward, gliding effortlessly like a dark swan. Petunia reached out and put a hand on her arm.

"Ravenna, remember he's a wedding guest."

"Hmm. Isn't that how all these things start? Either with an engagement or a birth?" Ravenna grinned, but it was more a baring of teeth than an actual smile. "Only the missed invitation isn't mine."

And it seemed that she'd taken Zuri under her dark wing.

Zuri peeped out from under the blankets. The poor thing was covered in green lesions, and Phillip remembered with alarming clarity exactly how much those things itched.

"Not that I don't love you all, but what are you doing in my room?" she asked. "Wait, who are you?"

"Darling, we'll discuss that later. We've come to make you better, isn't that right, Phillip?" Ravenna arched a brow at him.

"Trying," he mumbled.

"I really just want to dip myself in Benadryl and sleep for a week. Can I do that?"

Alec reached out but drew his hand back. "Yes, you can. I'll make them all leave. Then we can do some tests and figure out what's happening to you."

"Can you make yourself leave instead?" she asked.

"There it is, dear doctor. The patient asked you to leave. I suggest you do as she says," Ravenna said.

The godmothers fussed and fretted behind her, fairly buzzing with magic. All of them were. This was not the way to do this. Someone was going to explode and send their magic ricocheting around the room, and then where would Zuri be? Even more scared and confused.

"As far as I can tell, you don't even have a physician in this town. Look at her! She needs medical attention." Alec gestured to the lump on the bed.

Zuri sat up in bed. "Too bad you weren't this concerned about my health and well-being when you lied to me for three months."

"Zuri, I was confused. I didn't . . ." He looked around. "Can we not do this in front of everyone?"

"You're the one still talking."

Ravenna nodded in agreement. "He is, isn't he? We should make him stop."

He wasn't exactly sure what he could do to get Ravenna to turn it back a notch, but he had to try.

"Fine. I'm sorry, Zuri. I didn't mean to hurt you. I'll earn your trust again. I swear. Let's just get through Anna and Jordan's wedding, and then we can talk, okay?"

It seemed the godmothers must have sensed her will crumbling or something, because Petty kicked Phillip, Bluebonnet nudged him with her wand, and Jonquil just all out shoved him forward.

He stumbled and righted himself. "Not subtle," he said to the godmothers.

"If this was the time for subtlety, Prince Charming, I wouldn't be here." Ravenna put her hand on her hip.

"Don't call me that," he said.

"Yeah, don't call him that." Alec frowned. "Just because he's rich doesn't make him better for Zuri than me."

"There's lots of things that make me better for Zuri than you, but that's not up to us to decide, is it?"

"I'm going to leave you a bad review on Yelp," Alec threatened.

"Same to you," Phillip said.

"Oh, this is ridiculous," Zuri cried. "Stop it."

"Yes, it is. I'll take you out of here. Let me take you to Springfield or Kansas City, somewhere where they have a real hospital and can take care of you. If you ever believed anything I've said, believe that. Please."

Phillip actually believed that Alec wanted to help her. Only, he knew the cure wasn't in any hospital or research facility. Not in any kind of known medicine to the outside world.

"I understand you want to help her, and I don't want to get into a pissing contest with you—" Phillip started.

"You'd lose."

"Oh, for fuck's sake. Will you listen to me for one minute?" Speaking of losing, Phillip was about to lose his patience.

Alec snarled, but he motioned for Phillip to continue.

"Zuri has had a reaction to something local—"

"I knew he had to be one of those toxic frogs. I'm probably hallucinating all of this." She scratched at her arm, but Ravenna slapped her hand away. "If I'm hallucinating, why does it itch? Oh, don't tell me, I'm still out by the fountain tripping balls, and I'm getting stung to death by rabid mosquitoes that are going to drain me dry."

"We don't have mosquitoes in Ever After, dearie," Petty said.

Phillip sighed. "She's having an allergic reaction to some wildlife that is exclusive to Ever After. I can help her. My family has lived here for generations. We have a homegrown antidote, but we need you to—"

"If you think I'm going to trust her to some backwoods—"

"If you'll let me finish, if the cure doesn't work for her, and we'll know pretty quickly if it will or it won't, then you can take her, with her permission, to any hospital you choose."

"I will not—" Alec began.

Zuri interrupted him. "This isn't your choice to make. It's mine." She looked around to all the people who'd gathered in her bedroom. "I trust these people. I don't trust you."

"You would, if you'd let me explain."

"I don't know what there is to explain, Alec. Xander. Whatever your name is. You lied to me. You lied to Jenn." She held up her hand before he could speak again. "The fact remains you didn't tell either Jenn or me about what you were feeling. You would have married her that day without a second thought."

"I had plenty of second thoughts," Alec said.

"But you didn't share them with anyone. Please, I'd like you to leave. I said we could talk, but maybe after I'm feeling better. Even though, I'm not sure what else there is to say."

"Just that you'll give me a chance to prove myself to you."

"Right now, I'm really sick, and this is still about you."

"I just need you to listen."

Phillip recognized the plea in his voice. The need to be understood. The desperation to be told he wasn't the one who was wrong. He had no pity for the man. He had to learn his lesson the same as Phillip had. He had to choose to be a better man.

How could Phillip himself do that in this situation? He could continue to squabble, but he could see how tired Zuri was. He could see that she needed him to be, not her savior, but her support system. No one was listening to what she wanted.

The godmothers were wonderful, but they were waiting for a kiss that definitely wasn't going to come while the room was packed. He knew they were doing their best, and they wanted to be there to support him with proof when he told her about magic, and to support her when she realized how her world had changed.

Ravenna, he didn't know what she was doing, but he suspected Alec Marsh wasn't going to like whatever she had planned. He couldn't bring himself to feel bad for the guy.

"Come on," he said. "Everyone out. Let's give Zuri a minute."

Alec seemed like he was going to argue, but Ravenna glided over to him and grabbed him by ear. "Out, he said." She dragged him down the stairs.

The godmothers didn't hesitate and flitted toward the door.

"Call us if you need us, sweet peas," Jonquil advised.

He looked at Zuri. "I'll give you a moment, and I'll get you what you need."

"Thank you," she said softly.

When he opened the door to leave, he saw Zuri's mirror image standing there, her eyes wide as saucers, and a big smile on her face.

"You must be Zeva."

Her smile got bigger. "You must be Prince Charming." She wrapped her arms around him and kissed his cheek. "I am so happy to meet you."

A certain twinkle in her eye told him that she knew everything.

Relief washed over him. "You know, I think you might have arrived just in time."

"I think so, too. Twinning is helpful that way."

"Zeva? You're here?" Zuri called out.

"I'll leave you two alone for a minute." He knew they needed each other without being told.

Zeva grabbed his hand, her grip firm. "I can trust you, can't I? With my sister?"

"You can." Phillip squeezed her hand to reassure her.

She searched his face for a long moment. "I believe you."

The magic and warmth that radiated from Zeva almost made him forget that Zuri wasn't the one to break his spell.

Almost. Looking into Zeva's eyes showed him a future that didn't belong to him. Zeva wasn't going to be the sister he'd never had, and Zuri wasn't going to be his princess.

No matter how much he wished it could be otherwise.

Chapter 11

Zuri exhaled a breath she didn't know she'd been holding when she heard her sister's voice.

"You knew," she said.

"Of course I knew. I always know. This is what we do." Zeva crawled onto the bed with her. "Was that Alec I saw in the hallway?"

"Yes. He's the best man for a wedding I'm working on."

"What an insane coincidence," Zeva said dryly.

"Don't you start, too. Can't you see I'm sick?" Zuri grumped.

"And Prince Charming has the cure."

"Is that what we're doing?" Zuri drawled.

"It's not what I'm doing, but it's what you're doing. Oh, Zuri. Can't you see the magic at work here?"

Zuri held up her arms. "I see green rot at work." Then she narrowed her eyes. "You don't seem as upset for me as I think you should be."

"That's because I know that your prince has your cure."

"Why is everyone calling him a prince? Just because he owns a castle doesn't make him a prince."

Zeva took her hand. "No, his heart does. And, you know, he is."

"What are you talking about?" Zuri wasn't sure she wanted to hear this. She'd had some extra sense tingling at the back of her neck since she arrived, and she wasn't ready to put a name to it.

"Can't you see it? The magic in Ever After is everywhere. You've walked into a fairy tale."

"Zeva, I think maybe you might be having some secondary effects from my illness. You're talking like you think that magic is real. Not just, you know, the human experience, but like . . . magic. That this theme park–style little town is more than kitsch."

"It is. I know I'm not the only one who sees it. Your Phillip basically admitted it when I came in."

"Yeah, because *that* wouldn't benefit his business interests at all." She tucked her sister in next to her. "He's not my Phillip."

"He is. Maybe not right now, maybe not tomorrow, but he is." Zeva was annoyingly confident.

"Hush. You sound like the godmothers."

"You really didn't see how they sparkle? The one with the glasses leaves glitter everywhere she goes."

"Did someone spike your drink?" Zuri asked.

Zeva rolled onto her side. "Zuri, I'm telling you that this place is absolutely everything it says it is. I almost had a heart attack when I saw that dark-haired woman. She was every inch an Evil Queen."

Zuri knew Zeva didn't lie.

Except if Zeva could see it and Zuri couldn't, it meant magic was real for some people. Just not for Zuri.

Which had been Zuri's deepest darkest fear all along. She'd just said things couldn't get any worse, and she'd been given a definitively shitty answer that yes, they could. So why not this, too?

"Okay. I believe you. It's insane, but I believe you. What did it look like when you drove in?" She wanted to share Zeva's experience, too.

"Everything sparkled. It was like Strawberry Shortcake meets My Little Pony and with an extra helping of fairy dust. It was so strange. I thought I was hallucinating at first, but as soon as I trusted my instincts, it was like even more of this world opened up to me. I could see traces of energy from people I think are magic," she ended on a high pitch. "It's wonderful."

Zuri tried to be happy for her sister, and of course she found some joy, but she found sorrow for herself as well.

"Oh, but it's not wonderful for you right now, is it? I'm sorry." Zeva pulled Zuri into her arms. "I'm sure you feel terrible. We'll get Phillip back in here, and he's going to make you feel better."

"I don't think he will," Zuri confessed.

"Why do you think that, dumplin'?"

"You're even talking like the fairy godmothers, now." Zuri chuckled. "You're just infected with some magic mushroom that's a little more trippy than actual magic."

"Zuri, I swear to you."

"Pinkie swear?" Zuri asked.

Zeva held up her pinkie, and they hooked their fingers together. "Pinkie swear. I'm not tripping balls."

"That's both the best thing I've ever heard and the worst." Zuri pulled the covers higher.

"Why is that?"

"Because this is the first time we've experienced something major in different ways. It's like you're so far away from me now."

"And?" Zeva prompted.

"And . . . if magic is real, and you know it's real." She took a breath. "All these people are actually who I thought they were pretending to be, and that means it's real for only some people. Not for me, because I can't see it."

Zeva's happy grin slowly melted into a frown. "No, I don't believe that. I think you just can't see it *yet*. I don't know what's happened to me that it's different for me, but I think I need to find out."

"I know you do," Zuri said, but held on tighter. She didn't want to let go.

People didn't often get the chance to know when a moment was going to change their lives forever. It wasn't often that one could look and see where their new path diverged from their old one, but Zuri knew this was one of those moments.

After the moment passed, when she let go of her sister, everything was going to change.

She whispered the thought aloud, "It's all going to change, Zeva."

"I know, and I can't wait. I'm going to find a way to bring some of this magic to the kids at St. Marigold's." Zeva pulled away to look down at Zuri. "And you're going to find your way, too."

"I wish I was as confident about that as you are."

"Do you trust me?"

"Of course."

"Then believe me when I say that everything will work out. I can see it."

"Magic will make everything okay?" Zuri was skeptical. Neither she nor her sister had believed that in a long time. Not since the fateful night when their father didn't come home and all the wishing and hoping in the world hadn't been able to change the fact that he was dead.

"No, you will make everything okay."

Zuri was comforted momentarily. Then it hit her that Zeva had called Phillip Prince Charming. "Holy shit, is he really?"

"Who? The *charming* B and B owner?"

"That's worse than a dad joke, Zeva. That was awful." Laughter bubbled in the back of her throat.

"It was amazing, and I deserve so much credit."

"The Chicago judge gives it a negative ten."

Then Zuri remembered that Phillip had told her there were things he wanted to tell her but he couldn't. Not until she'd been in Ever After a while.

She found comfort in that, too. He hadn't lied to her. While he'd kept things from her, it was logical that he'd wait for her to be ready for what he had to say. If he'd just popped off with "Hey, baby. I'm Prince Charming . . . ," that wouldn't have gone over well. Zuri knew he'd been as honest with her as he could've been.

"What are you thinking about? Your charming prince?"

"Oh God, *stahp* already. I can't."

Zeva giggled. "Oh, but I bet you will."

Zuri giggled, too. "You're right. I probably will. As soon as I'm not green. Honestly, I don't know how you can lay next to me with all this going on." She motioned to her face.

"It's not contagious, I don't think." Zeva did a quick inventory of herself, holding up her arms and hands.

"We probably should've figured that out before you crawled into bed with the green plague."

"Phillip is getting your medicine. I'm going to go and see if there's an extra room for me."

"You can just stay with me," Zuri said.

"No, I can't. Not this time. You're going to need your space, but I'm still here. I'm not going anywhere." Zeva kissed her forehead. "I'll tell him you're ready."

Zuri considered telling Zeva not to be hasty. She wasn't ready for anything. Except to stop itching. Although, if that meant facing some fairy-tale prince she'd developed the hots for, she might just stick with the itching. It was easier.

She was already taken with him. His perfect hair, his perfect jaw, his ridiculously green eyes—wait. His eyes were an unnatural shade of green. They were *frog* green.

No.

That couldn't be.

Fate wouldn't be so cruel, would she?

A bitch might, she allowed. A bitch just might.

Today was the day where the hits just kept coming.

She definitely needed to go to the Pick 'n' Axe to throw

some axes and drink her mead. Zuri wanted to two-hand them both. An axe in each hand until she could barely lift her arms, and then flagon after flagon of that delicious mead.

Maybe some stew.

And some of Gwen's cookies.

Her mind wandered to all the pleasant places and things that brought her comfort. So it made sense that, much to her chagrin, it made its way back to Phillip.

To the drinking chocolate with him by the fire.

She heard voices at the door and the soft click as it was closed.

Phillip came up to sit in the chair where Alec had been perched earlier. He was actually too pretty to look at. It was unreal that someone as handsome as he was lived and breathed outside anyone's imagination.

"So you talked with your sister?"

"I trust her, but I have to ask, did you spike her drink? Did she kiss the frog on the way to the castle and now we're all tripping balls?"

Phillip laughed and looked down at his hands for a moment before raising his eyes to meet her gaze. "No. The frog isn't there after sundown."

"Oh God," she whispered.

"Yeah." He shrugged.

She swallowed hard and closed her eyes. "When I was talking to Zeva, I could still pretend this was one of our games. We used to make up our own worlds when we were kids. Whole universes with magic and portals and . . . I don't know if I can process this. I feel crazy for even considering it."

"I didn't want to tell you yet. You're not ready. I'm so sorry you're sick." He made to take her hand, but he pulled back before he touched her. "I have your antidote."

She peered at him, and he didn't seem to be holding anything. "What is it?" Zuri wrinkled her nose. "Please don't let it be any kind of nasty potion I have to drink."

"No, I can safely say that you don't have to drink it."

"Your tone says I'm still not going to like it."

"I don't know if you'll like it or not."

She was torn between demanding he just come out with it and deciding to trust him to lead her to it slowly. After all, a woman of sound mind could only process so much of this magic crap at one time.

"Since I'm not itching at the moment, can we start slow?"

His mouth quirked up in a half smirk. "As slow as you want."

His words made her body come alive, and she was sure that no matter what he had to say, things between them were headed to a fixed point on the horizon that was all carnal. What was going to happen after that, she couldn't say.

"So tell me. Tell me the whole truth about the castle. About your family. About your friend's skin condition."

His half smirk bloomed into a real smile, and she caught a glimpse of a dimple. How had she missed that?

It was as if slowly, inch by inch, more details were being revealed to her. More of the veil was being pulled away from her eyes.

Instead of being afraid, she remembered what her sister had said and let herself feel only the excitement at this new state of things. Maybe magic was for her, too.

Just maybe.

"So, to start with, I'm pretty old. Time used to pass differently outside of Ever After. So, wait, we agree that magic is real? Because you won't believe any of what I have to say without that basic foundation."

"Okay. Magic is real." The words tasted strange on her tongue, and for a moment, she doubted. Okay, for more than a moment. She wondered if this was a newbie prank they played on everyone who was new to the area, but Zuri didn't think that people as sweet as the godmothers would do that.

Only, that seemed more likely than believing in wands,

fairy dust, and . . . seven men of small stature who owned a bar and . . .

"Did I lose you?"

"No." She shook her head. "Yes. For a minute. I'm back now."

"There used to be more of us, but when love began to disappear from the world, so did our lands and our power. We stepped back from the mortal world and went about our business without interacting too much. The godmothers went back and forth, because it was still their job to meddle, as they so enjoy doing."

Zuri nodded. "Do they have wings? Because I just feel like they need wings."

"They most definitely have wings, but they hide them when normies are around."

This thrilled Zuri to no end.

"Anyway, our stores of magic began to run quite low, and—"

"Wait! Your parents. Your family. They didn't . . ."

He shook his head. "No, they didn't make the jump. They didn't want to change. They liked the old ways and thought that maybe it was time for magic to disappear."

"Phillip, I'm so sorry." She reached out for his hand.

His fingers were warm and strong when they closed around hers. "The same is still true as I said before. The town is my family. We've all had one another."

"I think that's more magical than wings, honestly."

"I do, too. I think we're very lucky the godmothers are who they are. Back to my story, though, if you still want to hear it." There was no judgment in his voice, just a calm curiosity.

"Yes, sorry. Go on." She looked into his eyes and couldn't help but wish he'd kiss her.

Not that he'd want to, since she looked like the creature from the black lagoon.

Oh God, her hair was probably a wreck.

Why was she worried about how she looked? Zuri decided she definitely needed therapy. She wondered if the health insurance plan from FGI covered it.

"You saw Ravenna, and you know the black castle is hers. She's a queen. Some would say Evil Queen, and the claim is not without merit. Alec is lucky she's trying to turn over a new leaf."

"She'd curse him for me? Really?"

"Really. She's the sort who might even put his heart in a box."

"You're not kidding." That was the kind of friend to have, though. Another woman to fix your crown, or your pitchfork, before anyone knew it was crooked.

"Not in the least. She wouldn't kill him, either. She'd make him walk around without his heart so he could learn what it's for."

Zuri wasn't sure if she was scared of Ravenna or had a massive girl crush. "Way to smash the patriarchy. And in those shoes." She sighed.

Phillip laughed. "You got it. That's Ravenna. A Gothic fashion icon, dark magic powerhouse, and a literal queen."

"You're a prince but not a king?"

"Ouch," he said. "But we'll get to that. Hunter is also a prince. It's not a skin condition. He made the mistake of crossing a witch, and he's cursed. He's a man wearing the skin of a beast."

"A werewolf?"

"No, no. We have one of those. Grammy. She's out at the ranch these days. She was bitten saving Red. We give her room to run. She doesn't bite anyone. Usually." He shrugged.

Zuri was even more gobsmacked. "I still feel like you're taking the piss, as they say on the BBC."

"Definitely not taking the piss."

"Okay. Okay. So. I have a feeling what's coming next, but I need you to say it out loud."

He nodded slowly. "I haven't had to confess this to anyone. Ever. Everyone here already knows. They've always known."

She nodded and took a deep breath, waiting for the words that were going to challenge everything she knew to be true.

"The reason I'm still a prince and not a king, aside from the fact we don't do that anymore, is that a cursed man can't be king. I'm the frog in the fountain." He held her hand tighter. "And I'm sorry as hell that you're sick because you tried to break my curse, and even sorrier that your kiss wasn't the one."

Chapter 12

He waited for the fallout.

Her eyes searched his, and he wanted to look away; Phillip wanted to hide from her scrutiny, but he forced himself to be present, to let her see anything she wanted from him.

"I am, too. I was sitting here thinking that it sucked that magic was real, because if it was, I was one of the ones who didn't get the Happily Ever After. Not everyone does. Obviously. Except, it's awful for you, too. You live with magic. You've always lived with it, and you're cursed. You must be bitter."

He shook his head, realizing that he wasn't bitter at all. He'd even found some gratitude for his situation. "I'm not bitter at all. Hunter told me that basically we were selfish assholes who got the opportunity to be better. Sure, we went kicking and screaming, but in the end, we're better people."

"Hunter sounds a lot like my sister."

"He's my best friend. He's a good man. I am sadder for him than I am for myself. His time is up. The deadline on his curse passed before he could find someone to love him."

"Oh no! Will that happen to you?"

"No. I don't think so. I'll have to ask Petty."

"Can she help you? I mean, I'm sure she tried, right?"

He knew the question he was dreading was coming, but he also knew that even if it didn't, he still had to tell her.

But he also knew all the understanding in her eyes would fade, and it would be a long time before she'd let him be this close to her again. He couldn't blame her. If he'd been in her position, he'd want to protect himself as best as he could, too.

"She tried. It's why she's doing that frog-kissing booth at the spring carnival. To try to help me break the curse."

"Who cursed you? What did you do?"

When he looked away from her, she spoke again. "You can tell me."

Phillip wanted to ask her if she wouldn't just rather have her cure. He could kiss her, and they'd surrender to this fire between them.

Only he knew the fire would be snuffed when she found out.

The old Phillip wouldn't have told her, he realized. The old Phillip would've taken what he wanted without any thought for the fallout.

The old Phillip was just like Alec Marsh.

If anything, Phillip knew he was a better man than that. A man who owned his mistakes. A man who valued other people and considered their feelings. A man who knew the value and the necessity of truth.

"I am how Petty got her nickname. Three hundred years ago, the sisters had not yet adopted their current incarnation. Not that they're not beautiful, but I just feel I need to open with that."

Zuri arched a brow and then casually started to scratch her hand.

"Stop that. It'll just make it worse. Believe me, I know."

"Wait, I got this from kissing you. Did you give me an STD?" Zuri demanded.

Phillip couldn't stop the gale of laughter that overtook him. "Oh my God, Zuri. No. *No*. It's just an allergic reaction. I promise."

"Are you sure?" She narrowed her eyes at him.

"I'm positive. No one else who kissed me got the frog pox."

He watched as realization dawned on her. "Oh, you've been kissed a lot."

He nodded. "Lucky me?"

"Wait, you don't have mono, do you? The kissing disease?" She wrinkled her nose.

He found the expression on her face to be ridiculously adorable. Of course, he wouldn't say that out loud. No one wanted to hear they were cute in times of distress. Yet, he found he was enamored with most everything about her.

"Zuri. No. I swear, it's just an allergy."

"But why am I allergic to you?"

"I don't know." He shrugged. "But if Petty says it's an allergy, then it's an allergy. She's been doing this a long time."

"Frog pox still sounds like something gross."

"I'm sure it feels absolutely awful."

"When do I get my antidote?"

"I'm getting there. You need to know the rest of this before I tell you what the antidote is."

She sighed. "This is part of the stuff you had to tell me, too, right?"

"Yeah." He nodded slowly. "It is."

"Fine. Let's get this over with." She crossed her arms over her chest.

He hadn't known Zuri very long, but he was sure she wouldn't want the antidote after he'd told her everything. Eventually, she'd accept it because she wanted to be done itching and didn't want to turn into a frog as well.

But she wouldn't want to kiss him.

He was pretty sure that was going to tear his heart out of his chest and shred it like filling for a street taco. Because even if she wasn't the one to break his curse—hell, maybe his curse was already permanent—he'd started to dream about building something with her.

"I was Alec," he blurted. "I mean, we weren't engaged or anything. But I courted Petty and Bluebonnet at the same time. When Petty found out, she cursed me. It's been this way ever since."

Zuri's mouth opened, and her jaw worked, but no sound came out. Then she snapped it shut and pressed her lips together.

She didn't need to say anything, though. He could see the betrayal in her eyes.

It was as if he'd taken the trust they were slowly building and dropped it to shatter like a glass globe on stone.

"I see."

"They've forgiven me," he said. "I'm a better man than I used to be."

"I suppose they have if they're trying to break your curse with the kissing booth," she said quietly.

Silence fell like a long, cold shadow between them. He didn't know what else to say.

She finally spoke. "Of course you're a better man than you used to be. You've had a long time to evolve."

"A long, long time," he agreed.

"So what's the antidote? Why do you somehow think I won't want it after finding out why you're cursed? Do we have to have sex or something?"

"Nothing that extreme. Just a kiss," he said as if it didn't matter. As if kissing her wasn't something he'd already thought about, longed for, and begged fate to give him the opportunity.

Not that he wanted it at her expense. He didn't want it to be something she had to submit to but something she wanted with equal fervor.

"A kiss that you ran away from last time?" She bit her lip. "Unless I misread that whole interaction."

"It was dawn. I was already changing back to a frog. I didn't think you'd enjoy that."

"You're right about that."

"So the antidote?" he prompted.

She exhaled heavily. "There's no other way?"

"You don't want to kiss me now? Is it because I'm a frog or because of what I did to Petty and Bluebonnet three hundred years ago?"

"That's not hyperbole, is it? It's really been three hundred years?" she gasped.

"Almost to the day. Will you answer the question?"

"I already kissed a frog," she said. "But that's my problem, isn't it? I keep kissing frogs expecting them to be princes, but even the one who really is a prince . . . he somehow isn't." She dropped her arms and sagged against the back of the bed.

"We all make mistakes, Zuri. No one is perfect."

"That's what Zeva says, but to me, that sounds like an excuse. It sounds like a push for me to settle."

His first instinct, even after all these years, even after all his lessons, was to remind her that he was a prince. It wasn't settling.

Except, maybe it was.

She wanted someone she could trust.

Obviously, Zuri didn't feel she could trust him now, and by all rights he couldn't blame her. Even if he did blame her, it still wasn't for him to choose who Zuri trusted.

"You don't have anything to say to that?" she asked.

"What am I supposed to say, Zuri? I've already told you my story. I told you I've changed, and I understand why you can't trust it, but that's it, then, isn't it?"

"I guess it is."

"You still have to kiss me if you don't want to be a frog." He hated that it had to be that way.

"Maybe I do want to be a frog. Is it easier?"

"Not really. I still remember some of what it's like to be a man. Although, that fades more and more every year. I can't connect with other frogs, even though I've made a couple of pals. Nothing you'd call ride-or-die. Not like Hunter."

The door was suddenly flung open, and the entire circus

of Ravenna, the godmothers, and Alec, along with Anna and Jordan added to the mix tumbled back in.

"We came to check on you," Anna said.

"Alec said you weren't getting care, and we wanted to make sure you're okay," Jordan added as he and Anna took in the scene.

Phillip pressed his palm to his forehead. "For fuck's actual sake," he murmured. "We were having a moment. Godmothers?"

Where was Zeva when he needed her?

"Why is she still green, Phillip?" Petty demanded.

"Well, I've had to do a bit of explaining, now haven't I?"

"Zuri, would you like to go to a hospital?" Jordan prompted.

"No, no. I'm fine. I'm sure I'll be feeling better shortly after Phillip is able to administer the treatment."

"I demand to see the treatment," Alec said. "This is ridiculous."

Anna put her hand on his arm and shook her head.

Alec sighed. "Zuri, it would make me feel a lot better if you'd let me be present. I'd like to make sure he's not giving you some kind of potion with batwings or something."

"We would never!" Ravenna snapped, obviously offended because of her beloved Esmerelda.

Bluebonnet looked at her wrist, where there was obviously no watch, but she tapped it with her finger anyway. "Time's a-wasting, Phillip. Tick tock."

"Really? It's almost like, hmm, no one will leave me alone long enough to get it for her," Phillip admonished.

"You know we're impatient, dear." Jonquil nodded.

"You've all signed off on this?" Zuri asked.

"Obviously, darling. We want you well," Petty said.

"I want to know why you told me to kiss that stupid frog in the first place." Zuri crossed her arms over her chest.

Phillip tried not to take offense at being "that stupid frog."

"You'd already been kissing one. What's the difference?" Ravenna asked. "Oh, except for the part where one is literally a frog and the other is . . . well. That." She looked at Alec pointedly.

"Ravenna," Phillip hissed. "Ixnay on the Rogfay."

Ravenna rolled her eyes. "Whatever. I think he just wanted me to drag him out of here by his ear again." She threw a look at Zuri. "Which I'm happy to do. If you want your cure?"

Why was Ravenna suddenly championing him? It didn't make sense. Unless she was trying to make sure she didn't have to deal with his pursuit.

It was getting hard to feel good about himself, what with all the rejection.

Phillip figured that was a big clue. He should probably just shut up and go sit in the fountain.

Ravenna smiled at him. "I'm trying to help you. This isn't a bad thing."

"After our talk the other day, I thought . . ." He shrugged.

"What talk?" Zuri asked. "Was it about me, because I've had enough of this."

"Maybe it was, maybe it wasn't. The crystal ball wasn't sure. Since you both are still having your same issues, my guess is it wasn't about you. Sorry, sugar." Ravenna shook her head.

"Will someone please tell me what's going on?" Anna asked.

"I will," a new voice called from the doorway. "Yes, hi. I'm Zeva. Yes, we're twins. Yes, our parents could tell us apart. Yes, we played the switch game when we were little. But what we're all going to do now is vacate my sister's room so she can rest." She cast a fiery look to Alec. "No, you're not going to argue. Because while your ex-fiancée set her dress on fire, I will set *you* on fire if you don't leave this room now."

Phillip had to admire Zeva's absolute take-charge attitude. She was not tolerating any of this, and he was entirely grateful.

Ravenna's bottom lip protruded in a pout. "I don't see why she gets to light things on fire."

Zeva linked her arm with Ravenna's. "You can light all sorts of things on fire. Even Alec, if you really want to. No one is going to stop you. Of course, it might make for a really bad review if you light the best man on fire for one of the weddings."

Ravenna curled her lip. "I suppose. I am actually trying to help, you know."

"We know," Petty said, and patted her arm.

"If you're sure, Zuri?" Anna asked her.

"I appreciate you looking out for me. But I'm okay. Or I will be, and it's my job to look after you. I'll be right as rain soon, and then we'll get down to the nitty-gritty of planning your dream wedding."

"Zuri, don't worry about the wedding. You're what's important," Jordan said.

It made Phillip wonder how a guy like Jordan was best friends with a guy like Alec. He supposed the guy had to have some redeeming qualities.

Phillip remembered the people who saw the good in him and believed in the man he could be before he himself did.

Looking at Jordan he was determined to help Zuri fulfill her promise to him, not just because it was good for business but because he wanted to help give Anna and Jordan their dream. They were a nice couple, and good people.

He'd watched those bridezilla shows to prepare himself for what they were going to have to deal with when they started booking these weddings, and he understood why people behaved the way they did. Sometimes, they were obsessed with making the ceremony perfect because they thought it was a reflection of how the marriage would be. Or it was something they'd dreamed of.

Anna and Jordan knew what they wanted, but they were willing to put it all aside so someone they just met could rest and recover.

"You guys, I promise, you're going to have your dream wedding. FGI knows exactly what they're doing, and I'll have Zuri up and around in no time. In fact, why don't we plan on a late dinner in the ballroom tomorrow, where we can finalize some plans? My chef makes an excellent filet."

"If you're sure," Jordan said.

Alec shook his head. "No, we're not listening to Blond Ambition over there."

"Yes, we are. Because Zuri is. Let's go, Alec."

"Yes, Alec. Let's," Ravenna said, and she shot her foot out when he took a step forward.

Alec stumbled and was unable to recover his balance and fell face-first onto the floor.

"You should make him mop the room with his tongue." Ravenna clicked her tongue.

Zeva laughed. "We should, but we can plot that later."

Zuri waved everyone out. "Go on. I promise, I'll be fine. No more health checks, though. I need to take the antidote, take a shower, and get some rest."

After everyone had finally left, Phillip went back up to the bedroom loft and shoved his hands in his pockets.

"So. You gonna take this cure, or what?"

"I don't have any choice, do I?"

"Of course you have a choice. I don't think it has to be a big deal. A quick peck and we're done."

"You know, Phillip, my reluctance isn't because I *don't* want to kiss you."

Something strange and unfamiliar twisted up his insides. "I suppose that makes it worse, then, doesn't it?"

Chapter 13

Kissing Phillip was something Zuri wanted and feared.
She wanted it because he was hotter than fire, but she was afraid of it because her heart was still tender and vulnerable.

Whether she wanted to admit it, she'd already developed feelings for Phillip. Except, that made no sense to her. If she felt all these things for him, why hadn't her kiss been the cure he needed?

It made her think once again that magic was for some people and she wasn't one of the lucky ones.

Her love wasn't enough.

Ohhhhhh no. She didn't love him. Did she?

Feelings were one thing. They were delicate, new buds. New growth, but it wasn't love. It couldn't be.

Only it didn't matter if it was or not, because when it was all said and done, Zuri wasn't enough.

She hadn't been enough for Alec. If she had been, he wouldn't have been seeing her on the side. She wouldn't have been a dirty secret.

God, what would that even look like to have had all of Alec? She couldn't picture it now.

But she could picture it much too easily with Phillip. Except those visions were all peach pie in the sky, because she wasn't the one. Zuri wasn't enough to break his curse.

Watching him standing there, with all his vulnerability on

his sleeve, she wanted to tell him that none of it mattered. Not his curse, not her frog pox, not the fact that she couldn't break his curse, because her heart wanted him, but that was dangerous territory.

He may have been Prince Charming, but even he couldn't live up to her expectations, could he? She expected him to have a perfect past, and no one did. Everyone made mistakes, but his mistakes were the ones she just couldn't get past.

Even though those he'd wronged had long forgiven him. Even though they wished him well and actively sought his happiness.

When Ravenna had mentioned their conversation, Zuri had felt a flash of jealousy, and that kind of green felt worse than frog pox any day. She wasn't the jealous type. Zuri didn't believe the emotion served anything.

Being jealous was a reflection of insecurity.

It didn't change anything. Jealousy of Ravenna, who was beautiful and powerful and fearless, all the things Zuri strived to be, wouldn't change what they'd talked about. It wouldn't change Ravenna's feelings, or Phillip's.

The only thing it could do was hurt Zuri.

Needlessly.

She wanted his kiss.

Wanted it more than she'd wanted anything in a long time. She didn't just want a quick peck, as he'd so carelessly put it. She wanted their lips to crash together like some sort of inevitable storm. She wanted to feel the wide expanse of his shoulders under her palms. She wanted to get lost in him.

Most of all, Zuri wanted him to make her feel something more than this pain, and this numbness that had begun to form like ice around her heart.

She knew his kiss would burn that wall down, it would singe her from the inside out. So yes, she wanted it, but she feared it, too.

"Zuri, I don't want you to be a frog," he said, when she still didn't say anything.

She didn't know what to say. *Kiss me? Come here? Give it to me?* They all sounded stupid to her. "Not even to keep you company in the fountain?"

"I hate that fountain," he said, moving toward her.

She realized then she didn't have to say anything at all. She held out her arms to him, and suddenly he pressed her down against the bed. His weight was a delicious sensation, and Zuri knew then she was in deep shit.

This wouldn't be just a kiss, not with the fire that still burned hot and wild between them.

She hadn't wanted a cold, impersonal peck, but she didn't think she was ready for this, either.

His body was so big and hard, a perfect contrast to her softness. He cupped her face with his hand, and he looked into her eyes for a moment that seemed to stretch into forever. Phillip brushed his thumb over the fullness of her bottom lip.

She could feel his reaction to her, his arousal, and Zuri wanted to get closer. She wanted to feel everything he had to offer.

"You're beautiful. The most beautiful woman I've ever seen," he said.

"I don't even know how you can stand to look at me like this," she whispered.

"A few itchy spots don't change the light I see in you."

Zuri wished desperately for that to be true.

She realized again that she was still in that moment of turning, that time when her path would change again.

Zuri had to kiss him to get well, but she had this sense that it was going to change everything. Including things she wasn't ready to change.

So she waited to close that distance between them. She let them both hang frozen in the moment, with his warm breath on her lips and the desire building deep in her core.

"Tell me how you want this."

The words she'd been unable to find came to her in a rush. "Kiss me like you want to forever."

He descended slowly, and her lips tingled with the anticipation of his kiss. She'd swear that a thousand years passed before they made contact, but when his mouth slanted over hers, it was easily a thousand more.

The man obviously knew what he was doing, and she supposed he'd have to, being Prince Charming.

The itching that skittered across her body changed to something else. Something even more intense. Her whole body burned with the want of him.

She wound her arms around his back and gloried in the feel of his sculpted body. Zuri moved her hands over him and touched him in all the ways she'd fantasized about while he claimed her lips.

His hand moved from her waist up to the edge of her pajama shirt, and part of her logical mind told her she should tell him to stop, but she didn't want him to stop. She wanted more.

Only, he made her make a conscious choice. His hand paused, his fingers warm on her skin. "May I touch you?"

"If you don't, I'll curse you again," she whispered against his lips.

He held her gaze while his hand traveled up to her breast and he cupped the weight in his hand, his thumb stroking over the engorged flesh of her nipple the way he'd stroked her lip. Carefully, with a designed purpose. To bring her body to life.

"May I taste you?" he whispered next, his mouth just at the corner of her lips.

She loved everything he was doing to her, but it gave him too much power. She couldn't surrender so easily. "What would you do if I said no?"

"Stop, of course," he said, and pressed his lips to her jaw.

"Tell me more. Tell me how you'd feel."

He moved his lips to her neck, and she was dizzy with her want of him.

"Which body part do you want to hear about first? The fact it would break my heart, or about the depraved things I'd do to myself in my room while I thought of you? Of this moment?"

"I like both."

He moved his lips down the line of her neck, down to her breasts. When he tugged her pajama top off, she was hit with a cold realization.

She couldn't do this.

Zuri wanted to, but this wasn't the way to fix her broken heart. It was a Band-Aid that wouldn't last long, and when it fell off, she'd be more devastated than before.

"Phillip?" she said, putting a hand on his shoulder.

He pulled back with a questioning look on his face.

"I'm sorry."

"Don't be sorry." He pressed another kiss to her lips, but this one was gentle and soft, with no insistence. "I'm not."

"I want to be with you like this, it feels so good. But it's not what either of us needs."

"It's definitely what I need." He flashed her a carefree grin. "But I understand. Any time you change your mind, you let me know."

Phillip eased away from her, and she felt cold and somehow abandoned. She immediately regretted her choice.

"I . . . I don't know what else to say."

"You don't have to say anything else."

"But I want to. I'm having so many complicated feelings." She gestured vaguely.

"I'm not going anywhere, Zuri. We have time. I said you could trust me, and you can. With your body, your mind, and your heart."

Somehow, that still sounded too good to be true.

"Can we have drinking chocolate again soon?"

"Anytime you like. What about if you let me take you for dinner? A real date."

"Where would we go? Pick 'n' Axe?"

"Why not?"

"I have to warn you, I really love those throwing axes."

"I'm game." He pressed his lips to her forehead. "Drink water. Sleep until you wake up. Don't worry about the wedding planning. The godmothers will take care of it."

"I assume you're going to report in?"

He nodded. "I have to let them know that their charge is cured and she'll be back in the fray tomorrow."

"Cured, huh? I never believed in magic dick, but here we are." She bit the inside of her cheek. Zuri hadn't meant to say that out loud. It had just sort of jumped off her tongue like a lemming.

"I guess it must be magic if it cured you without touching you."

"Oh, it touched me, Prince Charming."

He grinned again. "I guess you get to use the title."

"You guess?"

He winked at her. "Can I get you anything before I leave?"

She wanted to tell him not to leave, to get back in bed with her and finish what they'd started, but she did know better.

This was her making better choices.

Healthier choices.

A little voice in the back of her head said turning down what was probably going to be the best sex of her life was not a healthy choice.

Only, her heart felt differently. Her heart definitely wanted her to climb him like a tree, but these tender moments between them that weren't about the primal burn were better than any kind of superglue, and slowly, the pieces began to fit back together.

"If you see Zeva, send her in. I'm feeling much better."

"She probably knows you want to see her and is on her way." He went to the door, but paused to look back up at her.

Zuri was suddenly self-conscious about sickbed fashion, but he winked at her again.

"See you tomorrow, gorgeous."

"Same to ya, Prince Charming."

He opened the door, and right after he left, her ever-knowing sister came back in.

"Well, you look better. Only he wasn't here long enough to accomplish anything worth a sister conference."

Zuri cackled. "Curing me from the green plague doesn't count?"

"No."

"Come here anyway," Zuri pleaded.

"I would say I don't want to go up to that bed of sin, only I'm sure there wasn't enough time for any decent sinning to happen."

"Oh my God, Zeva. Plenty happened. Bring me a cookie from the kitchen, and I'll tell you about it."

"I can be bribed. I'll bring the box."

It wasn't long before Zeva was once again up in the bed with her and they had cookies and a pitcher of chocolate milk that managed to appear from somewhere.

Zuri had realized that the castle knew what she wanted and sought to provide it. Which was cool and scary at the same time, considering how often she thought about what she wanted to do with its owner.

"Okay, so tell me. What happened?"

"Well, he's a frog. But you knew that."

"I did."

"Kissing me was the cure."

"Was it everything you hoped?"

"It was more."

"Then why am I in here talking to you instead of Phillip?"

"Because we're taking our time. Because all this is a lot to process. How is it so easy for you?"

Zeva shrugged. "I don't know, but Petunia said she had something she wanted to talk to me about."

"How long can you stay?"

"Just a few days, then I have to get back to the kids. I was worried about you, Zuri. You scared ten years off my life."

"No, it was the twin thing that scared you. I did nothing."

"Fine, I suppose you're right, there. But it felt like you were deathbed sick."

"Phillip did tell me if I didn't take the cure, I'd turn into a frog, so . . ."

"We can't take you anywhere, can we?"

"Nope, guess not." Zuri ate a cookie.

"I love it here, Zuri. I love everything about this place. I met a . . . a person in the hallway. I got lost going to my room, and he's the most amazing . . ."

"Tell me," Zuri prompted.

"He's kind, generous, and strangely handsome."

"How strange? There are levels here, and I need to know."

Zeva laughed. "He's level ten. He's a cursed prince. Or he was, much like Phillip. His name is Hunter."

"Phillip told me about him."

"I think we're going to be friends."

"Oh yeah?" Zuri nudged her sister.

Zeva took a bite of one of the cookies. "Yeah. Just friends. He's got it bad for Gorgeous McEvil."

"Ravenna?"

"Yeah, that one." Zeva sighed. "Too bad for me, huh?"

"Maybe not. You never know."

"Well, I won't go into a new friendship wishing for him not to get what he wants so I can have a chance at what I want."

"You're a good egg, Zeva."

"I know. So are you."

They curled up together in the bed, and the lights dimmed of their own accord and little glow-in-the-dark stars appeared on the velvet canopy of the bed. It was so much like when they were children.

"See? Magic is real. You just have to be willing to see."

"Do you think zebras can change their stripes, Zeva?"

"I think that men aren't zebras. People evolve and change, but you must always take them for who they are in any given moment."

"Complicated."

"Yes and no."

They turned to look at each other and laughed.

"That's how I feel about Phillip. Yes and no."

"So you just need to figure out if it's more yes or more no." Zeva pulled the blanket up over them. "Even then, sometimes more no is still a yes."

"Not helpful."

"No, it isn't, is it?" Zeva laughed.

"I'm glad you're here."

"Me too. I wish I could stay longer."

"Be careful what you wish for. I think the castle has a way of anticipating wants and needs. You might find yourself trapped in the dungeon."

"With a terrible beast?" Zeva giggled.

"That would be the worst. Just the worst." Zuri sighed overdramatically.

"Whatever would I do?"

They dissolved into laughter.

"I wonder if Hunter has super hearing. Do you think he can hear us giggling?" Zuri asked.

"Maybe. If so, I should probably not tell you all the thoughts I had about his loincloth."

"He wears a loincloth? Good Lord."

"He has pillaging thighs." Zeva bit her lip. "And I quite like his eyebrows. They're very masterful."

"Masterful eyebrows? You're killing me."

"Fine. Your turn. Tell me something about the cursed prince. Yours, I mean."

Zuri considered. "Okay. I think kissing him is the closest I can get to heaven without dying."

"Whoa."

"I know."

"This is serious."

Then they looked at each other and were overtaken by another fit of laughter.

When Zeva stopped to catch her breath, she said, "Told you so."

"Nobody likes a know-it-all."

"You're stuck with me, wombmate."

Zuri found that the normalcy of these moments with Zeva was exactly what she needed.

Chapter 14

It had been a few days since he'd told Zuri about magic. Since they'd made their own magic with the kiss they'd shared.

A kiss.

That didn't begin to describe what had happened between them. How could something so extraordinary be described with only two words? It couldn't.

He'd thrown himself into helping with Anna and Jordan's wedding, and he'd gotten to spend a lot more time with Zuri. Especially now that he didn't have to hide anything about himself. They spent their evenings working until a late dinner, and then they talked over wine for hours, until neither of them could keep their eyes open.

He watched her across the Once Upon a Time Ballroom as the castle assisted her in hanging the soft, tiny flower bud lights Anna had wanted for the reception.

Zuri shook her head and directed the castle to move the latest string. She laughed when it obviously took her instructions way too literally. The string of lights jiggled at her in midair, and she continued to laugh. He heard her apologize to the castle for not being clear.

She. Apologized.

The castle was enchanted. It didn't have feelings.

Did it?

He was always polite to his home, but he'd never considered the prospect. Phillip had been living like this for three hundred years, and she'd discovered magic only recently.

Her heart was kind. It was the most beautiful thing about her.

She stopped what she was doing and turned to look at him. When her lips bloomed in a smile, he couldn't help but smile back.

He loved watching her work. He loved watching her do most anything, honestly. He was completely smitten with Zuri Davis.

She wiggled her fingers in a wave and turned back to what she was doing, although she tossed him one more sultry glance over her shoulder and shook her ass in a little tease.

He found himself for the first time imagining a future. Not just all the things he would do once he no longer had to spend his days green, but he imagined this. With Zuri.

Phillip liked working on the weddings. When he'd first opened the castle as a B and B, he'd thought it was going to be another tour in hell. Too many people in his space, too many people asking for his time and attention, too much to do.

Only the castle took care of everything. As the town's supply of love and magic increased, so did the castle's efficiency.

The guests mostly stayed out of his wing, and the castle kept them from bothering Hunter.

This new normal wasn't the way he'd imagined his life turning out, but that was okay with him. For the first time in a long time, he was happy.

One could even say content.

It wasn't that he didn't still strive for things, or he didn't want more, but he could see the path unfolding, and he wanted to take that journey with Zuri.

He'd never thought that about a woman before. Not even when he was courting Petty and Bluebonnet. He assumed he'd choose one of them, and they'd settle into a life. These feelings he had now were completely different.

He looked up again from his task of hand-lettering all the dinner cards, something he quite enjoyed, to watch Zuri.

Only instead of Zuri, he found Petty in his line of sight. She wore a dust cap with a few of her white curls peeking out from the lace, and a pink smock.

"Why do you look like Mrs. Claus?"

She raised a brow and crossed her arms. "You think you're funny, do you?"

He shrugged. "You're the one who left the house looking like that."

"I've come to finish the plans for the frog-kissing booth at the carnival." She looked down to his quill and ink. "Why don't you let the castle take care of that?"

"Because I like calligraphy."

"Hmm. Well, it's just going to have to wait. We need to talk about how to get your frog self to stay in the booth. We can't very well have people traipsing all the way to the fountain, unless we held the carnival in that little clearing, but I really wanted to do it in the town square. That way, it'll bring more people into the shops."

The idea of the kissing booth just seemed wrong now.

"I have a question."

"I might have an answer," Petty replied.

"Well, one would hope, since I'm asking you."

She cleared her throat and crossed her arms. "Well. One would. Do go on."

"Yes, well. If someone breaks my curse, that means I have to marry them, right?"

"One would assume you'd want to, since it's True Love's Kiss that's supposed to break your spell." Petty put her finger to her chin. "Good thing I've got my thinking cap on. I'm trying to remember the specifics of the curse. I don't think there's anything in there that says you have to."

His gaze was drawn to Zuri again. It was actually amazing

he'd gotten anything done, because all he could do was watch her, and he savored those secret glances between them.

"Hey. I'm right here." Petty snapped her fingers to get his attention.

"Sorry. I, uh, don't know if I want to do the kissing booth."

"Really? Okay. I mean, it would still be a really cute gig, and it would get you lots of smooch traffic you wouldn't otherwise get."

"This is probably not something you expected me to say, but I think I'm okay without it."

"Even if it would break your curse?" Petty asked.

He took a moment to really consider what that meant. He didn't want to kiss anyone but Zuri. "I've spent so much time trying to break the curse that I haven't stopped to consider what True Love's Kiss really means. Even if it's not true love, I don't want to kiss anyone else."

Petty grinned. "Phillip, that's really wonderful."

"Is it?" he asked, shaking his head. "I don't know. I might be shooting myself in the foot."

"Maybe, but that's the chance we all take."

"So what about some of the other frogs who hang out near the fountain? They might like to get kissed."

"That could work, but you're the only one I know personally. I can't recommend anyone just kissing a random frog. That's unsanitary."

"You wanna talk about unsanitary? Woman, I've been waking up with various insect legs in my teeth for years."

"Spiderweb floss does wonders for that. I can drop some off next trip." Petty picked up one of the cards and inspected it. "No offense to our delightful castle, but this really is top-notch work. You better be careful, or I'll have you enlisted for hand-lettering invitations on the other weddings."

"Trade you. I'll letter the invitations for the floss."

"Fair enough." She put the card back down on the table

carefully. "You know, it's quite something that you're willing to keep waking up with those wings and bits in your teeth for her."

Phillip considered. "It would be easy to say that I'm doing it for her, but it's not just for her. It's for me, too. It's a chance to really explore being with another person with no endgame in mind."

"Since you're telling the truth, Phillip, don't try to say you don't have an endgame in mind." She tapped his hand with her wand.

"I suppose I do have an endgame in mind, but it's for both of us."

"Tell me. What is it?"

"What, do you want me to paint you pictures of castles in clouds?"

"Why wouldn't you? You know this is what I do. This is my favorite part!" she pleaded.

"They're *all* your favorite part." Phillip didn't begrudge her. He was starting to see why.

She held out her hand, and a steaming coffee mug appeared. She took a long drink and sighed. "You're right about that."

"Fine. This. Right now. This is my castle in the clouds. Just being close to her while she does what she loves. It makes me love it, too."

She reached out and squeezed his shoulder. "That's good stuff, Phillip. By the way, have you seen Zeva today? I need to speak to her before she leaves."

"No, I haven't seen her."

"Can I tell you a secret?"

"About Zeva?" He looked at Zuri. "I don't know. I couldn't keep anything from her about her sister."

Petty rolled her eyes and sighed heavily.

"If you don't stop sighing, you're going to blow the castle over like the Bid Bad Wolf."

Then she snorted. "Zeva is a candidate for Fairy God-mother Academy. That's why she could see all the magic as soon as she hit town."

"That's huge."

"Right?"

"I noticed she had a fairy godmother kind of sparkle in her eyes when I met her. That's wonderful."

"She can say no, but I hope she doesn't."

"You know she's going to want to make sure all those kids are taken care of before she goes."

"I think you could help with that."

"Me?"

"Yes. So I have a plan."

"Oh no."

"Oh yes." Petty stomped her foot. "You haven't even heard my plan."

"Okay, let's have it. You want me to foster all those kids at the castle. Is that what you're going to ask me?"

"No. And yes."

"Have mercy. Out with it."

"Well, I know that Zeva loves each of those children like her own. It would be impossible for her to adopt them all. Unless, she could do it here. In the castle. And I know just who I want to help her."

He laughed. "Hunter? Are you serious?"

"He'd be a great father. The kids are all still young enough they'd accept magic more easily than adults."

"You want Hunter and Zeva to raise those kids together? Is he going to be a stay-at-home beast?"

"Well, why not?"

"First of all, he's head over tail for Ravenna."

"Ugh. I know, but that's not going to last."

"Because of your meddling?"

"Because Ravenna belongs with someone else. I've seen it."

"Maybe Ravenna doesn't see it that way. He's been to the castle for tea."

"Oh my. Things have already started to spiral out of control. I'm telling you, things are going to get ugly for them both if they don't get on the right track."

"What am I supposed to do, tell Hunter he shouldn't pursue the first woman he's been interested in in a hundred years?"

Petty opened her mouth to say something when Bronx, a fat red cardinal almost too fat for his own wings, flew into the hall and landed on her shoulder.

"Heya, toots."

"Hello to you, too," Petty replied.

"I bring news, and youse not gonna like it." The bird turned to look at him.

"Me? What now?"

"I got a message from the academy."

Phillip's stomach dropped, but he was careful to school his features.

"On the anniversary of da curse, it'll be permanent."

That wasn't so bad. Hunter's curse was permanent. This wasn't what Phillip had imagined for himself, but that was okay. He'd find a way to live with it.

"Not what I was hoping to hear, but okay." He took a deep breath. "I can deal with this. It's fine. I've been doing this dance a long time."

"Nah, Charming. There's more."

"Bronx?" Petty asked softly. "What do you mean, there's more? How can there be more? I didn't . . . oh no." She covered her hand with her mouth, and Bronx rubbed his head against her cheek.

"Excuse me? Can someone draw me a picture?"

"Youse gonna be a frog, my friend. Full-time."

Phillip had been hit with a wrecking ball. All his hopes, his dreams, his newly born visions of a future had been crushed with only a few words.

In a panic, he thought about the kissing booth, and his mind began reeling and spinning all his outs and options.

"This can't be right," Petty whispered. "We'll figure this out. I won't let this happen."

Phillip couldn't stand the sight or the sound of her at the moment. His blaming her wouldn't help, but now that the hope was gone, it had been replaced with a useless fury.

"Petunia, can you please give me a moment?"

"I . . ."

"Go, Petty."

He got up from his chair, and without a word to anyone, he made his way to his quarters.

Phillip was ever pragmatic, and he knew that his feelings for Zuri didn't matter any longer.

If he was forced to permanent frogdom, he wouldn't even remember them anyway.

His only choice was to somehow convince Ravenna to marry him and pray to all the powers in this universe and the next that it worked.

And convince his friend not to hate him.

He guessed Petty was right. Hunter wasn't supposed to end up with Ravenna, and the threads of fate had moved to decree it so.

That is, if he could convince her to say yes. She had zero reason to agree to his scheme. He didn't know what he had, what he could offer her to make it worth her while.

He scrubbed a hand over his face and realized before he did any of that, he had to tell Zuri.

It was the right thing to do.

Phillip supposed it was a good thing they hadn't consummated their feelings that night of the kiss. It would've only made this harder.

More painful.

Part of him wanted to rail against his fate. To lash out. To . . .

It was all useless.

Being angry wouldn't change anything. It wouldn't automatically mitigate the curse, or the finality of it all.

There was another part of him, a quieter part of him that told him the curse didn't matter. He'd lived a long—and mostly useless and privileged—life.

Wasn't it worth it to trade it for something that mattered? A few days with Zuri was better than an eternity without her. He could choose, after all. He could choose her.

In time, he'd be just another frog. He wouldn't remember any of this. So why not pass his time living with the good things he'd been given?

"Why not?" he murmured to himself.

Only, he knew the answer to that. It wasn't fair to Zuri to ask her to keep spending time with him, to keep building a bond that was going to be torn from them both either way.

Every single avenue of escape that lit up in his brain like neon always crashed in a dead end.

For a single moment, he considered marrying Ravenna, and then they could both go on about their business with the people they wanted.

Number one, Phillip knew magic wouldn't be appeased with something so simple.

Zuri wouldn't even consider that kind of arrangement.

Neither would Hunter.

He found it ironic that Ravenna would.

Maybe he should've been a dark prince, instead of Prince Charming. It would've been so much easier.

He wouldn't be about to become a damn frog for the rest of his life, that was for sure.

But he also wouldn't have met Zuri.

Damn it.

How did he tell her it was all over?

How was he supposed to tell her that he was choosing to break his curse over her? He couldn't do that to her, either.

This was the biggest pile of troll shit he'd ever managed to step in. Neck-deep.

When her soft knock came at the door, he couldn't face her.

"I'm not feeling well, Zuri. If I've caught a bug, I don't want to take the chance I'll make you sick."

"That's too bad, Your Royal Hotness. I was thinking we needed another kissing session. I guess I'll just see you tomorrow."

"Not if I see you first," he replied, and immediately hated himself.

"Can I bring you something?"

"No, love. Just get some rest. I will, too." He leaned against the door and wanted desperately to see her, to touch her face, to kiss her.

What he fucking wanted was a Happily Ever After, but no one was going to give him that, were they?

"Good night," she said.

He listened at the door until he could no longer hear the sound of her footsteps.

Chapter 15

Zuri had decided to spend the day with Zeva since she had to go back to Chicago early the next morning. Especially since it seemed she was doing most of her work for Fairy Godmothers, Inc., with Phillip in the evening.

Anna and Jordan had easily adjusted to the hours. The only fly in the ointment, so to speak, was Alec. He kept asking her when they were going to talk, but she just didn't have time.

She'd admit, it gave her a bit of a thrill to be the one telling him she just couldn't get away. Not that she wanted to.

Zuri realized she had nothing to say to him and she didn't owe it to him to let him speak. He could find closure in his own way. She just knew anything he had to say would be an attempt to push past her boundaries and weasel his way back in.

She wasn't tempted; she didn't want his excuses. So what was the point?

"You're awfully quiet this afternoon, Zuri. Daydreaming about your hot nights?" Zeva teased as they walked around the manicured gardens of the castle.

Zuri's cheeks warmed. "Actually, no. I was thinking about how I can't wait to be done with this wedding so I don't have to see Alec's face anymore."

"You're not going to talk to him? Isn't there anything you want to say to him?"

"I've had a chance to think about it, and no. I really don't." She waited on tenterhooks to see what her sister would say. If she'd argue with her.

"Good. I'm glad that you're moving on."

"It's funny how that works. It seemed like life was at a standstill, and now everything is barreling at me a thousand miles an hour."

"I know. Me too."

"Did something happen?" Zuri asked.

"Something amazing. Petty found a way to take care of the kids. They're all going to come to the castle. Phillip said they could stay. One of their godsons is a lawyer, and he's going to take care of all the paperwork." Zeva grabbed her hand. "How do you feel about being an aunt?"

"You're adopting all the children?"

"Yes. And I've said yes to Fairy Godmother Academy."

Zuri was stunned but happy. Zeva's joy radiated from her, and it was infectious in the best way. Tears gathered in her eyes. "Oh my God, Zeva. That's amazing. It looks like we both get to make magic in our own ways."

"They don't usually accept applicants my age, but since I've already adjusted to magic and because their numbers are so low, I'm in!"

"You're going to change the world in a big way, just like you always wanted."

"I'm probably not going to see Phillip again before I leave, since I'll be headed out at dawn. So can you thank him for me?"

"Of course. If I get to see him. He wasn't feeling well last night."

"Wasn't feeling well? Huh. I didn't think anyone here got sick. Except frog pox."

"Yeah, I didn't, either. But that's okay. Maybe it was a different kind of not feeling well." Zuri shrugged.

"Oh no. Here comes Dr. Jackass now."

"Zuri! I was just looking for you."

"What do you need, Alec?"

"Can you come to Rosebud's and look at my tux. I'm not sure if it's going to work."

"Rosebud is absolutely amazing. I'm sure she can tell you if it's going to work or not."

"Anna wants your opinion," he said with a helpless shrug.

"I can't right now." Zuri looked at her phone. "This is my off time. When I'm back on the job, I'll pop on over to Rosebud's."

"Sorry, she's busy." Zeva put an arm around Zuri's shoulder.

"Look, I know you don't want to deal with me right now, and that's fine, but Anna is stressing. Could you come for her?"

Zuri didn't want to tell Anna no, especially with how accommodating she'd been about everything else. "Okay, I can do that, but not this minute. Zeva leaves in the morning and we're finalizing some other plans. Personal and business."

"Okay. I understand. Rosebud did say that she could send the dresses and the tuxes to the castle later this evening, if that helps."

"Why didn't you open with that?" Zeva demanded.

"Because I'd rather she come now. The rest of us have multiple tasks to accomplish to make sure that Anna and Jordan have the wedding they deserve."

Zuri felt a momentary flush of guilt, but it was quickly washed away. "And they will. That's our job at Fairy Godmothers, Inc., to make sure they get the wedding of their dreams. Go on to your next task, and I'll see you in about an hour back at the castle."

"Fine. See you later," Alec said, and walked away.

"What did I ever see in him?" Zuri asked.

"Well, he is handsome. He's got a good job. He ticks everything off the list. Except for the personality part, and he hid that with charming manners."

"Do you think I'm making the same mistake with Phillip?"

"No. Phillip is nothing like Alec. But if you don't know that, maybe you should slow down."

"Thanks. You're right, and I do know that, I guess I'm just scared to believe it." Zuri sighed. "I suppose I should think about going in to work."

"Yeah, I think I should get a nap and pack. Or pack and then nap. Either way, somewhere in there I'm going to take advantage of the baths down in the dungeon.

"The baths?"

"There are hot mineral baths down there. Didn't you know? They're absolutely lovely."

"It doesn't hurt that you might stumble across a certain person?"

"We've chatted a few times." Zeva looked away. "Anyway, I'll let you do what you need to do." She hugged her. "I'll miss you, even though it won't be for long."

Zuri squeezed her back and then let her go.

After Zeva was gone, Zuri tilted her face up to the sun and let herself enjoy the warmth for a few minutes longer. The smell of the grass and the singing birds helped her to ground herself and just enjoy the moment

She decided to grab a shower and eat a light meal to fortify her to deal with Alec.

It was so wild to her that only two months ago, she'd been excited for any crumb of time he'd thrown her way, and now she couldn't wait to be rid of him.

Zuri enjoyed Anna and Jordan immensely, and was having a wonderful time working on their wedding, and really getting back into her groove and feeling confident about her work. Except for Alec's presence.

Surprisingly, he didn't make her doubt herself, and her irritation at having to deal with him had nothing to do with how she felt about herself professionally. He was simply a buzzing insect in her ear she couldn't seem to swat.

Zuri found strength in that.

After she'd showered and eaten a magnificent salad of field greens, chicken, bacon, hickory almonds, and a ridiculously large serving of crispy capers (her favorite thing) sprinkled on top with a ginger vinaigrette, she was ready to work.

She didn't know how she'd ever go back to not having a magical kitchen ready to anticipate her every need.

A travel mug with the Charming B and B logo appeared, and Zuri snatched it up to find it was a blond mocha with heavy cream. Exactly what she needed to get her workday off to a great start.

"Thanks," she murmured to the castle.

She felt a little silly speaking to it, but she thanked her maps app and all her smart devices. It just seemed like the thing to do.

The Once Upon a Time Ballroom was set up with tables and undying flowers in the soft blue theme that Anna and Jordan had chosen. Hansel was busy constructing the stage where the happy couple would act out the shoe scene, and she saw a place had been cleared for Rosebud.

In fact, it was almost as if half of Rosebud's shop had been transplanted in the northwest corner of the ballroom. Chaises and pillows abounded, with changing closets and mirrors, and even a small place for each person to model their clothes.

Rosebud was already waiting for Zuri and waved her over.

"I'm so sorry to have to bother you with this, but we can't seem to make a choice. I don't care for how the color turned out on the bridesmaids' dresses, or Alec's tux. I feel Alec's outshines the groom. The groom, of course, doesn't care."

Zuri took another sip from her coffee. "No worries, Rosebud. This is what I'm here for. Where would you like to start?"

Rosebud gestured vaguely, and Zuri understood exactly what she meant.

"Okay, let's start with the bridesmaids' dresses."

Rosebud called out, "Ladies, if you please."

One by one, the women stepped out from the dressing area, and Rosebud was absolutely right. The blue on the dresses was too dark, and it was the ugliest shade of blue Zuri had ever seen.

Somehow, it managed to be dark blue and brown at the same time. Zuri wasn't quite sure how any fabric could look like that.

"Oh!" she gasped. "Oh no."

"So it's not just me losing my mind? I've been in this business for a long time, but never . . . I'm afraid we might be too late. I could try to dye them, but . . ."

The bridesmaids all looked rather horrified and sad at this change of events.

"Don't worry, this is all under control," Zuri called to them. "We'll get them fixed. You all look lovely in the cuts and styles of the gowns you've chosen. This is an easy fix."

"It is?" Rosebud asked her. "Do you know something I don't?"

"We can ask the castle. If it can miracle me a mocha, I don't know why it couldn't change the color on the dress," she said under her breath.

"You're a genius!" Rosebud cried. "I don't know why I didn't think of that. Hmm. So," she began, as she pulled out a color wheel from her bag. "What do you think?"

Zuri considered and pointed to a blue silk sample that was two shades darker than baby blue but managed to complement the blue of the groom's jacket. "We should try this one.

"I was thinking that as well. With some pale pink rosettes on the sleeves and the waistlines?"

"And a pale pink insert in the trains."

"Perfect!" She looked up at the bridesmaids. "You can all go. Leave your dresses in the changing room, I'll take care of them, and we'll do another fitting soon. Thank you for your time!"

168 *Saranna DeWylde*

As they began to file out, Rosebud smiled at all of them, but when she turned back to Zuri she said, "I was losing my mind. My brain gave up and said no more."

"I totally understand. I'm sorry I couldn't come to the shop, I know that would've been easier for you."

Rosebud waved it off. "It's fine. I know you've got a lot to do, too. What with trying to put this together in three weeks? Even with magic, that's kind of a miracle."

"I think we're going to pull it off." Pride surged in Zuri's chest. "It's going to be beautiful. So, thank you for your part."

Rosebud smiled. "It's my job. And of course, there's the part where I do love it."

"So the best man's tux is a problem?"

Rosebud pressed her palm to her forehead. "Anna and Jordan said they could all choose their own styles. They wanted everyone to be comfortable, which is so thoughtful, but . . ." She turned toward the dressing rooms. "Alec, are you ready?"

Alec came out of the dressing area and stopped to stand in front of the mirrors, and it, too, was perfectly horrible.

He'd chosen a blue . . . well, it had breeches and a military jacket with tassels and . . .

"Doesn't that look exactly like Ransom Payne's look?" Rosebud asked her.

Thinking back, she realized it did. "What does the groom's tux look like again?"

Rosebud pulled out her laptop and showed her a pic of the groom.

The groom had chosen a royal-blue ensemble that was a fabulous choice for his build, coloring, and sense of style. It was elegant but understated.

The best man was flashier, and it definitely drew the attention away from Jordan and Anna.

"Can you turn to the side, Alec?" Rosebud called.

He did as he was told, and the tassels were just too much.

Zuri approached him, trying to decide if she should advise Rosebud to make alterations to this or if they should tell Alec he needed to start over.

At this stage in the game, working with what they had would be the best choice, if that was possible.

She tugged lightly at the tassels, and they came off without too much effort. It was still as if Alec were dressed as the groom.

"We may need to go with something else, if that's all right with you?" she asked him.

"Whatever you think," Alec agreed easily.

"Yeah, okay. Did you have any other choices? We can go through them and see what will best fit the theme of the wedding."

"Yeah, I have them in the changing room."

Zuri didn't think anything of following him back into the changing room. Not until he locked the door behind her and stood between her and the door.

"What are you doing?"

"Zuri, we're going to talk. I can't get you to talk to me any other way; we're doing it now."

"You know, I could just scream my head off, and Rosebud would come and let me out."

"Please just talk to me."

"We've already been through this. I don't want to talk to you. I don't care. It's over. It's done with."

"Not for me, it's not."

Instead of getting angry, Zuri said, "It doesn't always get to be about you."

"I know that. I was wrong. I love you, Zuri. Let me prove it to you."

"If you love me, you'd respect my space and my wishes. You'd let me do my job without locking me in a dressing room."

"Come on, you can't say there's anyone else you'd rather be

locked in a room with than me." He reached out to touch her face. "We had some good times. We can have them again."

"I can say there's someone else I'd rather be locked in a dark room with."

"Oh really? Name him."

"Phillip Charming."

A light exploded overhead, sending bits of spark and glass raining down on them, and suddenly everything was dark, and it smelled of must and age.

She reached out with her hand to feel the wall and realized she was no longer in the makeshift dressing room because the walls were stone.

Someone else was in the dark with her. Someone big, who sucked all the air out of the space. Heat radiated from him.

"Zuri?" Phillip asked.

"Oh, thank God it's you." She breathed a heavy sigh of relief.

"What are we doing here?"

"I don't know. One minute, I was helping Rosebud in the ballroom, and the next I was here. Wherever that is . . . ?"

She couldn't see much and reached out again. She found his solid chest, noticed that it was bare and his flesh was hot under her hands. It calmed the panic that had been rising in her throat, but stoked urgency other places in her body.

"I was just getting dressed and now I'm here. Might you have made any wishes?"

"What's with you and wishes? First the wish coin, and now this." Except, she had kind of made a wish, hadn't she? "Oh," she murmured.

"Oh, what? What did you do?"

"Don't blame me. It's your stupid castle that takes things too literally."

He rumbled with a laugh. "Okay, Zuri. But what did you say?"

"I was in the changing room—"

"Changing room?"

"Rosebud brought half her shop to the castle so I could help finalize some details. There were some issues with some of the fabrics. Anyway, I was trying to help Alec, and he locked us in together. He said he was sure there was no one else I'd rather be locked in a dark room with . . . and I might've said you."

Phillip laughed. "Oh God. Okay, you're right. The castle definitely takes things too literally."

"It delivers a great mocha, and I had the best salad for lunch, so I can't complain too much." She realized her hands were stroking over his shoulders, and his back, and she jerked her hands away. "I'm sorry."

"I don't mind. You can touch me all you like."

The idea appealed. "I'm supposed to be helping Rosebud."

"I'm supposed to be getting dressed to come help you help Rosebud. But here we are."

She dared to touch him again, her hands sliding down his sides. "How naked are you?"

He laughed again, and his hands covered hers, guiding them down to his hips, which were also bare.

"Good Lord," she breathed.

"We could always try telling the castle to let us out," he said.

She didn't want to be let out. "Or, you know, a door. Is there one of those?" But she wasn't really interested in a door.

"I don't think so. I've been here before. Once, I decided I wanted to hide from the world. I told the castle I didn't want to be found. It locked me in here for two weeks. Basically, until I'd gotten over my tantrum."

"But it still fed you, right?"

He laughed again. "Yeah, it still fed me. Do you want snacks? Or do you want it to let you out?"

"You keep saying to let me out. You don't want out?"

"Not really. I know what I'm supposed to say, and I know what I really feel."

"So you're feeling better from last night?"

"Not really. I got some bad news."

"Do you want to talk about it?" she asked him, still hyper-aware of her hands on his skin and the proximity of his naked body.

"No. Not until I decide what to do."

"You don't have to decide by yourself. I can be a good listener."

"I don't want to tell you where I can't see your face."

She stepped closer to him. "Maybe it's better that you can't."

"Maybe." He released her hands and pulled her even closer so she was flush against him. "I found out that if I don't break my curse, one of these next times I change into a frog, I won't come back."

His words stabbed her with a thousand knives. That just couldn't happen. She wouldn't let it.

"No."

"Straight from Fairy Godmother Academy."

"Phillip, we'll figure it out. The godmothers have to know some kind of loophole. This is what we do. You can't have a Happily Ever After as a frog." What she wanted to say, but knew it sounded selfish as hell, was that she couldn't have a Happily Ever After if he was a frog.

"I don't want to discuss it anymore, if that's all right with you," he said softly.

Zuri wasn't going to push. He'd opened up to her, and if that was all he wanted to give her, that was okay.

Except she had something she wanted to give him.

If they didn't have any time left, she wanted to know what it was like to be with him.

"Maybe we should go back to what we should be doing. Castle?" he asked.

"No," she said. "I don't want to go back. That can all wait. This can't." She wrapped her arms around his neck and stood on her tiptoes to press her mouth to his.

"Zuri, all the reasons why you wanted to wait are still valid."

"I don't care." She took his hands and moved them to her breasts. "Touch me, Phillip."

"If I was really Prince Charming, I wouldn't allow our first time to be in a broom closet like some bad fairy-tale fan fiction." His mouth closed over the tender part of her neck, and his hands tore her shirt off.

"Wait, wait," she gasped. "In the unsanitized versions of these stories . . ."

"No. That's not me."

"Oh, good. Carry on," she said, and arched back into him.

His hands were everywhere, and in just moments, she was bare to him. The room was cold, and she wanted his touch, his warmth. She'd never felt so naked being naked. So exposed.

So vulnerable.

Even though it was dark, she could still feel the intensity of his gaze somehow.

A small candle breathed to life as the room changed around them to accommodate their fantasies.

"In my whole long life, I've never seen a woman as beautiful as you are, Zuri. Let me worship you."

Who the hell could, or would say no to that?

He lifted her easily and she found herself reclining on the softest mattress she'd ever felt. It was like a cloud. But it could've been the stone wall for all she cared, because when he dipped his head between her thighs, she was floating anyway.

Phillip took her higher than she'd ever been before. She

pushed her fingers through his hair, and arched up to meet his mouth.

This was definitely better than anything else she had on her to-do list.

She wondered vaguely if elsewhere in the castle they were searching for her, but any other cares were washed away by the insistent flick of his tongue.

Zuri surrendered to the pleasure, to the waves of bliss, and it wasn't long before she was clawing at his shoulders while starbursts of ecstasy washed over her in a tsunami.

He didn't stop worshipping her. He kissed her thigh, her hip, her stomach, and blazed a trail up her body, back up to her mouth, where he kissed her hard.

She could taste her own pleasure, and his erection pressed hard against her belly.

"Do you still want this?"

Chapter 16

He searched her eyes, and waited for her answer.

Phillip wanted her permission again. He needed it, because he knew this might be their only chance to be together like this. He didn't want her to regret it, or him.

"Yes," she said simply.

"Are you on birth control?" he asked.

"Will the castle supply condoms, too, if we want them?"

"Most definitely."

"Do magical people get STDs?" she asked.

He laughed. "No, not unless it's a curse."

"That's an awful curse."

"Uh-huh."

"Well, I got tested right after I found out about Alec anyway. Clean bill of health. I have an implant. So no unplanned babies."

"Tell me again that you want me. Then tell me how you want me," he whispered in her ear.

"I want this more than anything, and I want it with no barriers between us. I want to feel all of you."

Her words drove him. Phillip hadn't thought he could get any harder, but at the moment, he was sure he could use his dick like a jackhammer and pound their way out of the room, if that's what either of them had wanted.

She wrapped her legs around his hips and he eased his

length into her slowly, until he was as deep inside her as he could get.

Her lashes fluttered upward, and she met his gaze. They drowned in each other, both utterly consumed.

He'd never felt so connected to another person. Her pleasure was his own, and he didn't understand how, by any definition in any universe, she wasn't the one.

Phillip shifted his hips carefully, moving in that age-old dance to a rhythm that was born with time itself.

It had been a long time since he'd been with someone, a century at least, but thankfully his body was in no hurry to betray him. He wanted this to last for as long as it could, to wring out every sensation, every bit of bliss.

Phillip committed every gasp, every sigh, and every press of her nails into his back to memory. He inhaled the coconut-apple scent of her lotion, her hair, and he couldn't get enough of her lips.

They moved together, their bodies in tandem striving toward the same goal of ultimate sensation. The world fell away in pieces, as did time and maybe even destiny.

Phillip wanted to stay there with her forever. He wondered how long he could make it last, until she pushed at his shoulders.

"On your back."

That was when he knew he was a goner, but he eased onto his back, and she straddled him, taking him deep. She grasped his shoulders and began to rock her hips.

She was a goddess of pleasure, both ethereal and earthy as she rode him, her heavy breasts bouncing as she took control.

He'd said he wanted to worship her but realized he'd fallen short. No mortal could ever give her what she deserved. Except, he reminded himself that he was no mortal.

And, he was the one she'd chosen.

It was that thought that sent him over the edge. His body

tightened, and he tried to fight it, but there was no fighting the culmination she demanded.

All he could do was surrender.

Submit.

Worship.

"Open your eyes," she demanded.

He stared deep into the dark pools of her eyes as culmination took him. Even after he'd spilled inside of her, he was still lost in her.

Phillip realized he'd spent before making sure she'd gotten hers a second time. He simply couldn't have that. He cupped her face in his palm for a long moment before pressing her back down into the mattress again.

She laughed, but said, "Oh my God, Phillip. What are you doing?"

"Making sure you get what you give, my lady."

"I got it. I promise."

"Oh, I don't know. I might need proof."

"You weren't counting? I thought you guys who prided yourself on being good lovers were extra vigilant about counting."

"I'll confess, you made me forget my own fucking name."

She laughed, obviously pleased with herself. "Good. That's how it should be. It shouldn't be a one-up competition. I mean, well . . . wait. That could be fun."

"How many?" He started kissing her neck again. Even though she arched herself to give him more access, she swatted at his shoulders.

"Three. Jesus. I call mercy. At least for the next twenty minutes."

He eased to his side, pulling her with him to keep her close. "I suppose."

It was on the tip of his tongue to speak words he'd never spoken before, but he stopped himself. It wasn't fair to her, and it wasn't fair to him.

No, he'd keep those close and quiet.

It was enough that he knew.

If he didn't speak them, maybe that would make it easier for her to forget him when she ultimately had to.

"You know, this didn't make me any more eager to get out of this room. I could stay here forever. The castle feeds us? What more do we need?"

The idea definitely had merit. "Nothing. Just this."

She stroked long, soothing motions down his spine, and he remembered having done the same to her on one of those first nights. She seemed to know exactly what he needed, what he wanted.

"Do you think they're looking for us?"

"You said Rosebud was here? She probably won't get worried until it's been a few days." He chuckled. "She'll corral everyone who isn't in the know and give them some plausible explanation."

"I suppose I'm not going to get any peace until I talk to Alec."

"Listen, we can . . . what is it the kids say? Yeet? We can yeet him so fast, his head will spin. And the godmothers can wipe all knowledge of Ever After from his mind, if you'd like them to do that. You shouldn't have to tolerate him if you don't want to."

"What about Anna and Jordan?"

"They can wipe their minds of Alec, too. They could make him disappear."

"You guys are like the mob with that shit. It's not that serious." She snuggled closer. "But it's good to know I'd be safe if it was."

"I'll tell him to leave you alone, if that's what you want."

"I appreciate the offer, but I'll take care of it."

"If you change your mind, let me know."

"Hey! How come you didn't tell me about the baths in the dungeon?"

"How did you find those?" he asked, curious. Sometimes he, himself, couldn't find his way down there.

"I didn't. Zeva did."

"That's interesting. You and your sister both are just full of surprises."

"Well?"

"Well what?"

"Are you going to tell me why you didn't want me to know about that little treat?"

He shrugged. "The castle decides who gets to use the mineral baths. Even I don't have control over that. Neither does Hunter. He loves them, but oftentimes, the way is closed to him. Which is really a burr in his butt."

"Your castle is as bad about matchmaking and meddling as the godmothers."

"You think it's trying to match Hunter and Zeva?"

"I wouldn't doubt it. Why else would they be running into each other in a place that's so hard to find?"

"You may be right about that." He wondered if the castle was trying to help both him and Hunter. "It's a good old girl, isn't it?"

"Do you think it's a she?"

"It must be. She takes care of us."

"Men can nurture, too," Zuri said.

"They can, but it's just a feeling I get."

"Since it's your home, I suppose you would know."

They lay there in silence for a long time, and Phillip felt each second that passed like a gunshot. He wasn't ready to let go of this, but dragging it out longer than its natural conclusion was just as painful.

"I really should get back. I don't want to, but I need to," Zuri finally said.

"Me too. I have some things to work out."

"I already said this, but it bears repeating. You don't have to work this all out on your own. I'm sure it feels like you do, but I can listen. I want to help you. I want to support you. The way you've supported me."

Ironically, her words just drove the dagger deeper into his heart. "I know. I want to talk this out with you, but I need to get it right in my own head first, if that makes sense."

"No pressure, Phillip. I just don't want you to think that I'm some delicate, breakable thing. I'm not. Even if I feel things deeply, or things hurt me, it's not going to break me."

He kissed the top of her head. "I know that, too."

"Good." She ran her hand down the wall of his chest. "It should actually be illegal for you to be lying here naked looking like that when I've got work I have to do."

"I thought you cried mercy?"

"That was twenty minutes ago. I'm good."

"Oh, really?" He was ready, willing, and able to run that gauntlet again. "Because I could do this all night."

Just as he was about to prove his point, the door to the room not only creaked open but also disappeared from its hinges, leaving them exposed to any passerby.

"Shit," she cried. "Looks like the castle has spoken."

"Indeed." He looked around the room for something to cover himself with, and the castle supplied him with a towel, which he tied around his waist.

She reached out and tugged at the knot. "Sorry, just needed another look at you before I have to go back to work."

"You can look any time you like." He was still looking his fill. He could look at her clothed or naked and never get tired of watching the way she moved, the curve of her hip, or the way she occupied her space.

She bit her lip. "Since our secret hideaway is kicking us out back to the real world, or as real as things can be in Ever After, I need to tell you one more thing. I understand that you may have to take measures to save yourself. I really do. I don't want you to lose yourself. Whatever that takes."

Zuri was stronger than he'd given her credit for, and

maybe, just maybe, she was stronger than he was. She'd just given him permission to break his own heart. He didn't know what her other feelings about the matter happened to be, but she'd given him a ticket off the guilt train, at least as far as she was concerned.

Which wouldn't be a hard thing to do if she didn't have feelings for him, but Phillip was sure that she did. Maybe that was naïve of him, but he couldn't have been feeling those things alone.

Could he?

But if he hadn't been, why hadn't the curse been broken?

He didn't understand any of this, and he didn't have the time to piece it together.

"Thank you," he managed. He forced a smile to his face that became real when she smiled back.

After she'd finished dressing, she closed the distance between them and kissed him with a fire that reminded him on a primal level that he definitely hadn't been feeling those things alone. Her kiss said everything words didn't.

When she'd gone, he was even more torn about his next course of action.

"You could dress me now. I need to find Hunter. Unless he's otherwise occupied," he said to the castle.

He found himself wearing jeans, a sweater, and a nice pair of loafers. A stairway leading down into the depths of the castle appeared, the darkness shredded by torches on the wall.

"Thanks," he said, taking a cue from Zuri, and headed down to find Hunter.

The stairs led him directly into Hunter's abode, and it could only be described as a man cave. He had pictures of dogs playing poker on the walls, a bar, ridiculously large leather recliners, which of course they'd have to be to accommodate his beastliness, and a projector screen where he was watching an old western.

"Seems like you and the castle are getting along nicely," Hunter said as he dipped his snout into a bowl of popcorn.

"You could say that." He went to the bar and grabbed himself a beer. Phillip noticed a tiny, delicate glass half full of champagne. "Been entertaining?"

"Zeva came by after her soak to watch that MMA fight."

Shit, they'd been in that room longer than he'd thought. Then he smirked because they'd been in that room longer than he'd thought.

"Nice! I really like Zeva."

"Good thing, I guess, since she's your girlfriend's sister."

Phillip sat down on the couch with a weary sigh. "Zuri's not my girlfriend."

"Oh, please, dude. You know that you two are stupid for each other. By the way, when do I get to meet her? She knows all about magic, right? So what's the problem? She doesn't seem like the kind who would have a problem with my . . . this." He motioned to himself.

"No, she's dying to meet you, actually."

Hunter put down the popcorn and turned to study Phillip. After a moment, he said, "You smell like sex, fear, and sorrow. You didn't come over just to hang out. What happened?"

He'd forgotten his friend's very delicate sense of smell. "Sorry, my bad."

"Whatever. So you had sex with Zuri, but . . ."

"I found out that my curse is going to be permanent. Only with added fun. One of the next times I turn into a frog, I won't be coming back."

"What?" Hunter roared. "That's bullshit. Seriously? Who told you this? Can we get a second opinion?"

"This came straight from FGA."

"What the hell do they know, anyway?"

"Well, I mean, they are the premier experts on magic and especially curses."

"This is crap. I mean, stuck the way you are now wouldn't be the worst thing, obviously. But why this?" Then he eased back and deflated a bit. "No, it's fine. You obviously love Zuri; she loves you. Curse broken, *voilà*. Yes?" Hunter looked at him. "No?"

"No. She kissed me when I was a frog and it did nothing. Curse not broken."

"I don't understand. The magic's broken or something. How do we fix it?"

"That's what I wanted to talk to you about. Hunter, I can't be a frog."

"Of course you can't. Who would expect . . . oh. I see." Hunter nodded slowly. "You're here because Ravenna is the only option you have left."

"I don't know what else to do."

"What do you want from me, here?"

"Your permission. Your forgiveness."

"Ah, fuck." Hunter pulled the lever so his big body could recline. "What did you think I was gonna say? *No? Fuck you, you have to be a frog?*"

Phillip shrugged.

"First, I don't own Ravenna. She can do as she chooses. I'm into her, but you're my best friend. Although, I have a question for you."

"What?" Phillip said miserably.

"Why should Ravenna agree to marry you? What's in it for her?"

"I have absolutely no idea. I have nothing to offer her. We're not even really friends. She has her own magic, her own money, her own castle . . . I don't know."

"You should think about that before you talk to her, if that's what you're going to do. And I don't think I have to tell you this, but I'm going to. Make sure you talk to Zuri. Because you don't just smell like sex. You smell like love."

"Love has a smell? Do I want to know?"

Hunter laughed, and his beast belly shook as he did. "My friend. Yes. All emotions have a smell."

"That might not be her scent. It's mine."

Hunter sat back up. "What? Did you tell her?"

"No, it seemed like a stupid and cruel thing to do knowing that we can't be together."

Hunter slapped a paw to his face. "I swear to the old gods, why I am the one who knows these things and I'm still an old bachelor beast all by myself, I'll never know. Tell her. Love isn't about what you expect to be, or do. It just is. Tell her."

"It's better if I don't. I know I love her."

"And you're still going to ask Ravenna to marry you?"

"She's my only hope of not losing my humanity. Of staying me."

"It's like you're not paying attention, Phillip." He shook his head. "But you do what you need to do. I've got your back."

"So now all I have to do is summon the courage to tell Zuri. She told me tonight she understands that I will have to take measures. She said she wants me to do whatever I have to do."

"Huh. That sounds a lot like love, doesn't it?" Hunter drawled.

"It does," Phillip replied. "But it didn't break the curse."

"If something that pure can't break it, why in the name of all that's Grimm would you expect an arranged marriage with Ravenna would?"

Chapter 17

Zuri finally agreed to have breakfast with Alec. When they'd spoken on the phone the night before, she was surprised that he'd not mentioned anything about the fact she'd disappeared from the dressing room mid-conversation. Zuri had a feeling that the castle wiped his memory for her.

Aside from more magic, breakfast was the only reasonable way to get him to stop demanding her time, trying to cause trouble, and basically interfering with her daily life.

Of course, she'd decided that if this didn't get him to stop, she was going to take Phillip up on his offer to zap him out of Ever After. Then she could say she'd tried everything before she'd resorted to magic, which she knew was supposed to be used for making people happy, not giving a lobotomy.

So she sat at a table in the large dining hall where a giant breakfast buffet had been laid out so all the castle guests and anyone from the town could come and enjoy pastries, sausages, pancakes, omelets, bacon . . .

She'd chosen a Belgian waffle along with an omelet to fortify her through this conversation.

Zuri was aware of him when he entered and watched him cross the room to her. She saw many a head turned to give him an appreciative look, but when she saw him, all she could think about was seeing the look on Jenn's face.

The betrayal.

The heartbreak.

The stoic determination.

She had wanted to be that stoic, and somehow, he'd been completely exorcised from her heart. Zuri realized now that anything she'd felt for Alec had been infatuation, mostly because, like others had said, he checked all the boxes in what she thought she'd been looking for.

Zuri realized she was lucky things hadn't progressed with him. Not that she was grateful he was a lying two-faced fucker, but the end had been something she'd needed. It had pushed her forward onto this new path that was taking her everywhere she wanted to go.

"Thanks for finally agreeing to talk to me."

"Before you start, we need to set some boundaries."

"Boundaries like I'm not allowed to say the things I need to tell you, you mean?"

She tried not to roll her eyes. "Alec, you can say whatever you need to say, but you need to know before you start, I do not want a relationship with you. Period."

"Without even hearing my apology? You're not even giving me a chance?" Alec asked her.

"No. You had your chance."

"I am willing to work to earn your trust again. Doesn't that count for anything?"

"Alec. I know this is hard for you to process, but the minute I saw how what you'd done affected Jenn, anything I ever felt for you died a sad and lonely death." She took a sip of her Bellini. "Why don't you go get a plate, and then you can say whatever it is that you wanted to say to me."

"You've already said that you're not going to listen. I don't know how to make you understand."

"Same," she said. "We've been talking in circles."

"I know, and I want to fix that. I'll listen to you, I promise. If you listen to me."

Zuri nodded, and Alec got up to go fill his plate.

When he returned, he had his usual spinach-and-salmon omelet with a cup of black coffee, and he eyed her plate.

"You shouldn't be eating all that butter. It's bad for you, love."

Zuri wrinkled her nose. She didn't need anyone telling her what to put in her mouth. She didn't care if he was a doctor. "I like butter."

"Don't we all?" He took a bite of his omelet and chewed.

She noticed he didn't seem to be enjoying his food.

"Is your omelet not good?" she asked.

"No, it's fine."

Had he always hated his food choices, or was this new?

Alec put down his fork. "First, I want to apologize. What I did was wrong."

"Then why did you do it?"

"The generic answer is I was selfish."

She nodded along, agreeing completely.

"The more nuanced answer is that when I met Jenn, she was everything I thought I wanted. She was smart, driven, real partner material. She made me be better. It didn't hurt that she was also gorgeous. If I could've written a list of what I was looking for when I was ready to settle down, she'd have ticked every box."

That sounded familiar. Very familiar.

"She also was like a spotlight on all my failures. Places where I didn't live up to her expectations or mine. I didn't know how to deal with that."

Zuri wanted to ask him if he was still a child, because while it sucked to be unable to live up to expectations, it was either take the loss or do better. She didn't understand why people had such a hard time with that.

"Okay, you're still listening." He nodded. "Then I met you. You were nothing like Jenn."

Zuri arched a brow. He'd just called Jenn all sorts of good

things, and then proceeded to declare her nothing like her. It was hard not to see that as an insult. She was driven and determined, too. Just about different things.

Then she reminded herself she wasn't in any kind of contest with the other woman.

"What I meant to say is, where she made me feel inadequate, you just accepted me for who I was. You didn't ask me for more time than I had to give you, or for me to be interested in your wedding stuff, and you showed passing interest in my job, but not so much I had to break down every bit of information and spoon-feed it to you. It was easy. Spending time with you was fun because you didn't ask me to be something I wasn't."

It occurred to Zuri just how much Phillip liked "wedding stuff." He was as into it as she was.

She realized that while she hadn't asked Alec to be something he wasn't, she had asked that of herself. She'd tamped down her enthusiasm for her job while she was with him. She'd created this little cocoon where it was mostly about the sex.

Compared to what she'd shared with Phillip, even the sex had been lukewarm and the experiences they'd shared had been tailored for the person she'd tried to be, not the person she was.

It was like getting hit in the face with a grapefruit when the epiphany struck her.

"I see," she said.

"I want that, Zuri. I want to be with you. I know I should've called off the wedding to Jenn, but it had already gone so far. She still fit me so well on paper, I just couldn't figure out how to untangle myself."

She looked at him for a long moment. "Is there anything else you'd like to say?"

"Only that I love you and I'm going to prove it to you. I

know I've been a little aggro, but I see now I need to give you some space. Time to process. I can do that."

"I know that you think I just need time to process, time to be angry and that when you think I've cooled down, I'll remember what a good catch you are. I'll remember how you ticked off boxes on my list, too."

"But you think that you won't?" he said this in a calm, even tone.

"I know that I won't. You said that you love me, but Alec, you don't know me."

"I know that your coffee of choice is a blond mocha with heavy cream, I know that planning weddings is your passion, I know that you hate it when your socks get wet, and I know that I can make you orgasm twice before breakfast."

"I made myself smaller for you, Alec. I acted like it was okay that you weren't as excited about my job as I was, I acted like it didn't matter that you didn't have the same amount of time for me that I had for you, and I acted like two orgasms before breakfast was enough."

His mouth dropped open but then snapped shut. "We can work on that. I want to know the real you. I'll try to care about weddings and stuff. Although, I think it's really not a thing that most men are into, but I'll give it a try if you let me."

"Phillip likes planning weddings."

"Trust me, he's faking to get into your pants." He held up his hand. "I know it sounds harsh, and I'm not trying to be cruel, but it's a fact."

"You don't know Phillip."

"I know men, because I am one. Trust me." He took a sip of his coffee.

"That's the last thing I would do, Alec."

"I'm trying to be honest with you. Something that this Phillip obviously *isn't* doing."

She was reminded that it was something he was doing. Even when there'd been roadblocks to what he could reveal to her, Phillip had been as open as he could be the whole time she'd known him. Even when it had come down to baring his mistakes, mistakes he thought would make her see him differently. Mistakes he thought would be the end of the spark that had sizzled between them.

"You don't know him, anyway," Alec continued. "You've painted him up like some knight in shining armor, and he's obviously been only too happy to let you. You're letting the kitsch of this place soak into your otherwise brilliant brain. Why don't you come back with me to Chicago and we'll give this a real shot? Complete honesty. Complete realism. See where it takes us, yeah?"

For a moment, her imagination wanted to consider what a future would look like. If only so she had a clearer picture of what she didn't want.

She could see herself withering away with him. Everything she was, everything she wanted melting into the background until her entire being was about him. Then as soon as it was, when he'd sucked the life out of her, he'd get bored and he'd start working late, and have so many conferences he had to go to, and she'd spend her nights crying into her pillow wondering why she wasn't enough.

Not only that, but if Zeva knew what she was thinking in this moment, even just for a glimpse, and she very well might've, her sister would smack the thought right out of the back of her head.

As she well should.

Then Zuri imagined what it would be like with Phillip.

How they'd be working long days, but together. How he shared her passion for giving people their dreams. How he really saw her. How he wanted her to shine as brightly as she could, for as long as she could.

She was reminded of how she could depend on him.

That he was trustworthy.

Honorable.

The way he'd agreed to host the children at the castle for Zeva.

The way he'd touched her.

That was the future she wanted.

"No."

Alec paused and put down his fork. "Why no? Everything here in Ever After isn't real. Not when you shine the harsh light of everyday life on it. I thought you were more pragmatic than that."

"Your views of the world are miserable, Alec. A life with you, for me, would be miserable. I love Ever After. My everyday life here is wonderful. It's magical in ways I can't even begin to explain to you because you wouldn't understand and you wouldn't believe it."

"Fine. Then I'll stay here, too. Would that convince you? They don't have a doctor. I'll go into private practice."

"I don't want you to stay here, Alec. I don't love you."

He looked stricken. "Isn't that a little hasty? I thought you were close to saying it before the wedding."

"No, I wasn't. I'd painted some pretty pictures of what I thought would happen, but I wasn't in love. You don't love me, either. You just don't like being told no."

"No one likes being told no."

She took another bite of her waffle. "And don't tell women what to eat. We can choose for ourselves what we put in our mouths."

"I was just trying to take care of your health."

"Save it for your patients. I'm a grown woman who doesn't need your opinion on my health or what I eat."

"Okay." He held up his hands in surrender. "You really are different from the woman I knew in Chicago."

"Yeah, I am."

"I'm still intrigued."

"You're still going to be disappointed."

He laughed.

"No, I'm being serious. I need you to stop. Or I'm going to have to stop working on Anna and Jordan's wedding. I don't want to do that. I want to give them their dream, but you're making it impossible for me to do my work. I gave you this meeting, but this is it. No more."

"You'd really refund them all their money and cancel their wedding just so you didn't have to speak to me?"

"Would you really keep harassing me knowing that I would cancel their wedding? Are you that selfish?"

"You must really have it bad for this Phillip."

"I do." She nodded. "I love him. I love him in a way I didn't know you could love another person. I see him, and he sees me."

Suddenly, emotion threatened to choke her.

"I don't want anything from him. I only want to give. Because that's what you do with love. You give it. The beautiful thing about it is that there's always more."

Maybe she could break the spell yet.

It was so long until dusk, she didn't know what she was going to do with herself until then. She had to tell him.

"Your head will always be in the clouds, won't it, Zuri? No one is ever going to be enough for you. I guess I'd say give me a call when you settle down and start thinking logically, but I don't know that it's possible for you."

Irritation swarmed over her like angry bees. "Why do you keep saying *settle down*? Settling? Being with someone isn't about settling. It's about adventures with your best friend."

"You've been reading too much of your own hype, sweetheart. That's not how this works."

"Alec. I'm done arguing about this."

"I can see I've reached the end of your patience."

"So will you stop?"

"I'll stop."

"Thank you." She got up to get another Belgian waffle and ignored her omelet.

"Are you getting another waffle just to spite me?" he drawled.

"I'm getting another waffle because I want one."

"Hell, will you get me one, too? I hate salmon."

"Then why do you eat it?"

"I don't know."

She grabbed him a waffle, and this time, for spite, she loaded it with so much butter each tiny square was a reservoir full of the melted goodness.

Zuri set the plate in front of him and he said, "Okay, the butter was for spite."

"You're right—it tastes good."

Without the threat of his romantic aspirations hanging over them, she was able to be present in the moment and talk with him about the wedding, about Anna and Jordan, and about all the banal things he said would shatter her illusions of Ever After.

They didn't.

Not in the least.

They only made her more eager for night to fall so that she could find Phillip and tell him that she loved him.

Chapter 18

When Phillip was once again a man, he was surprised to find himself without the taste of bugs in his teeth, or the stench of fountain water clinging to him.

He was sitting in the mineral bath with Zuri.

She was delightfully naked.

Scrubbing the water off his face, he said, "This is unexpected."

"I hope it's okay. Frog you was happy to hop in my basket when I went to collect him from the fountain before dusk."

"Interesting. He usually demands to be in the fountain. If you got him, I mean us, no . . . me. If you got *me* to leave, that's great." Then he went on high alert, inspecting her. "You didn't get frog pox again, did you? Are you okay?"

"I didn't kiss your froggy self. I'm fine. I might've enticed you with some strawberries, though, but I figured you wouldn't mind."

He ran his tongue over his teeth. "It's a pleasure to taste strawberries rather than what I usually deal with."

A new light sparkled in her eyes.

"What are you up to, pretty princess?"

She beamed at him and bit her lip. "I have something to tell you."

"Well, tell me."

"Not yet."

He laughed. "Okay, what am I doing here?"

"Besides taking a long, luxurious soak in the mineral bath?"

"Don't we have work?"

"Nope. Our schedules are clear for the next eight hours. So I expect you to make good use of that time."

He'd have to admit he liked the way her brain worked.

Phillip never thought he'd be as happy to stay in the water, but here he was in this hot mineral bath thinking he'd never leave.

At least, not until he had to.

He knew he should be talking to Ravenna, but what would it hurt to give himself one more night with his sweet Zuri? Especially after she'd gathered him from the fountain. He'd have to be crazy and stupid to leave her naked and wanting.

But he also had to be honest. "Zuri, last night you said you understood if I had to take measures for this curse."

"I do."

"I need to tell you what those are."

She looked down at her hands for a moment before looking back up at him. "Part of me wants to say that you don't have to, but you do, don't you?"

"Yeah. I do. Don't get me wrong, I want to be here with you."

"I know. So tell me. Then I'll tell you. We'll trade."

"I went to see Ravenna about the curse. Her crystal ball showed us a wedding, and it was Ravenna's familiar who escorted the bride."

He waited for the shock, the betrayal, to wash over her. He waited for her to change her mind about being with him.

Instead, she cupped his cheek with her hand. "That is not the answer. I am."

"What do you mean? Baby, you already kissed me, and not only didn't it break the curse, but you got sick."

"I didn't know then what I know now." She bit her lip. "I didn't *feel* then what I feel now."

"What?" The word almost got stuck in his throat.

Was this real? After all this time?

"You're the most amazing man I've ever met. You're kind, generous, warm, and open. You're honest. God, you're so honest. Even when it costs you something to be so. You're the kind of man who can admit you're wrong, who can own his mistakes and try to be better. You see me for exactly who I am, and you don't try to make me anything different. I want you to know that I see you, too. I love you, Phillip."

Emotion overwhelmed him. Dry, empty places inside of him that he'd thought were long lost burst to vibrant life. So did that little flame of hope. Hope for not just a future, but a future with Zuri.

He pulled her to him, and she wrapped herself around him. Phillip buried his face in the crook of her neck.

"I wanted to tell you last night, but I didn't think it would be fair to you."

"Tell me now."

He pulled back from her to look in her eyes. "I do see you, Zuri. You came to Ever After, and while this place is supposed to be magic, it's supposed to be a fairy tale, it's you that's magic. And I love you."

"This is True Love's Kiss," she said, before kissing him.

Phillip had no doubt, because he poured everything he felt for her into the collision of their lips, and he could feel the truth of her words in the way she melted against him, the passion of their kiss with its strange confident urgency.

It had all been worth it to bring him to this moment with Zuri. He'd do it all again, just for this.

Phillip couldn't quite believe that this stunning, smart, kind, funny woman loved him. She was everything.

He eased back onto the stone seat in the bath, and Zuri straddled him.

"Don't make me wait. I want you now." With no other

preamble, she eased down the length of him and took him fully.

"You can have me whenever you want me. However you want me."

"I like the sound of that."

She began to rock against him, and she felt too good. He'd never known how good it could be, how much higher having this intimate connection could take them both.

"You've got to slow down, or I'm not going to last," he warned her.

"I like that you think this is all we're doing tonight. I told you we had eight hours." Her voice was low and sultry, her breath warm against his ear.

"You're a cruel taskmaster."

"I'm just getting started, handsome."

Her words thrilled him and spurred him on. "Oh, you think so, do you?"

He lifted them together out of the water, and she squealed, but clung tight.

"No fair, you said I could have you however I want you, and I want you in the mineral bath. I'm going to ride you like the Kentucky Derby."

He laughed. "You're the one who said we had eight hours."

"We do, but this is a pregame snack."

Phillip eased them back down into the water. "You win."

"Good. When I win, you win, too." She began to grind her hips again.

"Don't I know it."

He managed to keep it together just long enough until her motions were no longer precise and controlled, and when she surrendered to the wild abandon of the heat between them, Phillip waited until the grasp she had on his shoulders became insistent, and she threw her head back while she found her bliss.

Phillip loved watching her like this. Loved that he could do this to her with his body. He let himself drown in the waves of bliss she'd brought him, spilled into her, and held her tight while earthquakes of sensation racked them both.

"I need to know if it's going to be like this every time. I think it requires much more research," she said.

"Much more," he agreed easily.

Her fingers traveled down the length of his arm, then back up again to his shoulder, down his chest and abs, then returned to his arm in a familiar, comforting pattern. "But I could stay here like this for a while, too."

"Uh-huh. Until you remember that the castle can give us anything we want. Just what will your imagination do with that, I wonder?"

"We're going to have to quit the wedding business because we're going to be much too busy to do anything except test this castle, and ourselves to the very limits," she promised him.

He laughed. "My love, as much as I'd love to take you up on that, you know that you don't want to give up the wedding business. Not for that long. Not for a second."

She grinned. "You're right. I love it."

"You made me love it, too."

"I made you?"

"Yeah. Seeing the joy it brought you, the joy you brought to other people, and these couples who are choosing us to make their dreams come true? I can't think of anything better."

"Stop being so perfect. It's honestly ridiculous." She floated off, away from him.

He swam forward to follow her. "I'm not perfect, I'm perfect for you."

"That's what my sister said."

"That I'm perfect for you? Of course." He shrugged and smirked.

"Ha. She did say she thought my future was with you

when we saw your picture on the Ever After website, but no. She told me no one was perfect but that I would meet someone perfect for me. That our angels and our demons would play well together. I wouldn't have thought that. Our angels, maybe. But not our demons."

"Zeva is pretty wise. She's going to make a fantastic fairy godmother. Although, I will say I'm glad our futures are set. We won't require any meddling."

"Set? You think?" She arched a brow and splashed him.

He dove for her and caught her, careful not to get her hair wet. "Don't worry. I know how mad you would be if I got your hair wet."

She laughed. "The castle oils and straightens my hair every morning while I sleep."

"Oh really?" He considered whether or not to dunk her, even as she clung to him, laughing.

"No, no. None of that. Tell me more about how our futures are set."

"If you don't think they're set, maybe I should keep that to myself."

"Tell me. What do you see?"

"Really?"

"Really."

"You might be disappointed."

"I might. But tell me anyway."

"It's not what you would call spectacular."

"No?" She was still laughing. "Tell me more, Prince Average."

He moved through the water with her. "It is average, and pretty wonderful. You. Me. Doing the same things we have been doing. Except my days belong to you, too. Running the B and B. Lots and lots of wedding planning. Maybe a couple of kids who look like their mama running around the castle. What do you think?"

"I think yes. All the yes. Yes, forever."

The castles in the clouds, the fairy tale, it was all solid and real. "You know, forever is something we can actually have in Ever After, so be sure you mean it."

"I mean it."

They made love again. He'd never used that phrase before, but it was the only thing that could describe what happened between them. The physical joining of their bodies was animal and primal, but it was transcendent, too.

Phillip couldn't believe that this was his life. This was his partner.

It was somehow too good to be true.

He tried to push that thought out of his head and be present only in the moment with Zuri. These were the memories that would build their life together. The foundation. Years from now, he could see bringing her down here to re-create the moment when they confessed their love for each other.

Phillip didn't want to remember feeling any doubt, or any fear.

Just the perfect trust that this woman who'd become his everything was his future.

Phillip supposed this was how the rest of the world did it, a person just had to trust and take that leap.

"What?" she asked him, obviously knowing something was on his mind.

"I just realized that being cursed was a gift."

"How so? I mean, aside from ensuring you always had your daily protein," she teased.

"Out in the rest of the world, you don't have any safety nets. You just have to jump. With my curse, all it took was a kiss. Other people have to invest years of their lives, their hearts, the tender parts of themselves they build walls to keep safe. Sometimes that other person catches them, sometimes they don't. Sometimes, they catch them for a little while and still let them fall."

"You're leaping, aren't you?"

"Phrasing." He eyed her. "I've been a frog for three hundred years. I've been leaping every day of my life."

She laughed. "Hey, I'm funny."

"Not even a little," he said, but he smiled anyway. "Not that I want to bring another man into our bed . . ."

Zuri snorted. "Yes, I talked to Alec. He said he understands. I told him if he didn't stop that I'd have to pull out of Anna and Jordan's wedding."

"Hardball. I like it. Of course, he probably said something to the effect of you would be that selfish or whatever to try and guilt you."

"He did. But I told him if he continued to harass me after I'd told him what I'd do, that he was the selfish one. We actually had a decent breakfast after I got him to accept our time together had the life span of a housefly."

"Good. Because I've had to tell the castle to ignore my feelings about that guy until after the wedding."

"To the dungeons with him?"

"And ruin our sanctuary here? Not a chance."

She laughed. "I still don't understand how someone like him could be such good friends with Jordan."

"I don't know. Not to root for the guy or anything, because I would never, but there were people, good people, who stood by me until I figured out I was a selfish asshole and got my shit together."

"I think that would be easier. You were already being punished. If someone turned Alec into a frog, I might be more inclined to listen to him."

"Then we should keep the FGs away from him. But now that I know he isn't a problem for you, I'm happy to forget about him."

"Hmm," Zuri teased. "Maybe you should make me forget about him . . . ?"

"Haven't you already?" He quirked a brow.

"Maybe I have, maybe I haven't. You should make sure."

"Woman, I'll make you forget your own name."

"Bring it on, Prince Charming."

And he did.

His single focus was her pleasure. He was determined that she wouldn't know whether to beg him to stop or beg him for more. Phillip wanted to drive her beyond reason, until she was a mass of raw nerve endings that radiated only bliss. He used everything he'd learned in his long life coupled with the love he had for her, and used it all for her glory.

When they were both spent beyond exhaustion, he held her close with a supremely male satisfaction.

"Let's go to your rooms and sleep," she murmured.

"Let's go to our rooms and sleep," he said.

"I love the sound of that." Although, she didn't move. "You wrecked me. You should carry me."

"It would be a pleasure to carry you."

Except when he moved to stand, he felt the familiar pull. The tightness of his skin and the heat in his limbs.

"Zuri?" he began, panicked.

"What's wrong? I . . . No, Phillip. No!" she cried. "I do love you. I don't understand. Phillip?"

He fled from the scene as the transformation took from him his hopes and his dreams and made a mockery of their love.

Chapter 19

Dawn was a bitch.

There was no other word for it. She was a home-wrecking, heartbreaking bitch of the highest order.

Or was that the lowest order?

Regardless, it was the absolute worst.

She didn't understand what had gone wrong. She loved Phillip. From the soles of her feet, to the crown of her head, and from the depths of her bones, she loved that man.

Why wasn't it enough?

Why wasn't *she* enough?

It was hard to get those thoughts out of her head. Hard to think that she wasn't the problem, but she knew her own feelings more than any stupid curse. What gave the magic the right to decide if it was true love?

She decided she was going to call Zeva, have a good cry, and then throw herself into her work. She'd made a commitment, and she had a job to do. Back in Chicago, she'd let herself be defined by her relationship.

Zuri refused to do that again.

She loved him. Her heart had splintered in half. But she wasn't going to fall apart.

As her nose tingled and tears gathered in her eyes, she sniffed. "Yeah, maybe you're going to fall apart a little bit."

Except Zuri knew she was more than this. She knew her love mattered. Phillip had made her see that.

She was determined not to give up.

Although, as soon as she had the thought, it occurred to her that when one gave the universe ultimatums, one was invariably tested.

Zuri didn't want to be tested anymore.

Why did she constantly have to prove herself over and over? When was it her turn to be happy?

When she got back to her room, she texted Zeva to see if she was awake.

You up?

Yeah. Getting my place packed up. What's up?

He's still a frog. I kissed him. And he's still a frog.

Her phone rang, and she answered it with a swipe.

"What do you mean? Didn't you get frog pox last time you kissed him?"

Leave it to Zeva to make her laugh when all she wanted to do was cry. "Yes, but the cure was another kiss."

"I know that. I was there, remember?"

"Yeah, well I talked to Alec and let him have his say. We had breakfast yesterday, and when I was talking to him, I realized that I'm in love with Phillip."

"Of course you are. Why is this a problem?"

"It's a problem because I told him. He said he loves me. We spent the night together." Zuri's whole body twinged with the aftereffects of such use. "Oh, boy did we ever."

Zeva giggled. "So what's the problem again?"

"He still turned into a frog. I should've broken his curse. I love him. He said he loves me. We planned our future together last night, Zeva. And this morning, he was a fucking frog."

"Okay, so his curse wasn't broken. Whatever. I thought you didn't mind his frog time?"

"Honestly, I don't. I mean, it's inconvenient, but if that's all it was, I could deal. Like you said, no one's perfect. But if he doesn't break his curse, it's going to be permanent. The frog part. Forever."

"Are you serious?"

"He just found out from Fairy Godmother Academy. I love him so much it hurts, Zeva. I know my love is true."

"No one doubts your love is true."

"Don't you think he does? That's supposed to be the key to ending his curse. But it didn't. So how can he not doubt me?"

"This is bullshit," Zeva said in an even voice. "And I'm not going to tolerate it."

"That's what I said, but it doesn't seem there's much I can do about it."

"I'm going to load the rest of my stuff into storage today, and I will be on my way to Ever After. I'm going to have a Come to Zeva moment with the godmothers. How dare they."

"How is this the godmothers' fault?"

"They let you have hope. They let him have hope. They mashed you two together like potatoes and butter and then left you with your butts in the wind. I won't have it."

Zuri laughed again. "This FG thing is really getting in your head. Just last week you would've said asses."

"I'm furious enough to say it."

"Also, who is the potato?"

"You know exactly what I mean, Zuri. This isn't fair. And the thing about fairy tales is that they're always, eventually, fair."

"Eventually?" Zuri sighed. "I don't know what to do."

"You take care of you, and—"

"Not about me, wombmate. I'm struggling, and my heart hurts, and I'm afraid. That's all true, but I don't know what to do for him. For Phillip."

"I'm going to figure it out, okay? I'll be there soon."

"It's dumb that you're always riding to my rescue. I should figure this out myself."

"No, you shouldn't. This is what your family and friends

are for. We all have to save ourselves, but we do it with our loved ones holding our hands. We'll figure this out. I promise."

Zuri was reminded she'd said almost those exact same words to Phillip.

"When it's your turn, Zeva . . ."

"I know you'll be there. That's what sisters are for."

Zuri took a deep breath. Just hearing her sister's voice fortified her and reminded her that she could do anything she set her mind to.

"Don't ruin your chances at the academy for this. I'll figure it out. I just needed to hear your voice."

"Zuri. If looking out for my sister, or demanding that people live up to their word will endanger my chances at FGA, I don't want to go because it's not the kind of place I thought it was. Get some rest, and I'll see you soon."

Zuri knew everything would look better after she'd grabbed a couple of hours of sleep. So she decided to take her sister's advice. "Okay. Let me know when you get here."

"I will. If you have time, do you think you could have Gwen make me some scones? The cherry ones? The more FGing I do, the more sugar I need."

"I'm on it."

They hung up, and Zuri lay down on her couch. She didn't want to lie in the bed, because she knew all she'd be able to do was think about Phillip and the kiss that cured her frog pox.

He'd been her cure, so she couldn't help but wonder again why she wasn't his.

Of course, he'd been the root of her illness, too.

God, that kiss had been a fantasy come to life. She touched her fingers to her lips, remembering.

Last night had not been a fantasy come to life, not at all, because she'd never dared to dream she'd have such chemistry, such fire with another person. She thought it was the kind of thing that didn't actually happen to people.

Yet, it had. It happened to them.

Zuri knew what was coming.

She knew that if he wanted to stay human, he'd have to marry the Evil Queen.

That was his only option.

She wouldn't and couldn't begrudge him that. Zuri meant what she'd said. She understood. It would grind every piece of her heart to a fine dust, but she understood.

There had to be another way.

There just had to be.

When she drifted off to sleep, she was haunted by nightmares of planning Phillip's wedding to someone else.

After she awoke, sobbing, she dried her tears. Phillip would never do that to her. He wasn't Alec. It was simply an anxiety nightmare, and if she did say so herself, she had in fact planned a beautiful wedding at the black castle.

Lots of candles, purple rose petals, and she and Rosebud had designed a beautiful tiara made of thorny black ivy. Zuri was confident she could plan a wedding to any bride's taste. Even an Evil Queen.

Checking her phone, she realized she had exactly twenty minutes to get down to the Once Upon a Time Ballroom to go over the torchier placement with Hansel. She understood why the castle was only allowed to help as directed in the guest wing of the castle. It made a bit more work for them, but no one needed normies wishing for their groom to be dressed in shining armor and to have the poor bastard suddenly bedecked in seventeenth-century jousting garb. With no practice moving in the stuff, that was surely a recipe for disaster.

Zuri realized she no longer thought of herself as a normie. Ever After had so quickly become her home.

The castle seemed to agree, because suddenly, she felt fresh as a daisy and realized her hair was completely perfect.

And she was dressed in a pair of houndstooth slacks, a soft

red cashmere sweater, and red heels so comfortable she felt as if she were walking on air.

"Good looking out, Castle. Thanks."

Her usual blond mocha appeared on her counter as well, and she'd never been more grateful.

She took a sip and let the warmth wrap her in familiar comfort.

"Got anything for the bags under my eyes, my friend?"

A mirror appeared, floating in front of her, with the words *Mirror, mirror* printed on the silver surface.

She peeked over and looked at her reflection. The mirror shimmied.

"Mirror, mirror?" she tried.

It didn't do anything, so she tried another tack.

"Mirror, mirror, in the air, get these bags out of here? Or something? Please?"

She watched as the bags under her eyes disappeared and a strange force moved her mouth into a smile. It would've been creepy as hell if not for the inviting vibe she was getting from the castle.

The castle wanted her to be happy.

So she smiled for real, and the mirror disappeared.

"I don't know what I did before you, Castle. Thank you."

She shot off a quick text to Gwen at Grammy's Goodies to order that batch of scones for Zeva before setting off to conquer her day.

She was armed with coffee, confidence, and hella great style when she went down to the Once Upon a Time Ballroom and found Hansel waiting for her.

"I hope you haven't been here long!" she said as she made her way over to him.

"Not at all. I was talking with the groom outside. It looks like we're going to pull this off after all. Not that I doubted the godmothers, but you know how it goes. It seemed impossible when we started, but this stage is almost ready, and the torchiers are the last thing we have to do."

"I know, it's incredible. You've done such an amazing job," she praised.

"It was my pleasure. I just started a long-term project helping Ravenna restore Castle Blackheart, and it's going to be a challenge. It's nice to have bite-size projects and get that immediate feedback from concept to realization."

She nodded in understanding. "I think it takes a special kind of person to be able to interpret someone else's ideas and incorporate them into your own thinking and then bring them to life."

"Yeah. You know exactly what I mean." He grinned. "So I had an idea for the torchiers. What would you think about a chandelier-style over here to symbolize the moon? Then we could re-create the streetlights, but keep the fairy-tale theme." He pointed to various places on the stage.

"That is absolutely perfect. I love it. I think Anna will love it, too. How soon can we get those put together?"

"I can have that done tonight, if you don't need the room for anything."

"I don't believe it's been booked for anything else. So it's all yours."

Things were coming together. It was all going to be okay.

"The main thing that's going to take a while is that chandelier moon, but we'll see what these torchiers look like in a minute."

Hansel set about doing a lite install and Zuri checked her phone while she waited. Zeva had sent her pictures of the kids making silly faces to cheer her up. It worked like nothing else.

Until she was reminded that she and Phillip had been talking about having children only the night before.

She pushed it out of her mind. Zuri had already told herself this wasn't how things were going to be done. She'd worry about what she could control.

And what she could control was the Markhoff wedding.

"Zuri, you ready?" Hansel called.

She looked up and saw the open flame in the torchiers, and for a moment, she flashed back to that day in Chicago when Jenn Gordon had lit her dress on fire.

But this wasn't going to be that day.

Anna and Jordan were utterly in love. They respected each other, and they were both excited to bring this day to fruition.

Note to self: Never plan another wedding where the groom doesn't show up for important things like meeting the wedding planner.

She supposed that should've been an obvious one, but here she was.

No, this was beautiful. Anna would descend the stairs and lose her shoe, just like Cinderella, and her groom would catch her and carry her up the stairs to the altar, where he'd present her not only with her shoe but with the ring that symbolized his eternal love.

Oh! She needed to catch up with Grammy and make sure she was still a go to officiate. After all, it was close to the full moon, and sometimes, she had a bit of excess facial hair that she needed extra time to have lasered off.

"They're fantastic, Hansel. You're a gem."

Suddenly, several strings of the tiny white lights they'd strung across the ballroom crashed to the floor and a fat red cardinal could be seen hanging upside down from one of the strings of lights.

"I told you it wouldn't support your weight. Your name should be Chonkey Boi instead of Bronx," a voice came from the corner.

"Listen here, I told youse, it's my winter weight."

"You look like a tomato with a beak."

"Shut yer snout. Delicate, you ain't," the bird said.

"Shut it for me. If your wings can carry you, Stubby."

"Esmerelda," Hansel called out. "Don't you do it."

Zuri saw who he was talking to, and it was an enormous flying fox. She was rather cute, and she realized this was Ravenna's familiar that she'd heard so much about.

The fat cardinal waved back and forth on the swinging line of lights that the flying fox continued to spin as the air currents from her wings spun him around. "I don't feel so good."

This was new for Zuri, but her boyfriend was a frog, so talking flying foxes . . . whatever. It was fine. It was all *fine*.

"Esmerelda!" Hansel demanded again.

"You guys, take it outside? Please," Zuri said.

"He said my mother had rabies."

"I take it back," Bronx cried. But then as the string of lights began to slow, he opened his stupid beak. "I meant yer sister."

The flying fox made a sound that could've been a roar, and she dived straight for the little round cardinal.

Bronx yelled and let go of the lights, sending him tumbling toward the ground. He managed to spread his wings and catch air, but he had to flap hard and fast to get any traction. Esmerelda gave chase, and Zuri was sure that she was going to catch him.

"Essie! You can't eat him. It's cannibalism," Hansel cried.

"It's the law of the jungle. I like a well-marbled chicken."

Bronx stopped flapping, obviously insulted. "Why, I oughtta—"

And he promptly fell out of the air, sinking like a brick toward their newly constructed stage.

Hansel darted to grab Bronx before the chubby little bird was nothing but a smudge on the stage, but Hansel crashed into Esmerelda, who was in a roll spiral heading straight for him. Hansel managed to catch the flying fox with one arm, and the loudmouthed cardinal in the other, but the tangle of wings and feet and inertia knocked over the torchiers.

And the stage that had taken Hansel so many loving hours to construct went up in flames.

Zuri guessed this was just like Chicago, but it wasn't a dress that had burned. It was the whole damn wedding.

Chapter 20

Petty could tell by Zeva's unexpected appearance through the specially designated Fairy Godmother Portal in their root cellar that she was angry.

Their whole cottage shook when Zeva propelled herself through the portal and landed among their jars of pickled garlic, habanero asparagus, and the ridiculous amount of cherry jams and jellies.

"I need answers, Godmothers. I need them now."

"What kind of critter bit her tail, I wonder?" Bluebonnet asked, following Petty down the stairs into the root cellar.

"I suspect it has something to do with Zuri," Jonquil said.

"You're right it has something to do with Zuri. How could you?" Zeva demanded.

Petty was confused. "How could I what?"

"You know very well what!" She stomped her foot, and bits of green fairy dust flew from her foot. "Oh, stop it," she yelled at her feet.

"Dearie, calm down and tell us what's the matter. We can't help while you're yelling, of course," Petty said.

"My sister. How dare you give her hope when there was none."

Petty's brows knit together with concern. "We'd never do that, Zeva. What's happened?"

"I think she needs some sugar," Jonquil said.

"Zuri was supposed to get me some scones, but I had to

see you first." Zeva huffed and blew more fairy dust out of her nose. "Stop it!"

"I hesitate to say this, but really, it's the only thing that works." Bluebonnet reached out a gentle hand to Zeva's shoulder. "But you need to calm down."

"When, in the history of ever has it worked when you told someone to calm down?" Zeva demanded.

"In the history of Ever After, or ever?" Jonquil queried.

Zeva suddenly looked as if she were about to explode.

"Not now, Jonquil." Petty took her hand and patted it, sinking to the dusty floor and pulling Zeva with her. "Will one of you please get this FG in training some sugar so she doesn't erupt?"

"I'm on it," Bluebonnet said, and trotted up the stairs.

Jonquil sat down with them and took Zeva's other hand. "Tell us. So we can help."

"Maybe let her acquire the sugar first to even things out," Petty said.

"Oh, right." Jonquil nodded. "I'm beastly if I miss out on my sugar."

"Too right," Petty agreed. "All of us are."

Bluebonnet trundled back rather quickly with a giant chocolate ice cream soda and handed it to Zeva. "Drink it all down. It's the best medicine."

"Wait, does this mean I can have as much sugar as I want and it won't all go to my ass?" She looked around at the god-mothers. "Or, is this why you're all padded so nicely?"

"Diplomatic way to put it," Petty said.

"I'm angry, not stupid," Zeva said. "Plus, you're all comfortably stuffed, if that makes sense. Comforting. Homey. Snuggly."

"Yep. It makes people underestimate us, and we get away with pretty much everything," Bluebonnet said with a grin.

Zeva took the treat and downed it in one gulp and then

exhaled heavily. "Okay, I actually do feel much better. Not as angry."

"Hmm. Yes." Jonquil nodded.

"Zuri called me this morning with terrible news."

"What's happened?" Petty was immediately concerned. Zuri needed to believe in magic more than ever. She noticed that Zeva was already out of her ice cream soda and Petty used her magic to conjure another.

"She's in love with your stupid cursed prince," Zeva growled, and slurped more of the ice cream soda.

Petty wasn't sure how one could slurp ice cream angrily, but Zeva managed to pull it off. Petty had never been more proud.

"Why is this bad? This is what we want, yes?" Petty asked.

"No more stupid Dr. Jackhole, right?" Jonquil nodded encouragingly.

"He's still a frog," Zeva managed.

Petty watched Jonquil's eyebrows climb up into her hair like caterpillars hiding in a begonia bush, and she knew her own had done the same.

"The synapses aren't connecting. How is that possible?" Bluebonnet asked.

Zeva gave another entirely rude slurp to empty the contents of the glass and then took a few deep breaths. "They spent the night together. They were sure they shared True Love's Kiss. They shared true love's everything, if you know what I mean."

Jonquil snorted. "We do know what you mean."

"You mean to say, that after all that, Phillip still changed into a frog?" Petty cocked her head to the side.

"I do. And Zuri is devastated."

Bluebonnet nodded. "I imagine she would be."

"She doesn't understand why her love isn't good enough. Why *she* isn't good enough. After what happened in Chicago . . ."

"Of course she's good enough!" Petty was getting mad now, too. "I cast that stupid spell. Who is it to judge what love is true?" Then the solution hit her like a lightning strike. "Girls."

"Hmm?" Jonquil and Bluebonnet looked at her.

"If the end isn't happy, it's not the end, right?" Petty asked.

"Right, right," Jonquil said.

"Is that what we're going with?" Zeva asked.

"It's the truth," Bluebonnet reassured her.

"So what's the problem?"

"The problem isn't Zuri, of course. It's Phillip," Jonquil said, obviously inspired. "We should know better, honestly."

"Do tell. What do we know?" Petty demanded, displeased that this time she wasn't the one with the answer. She didn't like feeling like she'd been left in the dark.

Jonquil reached over and opened one of the cherry jellies and began eating it with a spoon. "This is the part where Phillip has to stick to guns."

"What do you mean?" Bluebonnet looked at their sister.

"Happily Ever After is never just handed out like candy," she said between bites.

"You don't think all the self-reflection and work he's done in the past three hundred years is enough? I do," Petty said.

"Petty," Jonquil said after licking the spoon clean. "He's gotta prove it stuck. How do we prove who we are? Adversity." She waved the spoon.

"I see! A knight in shining armor is a knight who has never been tested!" Zeva said.

"Or he's just really a badass," Bluebonnet said helpfully. "Or . . . you know. Yeah. I missed the point, sorry."

"S'okay. We have to figure out what we're going to do, because obviously we can't tell him or Zuri. They both have to have faith. They both have to believe. They both have to pick love over everything else," Jonquil added.

"We can't tell Zuri?" Zeva sounded stricken.

"Oh, love. I know that's hard to watch her struggle." Petty squeezed her hand. "You want to fix it all for her because you're the big sister. I know. Believe me, I do."

Zeva looked at her. "This is what it means to be an FG, isn't it? I'm going to love all my charges like my own family."

"They are your family," Bluebonnet said softly.

"Oh, this sucks. I don't know if I can do this. I want to tell her. My mouth actually burns with the need to tell her," Zeva confessed.

"Of course it does. That's natural. You'll see in time that when you do things for them, they don't learn the lessons that they need to make the right choices. It's a very delicate weave, much like a spider's web. Strong, but delicate," Jonquil said.

"I need a drink," Zeva muttered.

"No, probably just more sugar," Jonquil said. "You're going to be a beast until your chemistry finishes changing. I'll get you another."

"Oh me, too," Bluebonnet said. "Meddling makes me thirsty."

"We're still going to meddle? I thought they had to choose themselves?" Zeva asked.

"We're definitely going to meddle. We don't make their choices for them, but we put them in situations where they have the opportunity again and again to make the right choices. It's not just one chance and fuck you, you're out," Petty said.

The sisters' eyes widened.

"This is a serious situation, and I think it calls for strong language," Petty said.

"I have to really work up to strong language these days. I don't like it anymore," Zeva said.

"Mmm. Yes. When you've been doing this a while, you'll be able to again. The academy is very stern about language. You'll see. Every word has immense power. Especially the swears. They're like curses, you know," Bluebonnet said.

"Like curses? They're literally curse words," Zeva said.

"And now you know how that came to be." Petty grinned. "Anyway. We need a plan. Because, as my sisters know, but I will clue you in, too, Zeva, Prince Dorkling went and screwed everything up by going to Ravenna to break his curse."

"Oh no," Zeva said as she accepted another soda from Jonquil.

Petty accepted her soda and sucked happily on the straw for a long moment as the sugar fortified her system. And superpowered her thinking cap.

"I know. I told him not to, but of course that probably made him even more determined. My bad. Anyway, he took Hunter—do you know Hunter?" Petty asked carefully, not wanting to give away too much of her side plotting.

"I met him. He's very nice."

"Handsome, in a beastly way, don't you think?" Bluebonnet prodded.

"Sure, but he's got it bad for the evil lady with the purple streaks in her hair," Zeva said. "Zuri was trying to hook me up with him. I guess she thought best friends and best friends are a good match."

"They are. They definitely are. Those are my favorite pairings," Petty said.

"Back on point, Pets. Daylight is a-wasting," Jonquil nudged.

"Yes, yes. Anyway," Petty began, and studied Zeva carefully. "He took Hunter to Castle Blackheart, and Ravenna had a vision or something of how to break his curse. A wedding. Apparently, to her. Or that's how the lot of them interpreted it. It totally screwed up the threads of fate."

"How so?" Zeva asked.

"Ravenna and Hunter aren't meant for each other. Ravenna and Phillip aren't meant for each other," Bluebonnet said.

"Isn't that up to them to decide?" Zeva asked.

"Up to a point. There are certain things fate wants to happen, and when she has to move the threads to get what she wants, often, it's rather uncomfortable and ugly," Petty said.

"So what are we going to do?" Zeva sighed.

"Well, we need to let Phillip make his choice. He has to prove himself. We can support Zuri, keep reminding her to have faith. To believe in herself. To believe in love," Bluebonnet said. "To believe in Phillip."

"Okay, I knew that part. You said we maneuver them so they get to keep making their choices. How do we do that?" Zeva asked.

"Phillip is probably going to propose to Ravenna. Or maybe the other way around. Yes, that's it," Jonquil said. "Ravenna is not ready for love. She's learning to love herself right now, in a healthy way. Not a selfish way. So she's going to be terrified of Hunter, and to make him not an option, she'll rush into this curse-breaking with Phillip as an excuse to hide."

Zeva sighed. "Zuri is going to be so heartbroken."

"And we have to show that to Phillip. We have to remind him that she means more to him than anything else. Even his future as a man. He has to be willing to trade it all for Zuri. I know that deep down, he is. He just has to be reminded," Jonquil continued.

"This has been kind of your baby from the start, hasn't it, Jonquil?" Petty asked.

"A little bit here, a little bit there. I was so happy to see the closure with Alec happened. Alec's not happy about it, but that's his problem." Jonquil grinned.

"I suppose it's a good thing I didn't Molotov-cocktail his Benz, then, right?" Zeva asked.

All four of them erupted into deep cackles, and Petty was struck again by how very close they were to being on the dark side of things. Of course, that didn't stop her from cackling. No, it made her cackle all the harder.

"I mean, maybe we could get away with eliminating his

ride," Jonquil considered. "You know, I'm feeling rather she-devil about the whole thing. We could make a list and then proceed to eliminate all he holds dear."

"Sisters. And Zeva. What have we learned from cursing Prince Charming?" Petty asked.

Jonquil sighed. "I know. It's fun to think about, though."

"We're so creative. It's just a shame to let those ideas go to waste," Bluebonnet said.

"You already nixed the carnivorous anal warts. After that, why bother?" Petty asked.

Zeva cackled harder. "That's beautiful! Oh my God."

"I thought so," Petty said.

The sisters sighed in unison. "No, we don't use our powers like that," they said to each other.

"But you could?" Zeva asked.

"We could, but there are consequences and repercussions," Petty said.

"Seems like it would be worth it," Zeva observed.

"Would it?" Bluebonnet asked. "This is a system of checks and balances. He'll get his. He'll learn his lessons. We just won't get to see it. Inflicting harm on him isn't really helping Zuri or anyone else. It's just letting us see his comeuppance and, while delightful, it's completely selfish."

"Ugh. Fine," Zeva said.

"See? Look. You were just offered the opportunity to keep making the right choices. To keep living your ethos. You chose correctly. So did we," Petty said.

"I see what you did there." Zeva shook her head. "Can't say I like it, but I see."

"This is why we meddle," Jonquil said.

"I think I need more sugar," Zeva said.

"Much more sugar will be consumed before this day is through, you can count on that." Petty perked and scratched the back of her neck. "My FG senses are tingling. Something's happened."

Zeva looked around the room. "Something . . . at the castle?"

"I think so. Good call. You're learning," Bluebonnet encouraged.

"We'd better go see what happened this time," Jonquil said with a sigh.

"Wanna try out your fairy dust, Zeva?" Petty asked.

"What if I blast us into Paraguay?"

"Eh. I haven't been recently. It'll be fine," Petty reassured her.

Zeva wiggled her nose, and with a burst of green fairy dust, everyone but Petty disappeared.

Petty looked around to make sure no one was looking, or listening. Then she muttered, "Oh for fuck's sake."

Chapter 21

When Phillip emerged from the fountain, he'd hoped against hope that Zuri would be there waiting for him, but she wasn't.

Instead, Esmerelda sat with her feet swinging in the fountain, and she used her wings to prop herself upright while she sang a little song of death and dismemberment.

He could smell the faint stench of char.

She turned her head as he dressed, and when he was done, she said, "My mistress would like to see you at Castle Blackheart, if you're available."

It was almost as if this were fate herself telling him what he had to do.

Except it went against everything in him. Every cell in his body rebelled at what he was about to do, but he didn't have any other choice, did he?

"First of all, why do you smell like a bag of burned garlic and kitty litter?"

Esmerelda snorted. "Some Prince Charming you are. A gentleman wouldn't mention it."

"A lady would've taken a shower."

She gasped. "So rude."

"But really. That stench is awful. Are you okay?" he asked.

"At least you're concerned for my welfare. I had a small disagreement with that awful Bronx."

"Seems like it was slightly more than small?"

"Fine." She splashed her feet some more. "He said some not so nice things about my mother and then my sister, and I kicked his ass for it. In the scuffle, we might've started a tiny fire. In the ballroom."

"What?" he demanded. "Oh no. I have to get to the castle and make sure everything's okay. You didn't totally trash the set up for the Markhoff wedding, did you? Zuri is going to be out of her mind."

"Oh, yes. Zuri did lose her mind. She's rather upset with both of us. So is Hansel. But Bronx started it. Little shit."

"Is she okay?"

"You don't have time for that. Mistress needs you now."

Phillip considered. Would it really be wise to ignore Ravenna's summons if he wanted a favor from her?

"Truthfully, I need to know that Zuri is okay."

"Yes, the godmothers showed up to help. She's fine. Frustrated and ready to pluck all the fur from my body, but she's okay. Are you satisfied?"

"If I find out you've been untruthful, I will be very upset," he warned.

"I don't lie. Contrary to popular belief. Everyone thinks the worst of me because I'm Ravenna's familiar. She doesn't lie, either. The truth is a much better and sharper weapon than any lie. Obviously." Esmerelda rolled her eyes. "So are you coming, or what?"

"Yes, I'm coming."

Although, Phillip wanted to be back at the castle with Zuri. Every step he took toward Ravenna and away from Zuri was physically painful, but still he followed the flying fox up the trail to Castle Blackheart, and its mistress, Ravenna.

He found her just inside the great room, pacing.

"Thank the dark powers you're here!" she cried.

He looked around the room, waiting for the crowd to emerge, for this to be some kind of a joke. Phillip had never seen Ravenna like this.

She was chewing her fingernails, her dress was . . . well, it was still magnificent. It lifted everything to its best advantage and clung in all the right places. Only, her dark lipstick was smeared and her hair was in matted tangles.

Someone had definitely tampered with the Evil Queen, and he didn't know how to process it.

He wasn't sure if he was supposed to comfort her, offer to get his shining armor, or what exactly she wanted from him.

"What do you know?" she demanded.

He wondered if she might've inhaled one too many of her own potions. "About what?"

"Your castle did this to me. You must know."

"Did what? Ravenna, I don't understand."

"I have been locked in your dirty dungeon for over twenty-four hours."

"Why?"

"That's what I'm asking you. It's your castle, isn't it? I came to talk to you about this curse thing, and one minute I was knocking on the door, and the next I was on the Slip 'N Slide to hell."

"I'm Prince Charming, remember? I don't do that."

"Your castle does. It locked me in a sex dungeon with your castle beast."

"Whoa, whoa. Calm down. Castle beast? You did not just call Hunter my castle beast."

"I did! That's what he is. He kept me in that dungeon and ravaged me." She blushed. "I mean, he asked permission. But the castle wasn't going to let us out until we did. All manner of sex toys appeared and disappeared like your castle was caught in some sort of magic porn loop."

Phillip coughed and tried not to laugh. Hunter, for all his beastly appearance was a good man, and a gentleman. He tried to imagine his friend being bombarded with sex toys while with the object of his affection. Well, not object. Ravenna wasn't an object. But . . .

"You think it's funny? You try it," she snapped.

"Are you hurt?" he asked.

She stopped pacing and chewing on her nails to look at him. "No. I'm fine. Just, terrified. I can't have this. I really can't."

"Can't have what? Being locked in the castle for twenty-four hours? I understand. That's awful, and I'm so sorry. I'll have to reiterate with the castle that guests' desires are to be fulfilled by verbal request and not . . . that."

"Desires? Are you implying that I wanted to be locked in with him?"

"No. I'm saying that you did want him, and he wanted you. The castle responds to desire." He shrugged. "As long as you weren't hurt—"

"But I could've been hurt. I could *be* hurt!"

Phillip didn't understand what she meant. He could see her being angry about the castle trapping them together, but being hurt? He didn't see . . . oh. She meant emotionally.

"Do you have feelings for Hunter?"

"No. I mean . . . not that kind. Well, that kind, but not that kind."

"You are making zero sense, Ravenna."

"He was a good time in the sack, and I'd like to do it again, which is why I can't. Get it?"

Surprisingly, he did. "Oh. Yes, I understand very well."

She sighed. "I don't usually say things like this, but I am sorry you understand. All of this with the feelings. It's completely unreasonable. I don't like it."

"It's not so bad," he reassured her.

"Even when it sucks? Because it's bound to suck, right?"

"Not always. But yeah, the bad comes with the good. The good is worth it, though." It really was. Even though he had to say goodbye to Zuri, and the very idea of letting her go made him miserable, he still wouldn't trade the time he had gotten with her.

"You have to say that. You're Prince Charming. It's your job."

"Kind of. But I don't get my Happily Ever After, either, it seems."

"What?" she shrieked.

He held up his hands. "Whoa, I didn't realize my Happily Ever After was important to you."

"Don't be stupid. It's important to everyone. If you don't get yours, how will anyone, ever? You kind of wrote the book, you know what I mean?"

He shrugged. "This time isn't like the stories. It's all shit."

"Tell me."

"If I must," he sighed.

"You definitely must. This is unacceptable."

"You weren't this upset when we came to you for help with the curse."

"Things were different then. I thought you'd have figured out who the bride was. It obviously wasn't me. Evil Queens don't get the pretty weddings at the white castle."

He took her hand. "Why don't they? The fairy godmothers are always saying that love is for everyone. Why isn't it for you?"

"You're not going to turn this around on me. I've had enough of that today, thank you very much. Just tell me what happened to you."

"Fine. I'm in love with Zuri," he began.

Then, the Ravenna he knew was back. "Well, obviously. Let's move on to new territory."

"She kissed me. It was supposed to be True Love's Kiss, and I'm still a frog."

"That's impossible."

"Obviously not," he tossed her own sarcasm back at her.

"Oh, right. Sorry." She let go of his hand and began pacing again. "Something is wrong in Ever After. We have to fix it. I don't know what or how, but everything is coming unraveled."

"That's exactly what the godmothers said would happen when I told them I'd been to see you."

"Old bats," Ravenna murmured, but there was affection in her voice. Whether she knew that's what it was or not.

"I don't know who else the bride could be in your vision if not you. Who else would Esmerelda want to escort down the aisle?"

"I absolutely cannot imagine." Ravenna worried her bottom lip between her teeth for a long moment. "Well, it seems we're both in a bind. I say we dare Ever After to fix its shit."

"How would we do that?"

"We should go ahead and get married."

"What? Why?"

"Don't you want to, dummy? To break your curse? If you really think that's me in the vision?"

"I mean, yes. That was my plan. To come here and beg and plead with you to marry me, but why would you want to?"

"Obviously to close the door on Hunter and any romantic ideas he has about me. The only way to do that is to marry his best friend."

"Holy shit, you're diabolical."

"Only when I have to be. I already tried a potion. I blew an ardor cooling powder right in both of our faces to fix our problem and nothing. It didn't work. That's never happened to me before. Ever. My magic always works as I intend."

"I'll be honest, Ravenna. This seems like our only out, but it feels so wrong."

"I know, but I don't see how we have any other choice."

She was right. This was what he'd intended to come here to do, to convince her to marry him. But she didn't want to marry him. He didn't want to marry her.

Moreover, he didn't want to be a frog.

And she didn't want Hunter to break her heart.

What a fine mess they'd made of things.

Just like what Petty had told him would happen.

Rude of her to be right.

"Are you going to ask her, or what?" Esmerelda chirped.

"Mind your business," Ravenna snapped back.

"Just trying to help," Esmerelda said.

"I think you've helped enough today," Phillip advised her.

"What did you do?" Ravenna turned to look at the shrinking Esmerelda.

"Nothing, really. I mean, I helped rescue you." She kicked her foot.

"Why do you smell like you've been flying through smoke?" Ravenna narrowed her eyes.

"Apparently, a certain cardinal told her that her mother or her sister or something had rabies and those were fighting words. There's been a fire at the castle. I haven't been to inspect the damage yet."

"Oh, by the darkness!" she swore. "I suppose since my familiar made the mess, I should see what's needed to clean it up. Or offer a favor to whoever did clean it up."

"The godmothers handled it. I think," Esmerelda said. "I'm sorry, but he just infuriated me."

Ravenna sighed and scratched Esmerelda behind the ears. "It's okay, my love. I understand. Bronx can be such a little fucker sometimes. He thinks he knows everything. And he thinks that accent is cute, but it's not."

Esmerelda nodded and leaned into her mistress's caress.

"Did you bite his head?"

"I did. I ate him, but Hansel made me spit him out. I almost had him down my throat, too."

"Oh, that's a good girl. Maybe he'll think twice about saying nasty things about your dear mama," Ravenna cooed to her.

"Hate him," she grumbled.

"I know. It's okay. Why don't you go get some strawberries from the kitchen and curl up in your den?"

Esmerelda flew off in search of her treats.

"I didn't know she swallowed him whole."

"Eh, she spit him back out. That's what matters, right?" She flashed a wicked smile. "But she was right. We should make a choice."

"Are you sure this is what you want to do? You could always see where this goes with Hunter."

"I'm insulted you would say such a thing. He's wonderful. He's kind. That's not for me, Charming. You should know that by now."

Phillip couldn't help but laugh. "So what does that say about me? You think I'm some kind of asshole?"

"I know you used to be, but no, you're all that rot, too. But you're not interested in me. We could have a lovely arranged marriage based on mutual goals. Me, not getting my dark little heart broken, and you not staying a frog for eternity. We wouldn't even have to cohabitate or really deal with each other except for royal functions. Ever After doesn't do many of those anymore anyway."

"Okay, Ravenna. I know you have your own reasons, but thanks for helping me."

She studied him for a long moment. "You're welcome."

"So, uh, you wanna get married?"

"That is the worst proposal I think I've ever heard."

"At least I didn't text it to you."

She rolled her eyes. "Yes, Charming. I'll marry you."

Then they looked at each other, each obviously wondering just what they'd agreed to.

"What's next?" he ventured.

"I suppose we have to tell the world about our decision."

"And start planning the wedding."

"Do you need to tell Zuri before we make an official announcement?" she asked.

"Yes, I'd like to speak with her before we make it public. Although, she does know it's coming. I wouldn't do this behind her back."

"Good. I don't want to hurt her. She seems like she's already been through enough." She narrowed her eyes. "And not because I'm going soft or anything, but because she's a woman. We women have to stick together."

He held up his hands. "Hey, no judgment from me. Hunter is expecting it, too. But I still want to tell him as well."

"Thank the dark gods you're going to do it, because I just can't."

"I know. Think of it as my wedding gift."

"Whatever shall I get you?" Ravenna asked.

"I don't know. You'll figure it out, I'm sure."

"The godmothers are the only planning game in town, but since your Zuri is working with them . . ."

"We'll talk to them and figure it out."

"Oh, that's going to be fun," Ravenna said in a dark tone.

"Basically like everything about this wedding."

"Except for the part where we break your curse."

Although, Phillip wondered if it was worth it.

He could have another eternity of living the way he had before Zuri, or he could spend the few days he had left with Zuri and cram as much love and living into those days as was possible.

"Already having second thoughts?" Ravenna asked.

"Honestly? Yes. I'm wondering if it wouldn't be better to just spend the time I have left with her instead of trading her for an eternity of nothing."

"You already know what I'd choose, but you're not me." She shrugged. "Just promise me, if you change your mind, you'll tell me."

"Of course. We're friends now, right? Friends don't do that to each other."

"Why do you do-gooders always want to be friends?" Ravenna sighed heavily. "Fine. Ugh. I guess we're friends. I guess that means we have to play board games or something."

"Is that an invitation?"

"I suppose. I have Pretty Princess, Dungeons and Inquisitions, and Cards Against Fairy Tales."

"If you also have a good bourbon, I'm down for Pretty Princess."

"Fair warning. I always win."

"Only because you always play with Esmerelda. She lets you win."

"Nobody lets me win. I win because I'm ruthless."

"Is it any fun to win that way?"

"Of course. Why else would I keep doing it?"

The idea of winning brought his thoughts back to Zuri. He wanted to see her. Touch her. But if he did, he knew he wouldn't go through with this farce of a wedding. Phillip wasn't sure he wanted to win. He needed to know that winning was the right thing to do.

"Because you're afraid to lose?"

"No, we're not having any of that introspection nonsense tonight. It's only alcohol and board games. Maybe a pizza. Chuck the rest of it out the door."

"Double pepperoni?"

"And pineapple," she said with evil glee.

"If you think I'm going to argue, I'll see your pineapple and add bacon."

"No one on the light side likes pizza like that. I just thought you should know. Maybe you were assigned the wrong side at birth. You should've been a dark prince. You have the hair for it."

"I look like an angel of the Lord, what do you mean?"

"Exactly. In some cultures, hair as blond as yours is the marker of a villain."

"You'll think villain when I'm wearing the Pretty Princess crown."

It was nice to do something that didn't have any long-term implications. With Ravenna, it was okay if he wasn't Prince Charming.

He knew it was okay with Zuri, too, but Zuri made him want to live up to the hype.

And Ravenna couldn't care less.

There was a freedom in that, and it was a strange kind of painkiller for his broken heart.

Chapter 22

Zuri had been avoiding Phillip.

She knew what was coming, and she wasn't ready to hear it.

As long as she avoided hearing the words, it didn't have to be real.

She supposed it was childish in the extreme, but she wasn't ready to tell him goodbye. Even though she knew she was wasting time she could have with him. Part of her wanted to ask him for just one more day.

Although, it reminded her of going on a theme park ride she didn't want to be over. Doing anything to get one more turn, even though she was already tired and done for the day, but knowing that when she left, she'd never get another turn.

Not that Phillip was a ride—she blushed. Well, he kind of was, but that wasn't what she meant.

"What do you think?" Anna said as she emerged from the dressing room.

Anna looked nothing short of stunning. Rosebud had definitely outdone herself. The blue and pink rosettes in the veil were nothing short of art.

"It's perfect," Zuri managed.

"It's amazing that you've managed to bring everything together. Even having your Hansel rebuild the stage after that crazy fire. You're a miracle worker," Anna said.

"More like magic," Rosebud mumbled.

Zuri gave her a tired smile. "If everything is perfect, this will be your last fitting. We're so close. Are you ready for your fairy tale?"

"I've already gotten it. This is just so everyone else knows it's our fairy tale, too."

Rosebud put a hand over her heart and sighed. "Oh, honey."

"This dress is perfect. Everything is perfect."

After that fire, it almost wasn't perfect. Zuri wasn't sure how she would've pulled everything together if Zeva and the godmothers hadn't shown up.

Of course, Zeva hadn't done her usual sister thing. This time, she'd just told Zuri to have faith in that irritating way that the godmothers had.

She supposed that was to be expected since Zeva was an FG in training, but she hadn't thought as her sister she'd get that treatment, too.

"Zuri?" Rosebud nudged her.

"Huh?"

"Anna wanted to know if we need anything else."

She looked at the expectant bride, who blushed with obvious joy. "No, Anna. We're almost there. I don't think we'll need anything else from you until the rehearsal."

"Thank you. Thank you for everything."

It was then that Zuri realized how tired she was. Yes, she loved wedding planning. It was her passion, but passion took a lot of energy. A lot of fire. Zuri realized that her fire was slowly burning down to quiet embers and she needed a break.

Perhaps she should've taken a break between Chicago and coming to Ever After.

Zuri knew she still wanted to be a wedding planner, but she didn't want to stay here and watch her future with Phillip unfold with another woman.

She wasn't angry with him, none of this was his fault.

Perhaps it was hers because she simply wasn't enough.

Have faith, Zeva had said. Faith in what? In the magic that had done her dirty since day one?

Zuri was grateful for her time in Ever After, but she wondered if maybe it was over.

She began packing up her satchel.

"Hey, do you have a second?" Rosebud asked. "I have something for you."

"For me?"

"I have a sense about things, sometimes. Usually, it has to do with dresses. I made this last night, and I knew it belonged to you."

Rosebud went to a rack and pulled out a lavender dress that seemed to be made of glitter and sea-foam. It was slinky and sexy, with a slit up to just above the knee but still with a long train in the back that glittered just so when it caught the light. The neckline was high, but it would accentuate her high cheekbones and jawline.

She couldn't stop staring at the color.

"You made that last night? From what? Air?"

Rosebud smiled and pushed it toward her. "It's yours. With my compliments."

"I couldn't possibly accept this."

"You couldn't possibly not. It was made for you. Literally."

"Rosebud, where would I ever wear this?"

"I don't actually have any idea. I just know that you will. Please. Take it."

"I . . . I don't know if I'm staying in Ever After," she confessed. "I feel like I'd be lying to you if I accepted such a gift without telling you."

"Honey, I don't know where the wind is going to take you, but I do know you'll be wearing that dress. Wherever that happens to be."

Zuri hugged her.

"If you do end up leaving, stay in touch. And don't forget that you can always come back."

"Thank you," Zuri said, and scrubbed a hand over her face.

A new voice interrupted them. "Leaving? Girl, you just need a break. Let's go throw some axes."

Zuri looked up to see Gwen standing there with one of her red boxes. "What are you doing here?"

"You're hard to track down. I have your order of scones for Zeva. I thought I'd deliver them personally. I heard through the grapevine that you're having a hard time."

Rosebud nudged the box open to inspect the scones.

"You're as bad as the godmothers, Rosebud." Only Gwen produced another box. "Here. I made you some wedding cake cupcakes, since I know how much you like them."

Rosebud squealed. "You're the best."

"I know." Gwen grinned. "So listen. My little monsters are spending some time with our neighbor. They seem to like him." She shrugged. "Wanna go throw sharp things and get loaded?"

Zuri found she wanted nothing more at that moment than to go throw sharp things and get loaded.

"Maybe some of that good brown bread and honey butter, too," Rosebud suggested.

"You should come, too," Gwen suggested.

"Oh, I . . ." Rosebud paused and looked around the shop. "I should. Let's go."

The three of them walked over to Pick 'n' Axe and Shandy, one of the brothers who owned the bar and had rubies braided into his red beard, got them set up in one of the throwing lanes.

"All right, lassies. You be knowin' how ta throw, do ya?"

"We do," Gwen said. "Thanks." She grabbed one and sent it sailing through the air with an expert turn of her wrist, and the head of the axe fixed itself squarely in the center of the bull's-eye.

"I see. Man trouble, then?" he asked.

"Off with you, Shandy," Rosebud shooed him away. "But come back with some of that bread."

"No salads tonight, eh, lassies?"

Gwen scowled at him. "Mead!"

"Water, until ye be done with the axes," he corrected.

Gwen slouched. "Fine."

"I like to keep me fingers," he said.

When he was gone, Gwen scowled again. "Men. Even enchanted ones. Bah."

"Bah," Zuri agreed, and grabbed one of the axes and threw it clumsily. The axe head didn't even hit the target with the sharp side, but it was still satisfying to hurl it through the air.

"Don't forget it's in the wrist," Gwen reminded her.

Rosebud grabbed two axes and double-handed her throw, both of her axes landing exactly where she'd aimed them. She grinned. "I've been doing this a long time."

Zuri grabbed another axe, and this time, she breathed and remembered what Gwen had taught her, and she knocked Gwen's axe out of the center of the target.

"Fantastic!" Gwen cheered her on.

This was what she loved about female friendships. They could be competitive with one another, but the right friends were supportive. Gwen wasn't threatened that Zuri had knocked her axe out of the target. She was happy for her that she was learning to throw and improving her skills.

"You want to try two-handed?" Rosebud asked her.

"Yes!"

A deep voice sounded from the edge of their lane. "You're gonna make her a first-class marksman in no time."

Zuri looked over to see a man, no he was more like a grizzly bear and a lion. He stood as tall as a grizzly on his hind legs, anyway. His appearance would be fearsome, except his bushy eyebrows made him look a bit like a cartoon.

He smiled at them, baring sharp predator teeth, but Zuri

felt an instant kinship with him. She had the sudden urge to hug him tight.

Zuri could feel his heartache as if it were her own. Although he didn't wear it on the outside, she felt it intimately. She wasn't sure if it was because Zeva felt it, but it was all she could do not to cry.

She searched for the right words to say but couldn't seem to find them.

"Have I startled you?" he asked.

"No, no!" She bit her lip. "I just want to hug you."

"If you say it's because I look like a teddy bear, I'll . . ."

"You'll what?" Rosebud dared. "Be a teddy bear and let her hug you?"

He slumped. "Yeah, I guess."

Zuri laughed. "Oh, you're wonderful. Can I?"

"Fine." He held open his big, furry arms.

She hugged the big beast tight, and although his fur tickled her nose and her face, it gave her such comfort to hug him. To be close to him.

Then she realized why.

Zeva. It wasn't just that Zeva cared about him. It was so much more. So much deeper.

"It's so good to meet you, Hunter."

"My reputation precedes me?"

"Kind of."

"Who? Phillip or Zeva?"

"Both. So you knew I wasn't Zeva? A lot of people can't tell us apart, you know," she said.

"Then they don't pay attention. You're completely different," Hunter said.

She liked him better and better.

"Wanna throw axes with us?" she asked.

"I would, but they don't let me. I usually throw them through the targets." He shrugged.

"How about you have some honey mead with us after we're done?" Gwen offered.

"I'd like that. Today was kind of crappy. Time with friends is just what I need."

"Why did you have a bad day?" Rosebud asked.

"Eh. I was locked in a room in a castle with Ravenna for more than twenty-four hours." He shrugged again.

"Holy shit, why?" Rosebud asked.

"I'd rather not go into it."

"Oh. We'd rather you not go into it, too," Rosebud said.

"I figured."

Gwen threw again. Then Zuri. Rosebud took her turn.

Zuri tried two-handing the axe throw, and she got it on her first try.

"You're a natural!" Rosebud said.

Hunter sat with them while they continued throwing until their time on the lane was up, and then they moved to a table, where they all shared the brown bread and several flagons of mead.

Gwen drank as much mead as Hunter.

"Do you think you might want to get a burger or something with that, cookie lady?" he asked.

"Please, I was a PTA mom. I'll need another flagon before I feel it," Gwen replied.

"Fair enough," Zuri said.

Hunter pushed the rest of his flagon toward her. "For the cause," he said.

"For the cause," Gwen echoed, and chugged it.

Hunter put his head down on the table and sighed miserably.

"Oh, fine. Tell us why being trapped with Ravenna was so bad," Rosebud caved.

"Because I like her. I like her a lot."

"Why is that bad?" Gwen asked. "And listen, if you tell me

it's because you don't have those kinds of feelings, I'm going to whack you on the snout with a newspaper."

Hunter wiggled his nose in what seemed like anticipation. "Listen, I'm not a dog. I'm a . . . Hunter."

Gwen snorted with laughter. "I'm sorry. Go on. I just get tired of that crap. We all have feelings."

"Right? I wish you could get Ravenna to understand that. She's the one who's all no . . . feelings, I can't," he said in a high-pitched voice.

"I don't mean to be cruel, but it doesn't seem like she has any other prospects. So what's her problem?" Rosebud asked.

"Oh, but she does," Zuri drawled, the honey mead having loosened her tongue just a fraction. "She's going to marry my true love."

Hunter sighed heavily. "Yep."

"Did he tell you?" Zuri asked him.

"Not in so many words. He said he was going to ask her, but . . ." He shrugged and sagged in his chair.

"He told me he was, too. But silly, stupid me, I told him he didn't have to. I told him I could break the curse. But did I? *Did I?* Ask me. *Did I?*"

"At the risk of being the jerk here, I don't imagine you'd be out drinking with us if you had," Gwen said.

"No, no I didn't. I kissed him. I know it was True Love's Kiss," Zuri said miserably. "Love can suck it. What's it good for?"

"Magic, I think," Rosebud said, scrunching her nose.

"What has that ever gotten anyone?" Zuri asked.

"I don't know." Hunter shook his head.

"What a bunch of sad sacks we are, eh?" Gwen asked. "I'm divorced; Rosebud's not looking; Hunter and Zuri both had their hearts broken . . ."

"You know what?" Rosebud slurred. "Hut-ner . . ." She laughed. "Hut-ner . . ." She laughed again. "Hunter and Zuri should hook up. Show 'em what they're missing."

"No more matchmaking," Gwen said.

"But it's kinda fun," Rosebud said.

Hunter and Zuri looked at each other and then shook their heads. They seemed to silently agree it was a bad idea.

Zuri would never do that to Zeva, or to Phillip, or to herself.

That was when she realized she had to face it.

Him.

And the reality that he wasn't her Happily Ever After, as much as she wanted him to be.

Yeah, she definitely had to get the hell out of Ever After.

Even though she'd just started to think of herself as a local. She didn't know how she'd fare in the outside world, but she'd figure it out.

And miss her new friends, and the life she'd started to build for herself, every step of the way.

Chapter 23

"Are you ready to do this?" Phillip asked Ravenna as they stood on the moonlit sidewalk outside the doors to Fairy Godmothers, Inc.

"Not really, but we might as well rip the Band-Aid off, right?"

"Right."

Wrong. Wrong. Wrong. He was still a raw, aching wound, and he'd yet to put a Band-Aid on it.

Zuri had been avoiding him, and he realized it was because she knew what was coming. He didn't blame her for not wanting to hear it. He didn't want to say it.

Every time he thought of her, he thought of the beautiful future they'd dreamed of together, and now it was gone like so much dust and ash.

As soon as they walked through the doors, Zeva took one look at them and said, "No."

"You don't even know why we're here," Ravenna said soothingly.

"Yes, I do. The answer is no. You're not getting married."

"Oh, so you do know." Ravenna pursed her lips.

"Zeva, be reasonable. Your sister understands, why can't you?" Phillip asked her.

Zeva huffed. "No, you're the one who needs to understand. You're about to make a huge mistake."

"Are you threatening him?" Ravenna asked casually.

"Sure. You could call it that. I'm not going to do anything, but you have to live with the fallout of your choices. Are you prepared for that?" she asked.

Petty came out from a back room. "What's the fuss?"

"These two idiots think they're getting married."

"Oh. Hmm. I wonder," Petty said, pressing her wand against her temple, "if you'll recall what I told you about fucking with fate?"

"Petunia, if you'll recall, the message we got from the FGA about my situation. I refuse to believe it's my fate to be a frog forever."

Everyone looked at Ravenna, who only managed to say, "Yeah."

"Don't be angry with me, Zeva. I don't know what else to do."

"I'm not angry with you. I just know you can make a better choice," she said.

Ravenna turned to look at him. "She's not mad. Just disappointed."

"Ravenna," Petty warned.

"What? We came here as a courtesy since you're the only wedding planning service in Ever After."

"Would you really—" Zeva began.

"Of course not," Ravenna answered. "We just wanted to let you know. We'll figure out the details ourselves. I need you to know, it's not my intention to hurt your sister. I do enjoy her."

Phillip expected Zeva to have more to say than that. To tell her that if she enjoyed Zuri, she wouldn't marry him. But Zeva said nothing.

"Well, it seems you both have thought this through. I suppose there's nothing left to say except congratulations." Petty shrugged. "If you want to use any of the services, I can give you the price lists and everything. Although, I don't think many people will attend."

"We don't need many people to attend. We just need to be married. But we do need to talk to Grammy about officiating, as she's the only one who can marry us, except us."

"Oh, we could do that. By royal proclamation?" Ravenna suggested. "Save us the trouble?"

"Good idea," he said.

"Oh, it's them," Bluebonnet said from the door. "Dumber than two boxes stuffed full of hair, I say." She shook her head.

"Come now, Bon-Bon," Phillip said.

"Don't Bon-Bon me. That just gets you in trouble, if you'll recall," she said.

"As if I could forget," he reminded her.

"Phillip?" Petty called. "Before you do this, make sure you speak to Zuri. I know she's made herself unavailable, but I think she'll be ready to talk."

"I will. Of course I will."

"Do it soon," Petty prompted.

"Ravenna, dear, can I talk to you?" Bluebonnet asked.

"Not if you're going to tell me all the reasons why I shouldn't marry Phillip."

"Nope, none of that. Promise."

Phillip didn't know what he was supposed to do with himself while Ravenna was in the back talking to Bluebonnet. He'd not been uncomfortable around Petty in at least a hundred years, but he suddenly didn't know what to do with his hands.

Or his feet.

Or his bottom.

He wanted to sit down but had the distinct feeling he wasn't welcome.

"Do sit down, you're making me nervous," Petty snapped.

He sat and still didn't know what to do with himself.

"You know, if you're feeling out of alignment, that's because you are."

"Petty. Give it a rest."

"I can't. Not until you stop screwing this up."

"How am I screwing it up?"

"Saints and apple pie, son! If I could tell you how you're screwing it up, I would. But I can't. It's against the rules. It doesn't count if you don't do it yourself," Petty cried. "But seriously, you're making my hair fall out. My head is as bald as a baby's bottom. I can't take this stress."

"Don't guilt-trip me. I know all your tricks."

"You think I'm kidding?"

"I think you'd never let your hair fall out. You're too vain."

Petty grinned. "Okay, fine. You're right about that. But if I wasn't vain, my hair would fall out."

"Any chance you're going to tell me what Ravenna and Bon-Bon are discussing?"

Petty snorted. "You know better than to ask."

They sat there in awkward silence for a long time before Petty spoke again.

"Okay, I can tell you this one thing. Zuri loves you. She loves you so much she'll step aside while you marry someone you don't love to break your curse."

"I know that."

"Then how are you going to let her live the rest of her life thinking her love wasn't enough?"

"I have no control over that."

"Don't you?" Petty asked carefully. "There's always a choice."

He didn't want to think about her words. He didn't want them to echo through the marrow of his bones or tattoo themselves on his brain.

He could choose not to rail against his froggy fate. He could choose to trade an endless but empty existence for a finite one full of moments with her.

He could choose Zuri.

He could choose not only for her love to be enough, but to give her the indelible knowledge that *she* was enough. She always had been. Curse breaker or not.

He could choose, but it wasn't Zuri he doubted. It was himself.

Phillip just nodded, and Petty finally let it drop.

"By the way, we're still doing a frog-kissing booth at the spring carnival," she said.

"What if someone gets frog pox?"

"We've inoculated all of them, except you, of course. But that's not going to be a problem, anymore, is it?" she said.

Okay, so maybe she hadn't dropped it at all.

Finally, Ravenna emerged from the back and her eyes were rolling so hard, he was surprised they hadn't fallen out of her head and rolled all the way back up to the castle.

"Can we please go?" Ravenna asked him.

He was more than happy to oblige.

On the walk back to Castle Blackheart, he asked her, "Care to tell me what you and Bon-Bon talked about? Petty wouldn't tell me."

"I'd rather not tell you, either, if you don't mind?"

He nodded, and they walked in silence for some time, until she said, "Have you ever thought about what it would be like to live out in the world? Away from Ever After, I mean."

"Live there? No. Not really. I've thought about visiting, though, now that we can come and go."

"Where would you visit, then?" Ravenna asked.

"Somewhere new. Somewhere completely unlike Ever After. Nothing in Europe. Maybe Thailand."

"Thailand. That could be good. I have no idea where that's at, but I like the way the word feels on my tongue. It's pretty."

"What about you? Have you been thinking about traveling since we opened our borders?" he asked.

"I have. Quite a bit. I want to go to the North Pole and build myself an ice castle. Like a holiday cabin. No one would be able to see it, of course. But I think it would be quite something to watch the northern lights from my bedroom."

"That sounds like a fantastic trip."

"Esmerelda isn't too excited about that. She doesn't like the cold."

"You could enchant a polar bear."

"Hunter said he'd go with me to keep me warm." She turned to look at him. "Not like that."

He held up his hands. "Even if it was like that . . ."

Ravenna sighed. "I forgot to ask, was there anything you needed from me to cover the damages from Esmerelda?"

"Aside from the fact that Bronx needs therapy, no."

"Does he, really?"

"Oh, yeah. He's afraid to leave his nest, now. Rosebud tells me that he's not coming to work. He just sits in his nest eating Cheetos and binge-watching *Queer Eye* and *Project Runway*."

"Well, that's a kind of therapy." Ravenna grinned. "I didn't want him to be permanently damaged, but he's been harassing Esmerelda for quite some time. Her retaliation didn't come out of nowhere."

"You should've let Rosebud know. She'd have talked to him and set him straight."

"Rosebud and I aren't on the best of terms."

He walked her the rest of the way to the door. "I suppose here is where I say good night."

"You could come in, if you wanted. We could play another board game?" she offered.

"On another night, I'd like that. Tonight, I need some time. You know?"

"Yeah." She nodded. "I do." Then she sighed. "No, what you need to do is talk to Zuri."

"She won't see me."

"Honestly, I wouldn't, either. Not if I knew you were going to tell me what you have to tell her."

"Maybe I could just tell her that I love her."

"Maybe you could." Ravenna stepped inside. "I hope it goes the way you want it to."

"Look at you, Ravenna Blackheart. Kindness after all."

"I've always had kindness to give. No one wanted it."

"Can you blame them? You're kind of scary."

She snorted. "Are you afraid of me?"

"A little, if we're being honest."

"A man should be a little afraid of his wife." She winked at him and closed the door behind her.

He traipsed the path back down through the Enchanted Forest until he found the fork that led him to his own castle.

His life had changed so quickly in these last weeks. He found himself in situation after situation he'd never imagined.

He never thought he'd fall in love.

He never thought he'd get married.

He never thought that the two would be mutually exclusive.

At least, not until after he'd been cursed.

Zuri, Zuri, Zuri. Her name was a mantra, and the chant echoed in his brain beneath every thought and every action.

He checked the position of the moon and realized it was late. Probably too late to go creeping around her door, but he had to give it one more chance.

He had to talk to her.

Then he remembered what she'd said about Alec. About how his need to explain things was only about him and not about her at all.

She'd told him time and again she didn't want to speak to him, but he'd continued to pursue her anyway.

Was Phillip pulling an Alec?

He stopped to consider his motives and decided he'd try

this one last time. If she still chose not to speak with him, he'd leave it be.

When he entered the castle, it was obvious it sensed his distress. It tried to send him down to the mineral baths, because it knew that's where his heart wanted to be. Down there with Zuri.

"Stop," he whispered. "This is something we have to figure out for ourselves. No locking us in together."

The magic in the air dissipated.

"Thanks."

He loved how she thanked the castle and treated it as if it were sentient.

He loved how she did most everything.

He loved her.

Phillip walked slowly to her rooms. On the way, he noticed little things had changed in the castle, and he realized they'd changed to accommodate her.

She'd remarked once that she didn't like the suit of armor that stood not too far from her door. It had been moved nearer to his door.

She'd commented how much she loved the old tapestries, and they'd all been refreshed and hung in the stairwell up to their rooms. Tapestries he'd never even seen before had been resurrected to please her.

The stone steps were covered in the red carpet that spilled down the outer entrance to the castle because she'd said she thought it was nice.

Drinking chocolate found its way into her room, and he knew from the warmth in the walls that the fire would start itself before she returned to her room.

He'd changed to accommodate her, too, but not in a shallow way. It hadn't been with the intention to accommodate or impress her. It had simply happened.

As a prince, he'd never cared one way or another for social functions. Weddings had always been matters of state, and he'd never been moved in the planning or preparing of them. Yet, he loved working with her. He loved running the B and B. He liked having the castle full of tourists, and the castle liked having people to care for.

He never thought he'd be excited to fill the castle with other people's children, but being able to offer that to Zeva and knowing the magic those children were going to experience, it was a gift he was happy and ready to give.

Zuri'd changed him in so many ways.

She made him want to be better because he liked who he was when he was with her.

He'd mistakenly thought Ravenna's indifference was a kind of freedom, but it wasn't. Or it wasn't any kind of freedom he wanted.

He liked Zuri's expectations of him.

She expected him to be every inch the man he'd promised he'd be with no exceptions.

It was with that thought in mind he knocked on her door.

Chapter 24

Z uri could tell from the cadence of the knock that it was Phillip who stood outside her door.

She knew it was time to face him.

To face the loss of all her dreams once again.

It would be easier if she could be angry with him, but she wasn't angry at all. Just heartbroken.

She pressed her cheek against the door and sighed.

"I know you have all the drinking chocolate," he said softly.

Zuri opened the door.

Still, even though she knew it was him on the other side of the door, she hadn't expected the sight of him.

That sounded stupid.

But seeing him twisted things up inside of her. He was just so . . . perfect. Not a hair was out of place. No five-o'clock shadow. He was always so perfectly groomed. She knew part of that was the castle, but she wanted to see something that reminded her he was real.

Just a bit of stubble.

And just like that, he had the beginnings of golden scruff.

Why had she done that to herself? It made him hotter.

He reached up and ran his hand over his cheeks.

"So, you want the ruffian look tonight. I can deal with that." He gave her a gentle smile. "The castle obeys you in all things."

"She's accommodating." She opened the door wider so he could come in.

He smelled so good. She wanted to throw her arms around him and retreat from the outside world. To find someplace where they could just be together.

Zuri knew it was time to shake all those thoughts out of her head.

Two cups of steaming drinking chocolate appeared on her counter. "She knows us well, it seems."

He accepted the mug, and she tried not to think that this was the last time they'd share their late-night drinking chocolate.

"She does." He didn't seem inclined to do anything except stare at her.

The tension built in the room, and they were awkward around each other. Something they'd never been before. Zuri didn't like it.

"Things weren't even weird like this when you gave me frog pox."

"Ah, but I didn't give you frog pox. You caught frog pox."

She arched a brow. "The difference?"

"You had to chase me to get it. I was just hanging out in my fountain doing my thing, and you snatched me up."

"I beg your pardon, I did no such thing. You approached me. You kept staring at me with your sad little froggy eyes, and I finally caved. But I didn't snatch you up. I offered you my hands and you jumped."

He laughed. "Okay, I'll let you have that one." Phillip took a deep breath. "I've got only three days to break this curse."

"Three? That's all? Oh, Phillip. That's awful. You must be so scared." She went to him and surrendered to the urge to hug him tight. "I'm sorry I've been avoiding you. It was selfish. I just wasn't ready to face what I know you're here to tell me."

His arms closed around her. "I understand. This isn't . . . what does that stupid curse know anyway? I don't love Ravenna. She doesn't love me. But I do love you."

She hadn't expected those words again. They were like a deluge of cool, crystal water, and her heart was a dry, cracked desert.

Zuri allowed him to comfort her. Inhaled the familiar scent of him. "I'm sorry my love couldn't break the curse. It is true, you know. I hope you don't doubt that."

"I don't doubt that, Zuri. Or you."

"It's just not good enough," she murmured.

"It is. Don't you doubt yourself."

"Phillip, the fact remains. If I was enough, your curse would be broken. But it's not. You're going to marry someone else."

"It'll be a marriage of inconvenience," he said quietly.

"That's miserable. No one should have to live that way, and I can't imagine that's something that any kind of magic would subject either of you to."

"Maybe it's not the answer, but I don't know what is," Phillip said. "And my time is up."

"I know. So is mine," she confessed.

"What do you mean?"

"I don't want to be in the way here, and I would be." She pulled back from him and shook her head when he rushed to reassure her she wouldn't be in the way. "I need to leave. I need to heal and recharge. So after the Markhoff wedding, I'm leaving Ever After."

"No. This isn't it. It can't be."

"But that's why you're here. To tell me this is it. You can't . . . Phillip, that's not fair."

"I know. I'm a bastard. Just let me see you one more time. Let me see you off."

"Only if you promise not to make it hard."

"It's not me that makes it hard, beautiful," he teased.

"This is not the time for dick jokes." She sniffed. But then she laughed.

"See? What better time?"

"I don't know if I can make that promise. It's too much. It would be better for both of us to say our goodbyes now," she said.

"Would it?" He kissed the top of her head. "Or would it be better if I could see you leaving for something better and know that you're going to be happy again, and you would know that I'm still here?"

"Why is it good for me to know you're still here? I mean, aside from the fact I don't want you to turn green forever?"

"Um, that's it, really?" He chuckled. "I just want to see you. Yeah, I guess it's still selfish."

She could give him that, couldn't she?

"Plus, what if I see you after tonight? If we've already said goodbye, then it's awkward, right?"

Zuri laughed again. "It'll be awkward anyway, won't it?"

"I don't know. I've never done this before."

"New territory for us both. Oh, wait. That's a lie. I've been somewhere similar," she managed to tease.

He stumbled back from her and clutched his stomach over-dramatically. "Shots fired! A gut wound. It'll take me hours to bleed out."

"I guess you better think about where you want to spend your last hours. Will it be drinking honey mead at Pick 'n' Axe? Will it be picking out your funeral finery with Rose-bud? What do you think?"

Had she just really compared picking out his tux to marry Ravenna to funeral finery? That hadn't been what she meant, but that's where the analogy easily led.

He was silent but seemed to brush it off. "Right here. An exchange of witty barbs to my last!"

They were silent for a long moment.

"Where are you going to go? Tell me your plans. Zeva is going to be at FGA, you're going to be out in the world without your family."

"I . . . hadn't gotten that far yet. I only just decided I'm leaving. I haven't told the godmothers yet. I told Rosebud and Gwen. You should know I met Hunter. We all went axe throwing and got shit-faced. It was a good time."

"Hunter is great. I'm so glad you got to meet him."

"Gwen suggested he and I hook up to get over our broken hearts." She didn't know why she'd said it. Maybe it was to hurt him. "I'm sorry, I shouldn't have told you that. It was funny when Gwen said it because you should've seen Hunter and me look at each other and turn up our noses."

"If you and Hunter could be happy together, I wouldn't begrudge you. It'd be no less than what I deserve, honestly."

"Why do you think that? You talked to us both before you made this choice. You've been completely honest. It's not like you betrayed either one of us."

"I feel like I did."

Zuri closed her eyes and took a deep breath to steel herself for the words that were going to be so hard to say even though she meant them. "I've decided what I want in trade for letting you see me off."

"I can already tell I'm not going to like it."

"Well, that's my price, so you're either going to have to agree or suck it up."

"Zuri, you know I'll give you anything you ask of me."

"Anything?" she asked softly.

"Anything."

"Then I want you to try to find some happiness in your arrangement with Ravenna. Try to help her find her happiness the way you did with me." Tears threatened, but she stuffed them down. She could have them later, when he couldn't see.

"Jesus, Zuri. I know why it didn't work."

"What? You better explain yourself quickly, because I'm about to kick you in the shins."

He sighed, long and deep. "Oh, baby. It's not because you're not enough. It's because I'm not. I don't deserve you. Or your love."

"Shut up. That's trash. Yes, you do. We deserve to be happy. Both of us."

"You're not getting out of telling me your plans, you know."

"I told you, I didn't quite have any plans."

"I don't like you being out in the world without Zeva." He looked away. "Or me."

"I'll be just fine."

"Financially, are you okay?"

"If I said I wasn't, what would you do? Throw your money at me? Which I definitely would not take. I don't want your money."

"It would make me feel better to know you had it."

"I'm fine. I don't need it."

"Would you take a credit card, just in case of emergencies?"

"Phillip."

"Zuri."

"Do you even have a credit card that works out in the real world? I mean, you're a fairy-tale prince, can you really have a good credit score?"

He snorted. "Of course I have a good credit score. I wouldn't be a fairy-tale prince with bad credit, now would I?"

"Maybe. Money isn't everything." She lifted her chin.

"No, it's not everything. But I'd rather cry in my castle than . . ." He trailed off.

"Than in a fountain?"

"That's not fair," he whispered.

"You're right. It's not. I'm sorry. It just . . . you know how when the banter gets started I just say whatever pops into my head. Today, it was that."

"It's okay," he said. "Take the card to make it up to me."

"And what, your wife will be okay with you paying my bills like I'm your mistress? Is that what you're trying to do because that's . . ." She sagged. "God, I wish that's who we were."

"I already thought about that. Believe me. But I knew that wasn't who you were or who I want to be. Not that Ravenna would even care. She likes you, you know. She wanted to make sure we weren't doing anything behind your back."

"I don't have the gifts that my sister has, but I can see Ravenna. She doesn't have a black heart at all. She only wishes she did. Her heart is like a pearl, encased in all that darkness."

"Made just like a pearl, too. Something got inside and irritated her," he said.

She couldn't help but laugh again.

"So the card?"

"Phillip, I have my own good credit score. Plus, I don't trust myself. What if I decide to go on a shopping spree to mend my broken heart? Or what if I want to go to Monaco?"

"I hear that Ransom and Lucky are still in Monaco. You could visit them."

"I just said I was going to spend all your money and you don't care?" she teased.

It was easier to pretend this was just a game. It was easier to fall into the cliché of telling him she'd max out his credit card to make him pay for her broken heart. It was easier to pretend that after this wedding, and after she left Ever After, she had a plan for the healing she talked about.

If she were the strong woman she wanted to be, she'd already have a plan for putting her life back together like Jenn. She wouldn't need to go bury herself somewhere and hermit.

Of course, if she was going to bury herself somewhere, it

wouldn't hurt to not have to worry about dipping into her savings.

"I don't give a shit," he said. "Even if you never use it. Even if you tuck it away in a vault somewhere and never look at it again. It would be nice to know in an emergency, I could still help you. Or treat you to a spa day."

"And if I did that, how would I ever forget you?"

"Another gut shot." He shook his head. "Can you say you'll ever forget me? Do you want to forget me?" he rushed on. "I will never forget you."

"You're the worst. This romance crap sucks." She sniffed back tears. "You are not allowed to keep being romantic after we're broken up."

"I'm Prince Charming, baby. That's just how I'm wired."

"Maybe you could go back to being a philandering jerk?"

"Don't tempt me. I want to kiss you right now more than anything else in the world."

"Anything?" She almost asked him if he wanted it more than he didn't want to be a frog, but that was unfair, and it would sound like she was asking him to pick her instead of his own life. That wasn't something she wanted him to choose.

Sure, she wanted the validation that he loved her more than anything, but the fallout wasn't worth the price. She'd rather know that he was himself, and hopefully finding some measure of happiness because she would try her very best to do the same.

"Anything," he said, taking her chin with his thumb and tilting her face up to his. "Ask me for what you want from me."

Zuri shook her head slowly. "No. Because it's not fair to any one of us."

"A woman of her convictions to the bitter end. It's part of why I love you, Zuri. Part of why I will always love you."

She grabbed his hands. "Don't let this be the bitter end. It doesn't have to be. You promised you'd try to be happy. I know it seems impossible now, but we weren't meant to live in a constant state of sorrow. I believe that with every fiber of my being."

"Is that what you're going to do?"

"I'm going to try my damnedest."

He kissed the inside of her wrist. "All right. I'll try. Don't forget your promise."

"I won't," she said on a shaky breath.

When he was gone, she turned and walked up the stairs to her bedroom loft and stared longingly at the lavender creation on the dress form in the corner.

Even though her heart was breaking, she'd pack that dress away, and someday, she'd wear it. Someday, she'd be happy again.

Someday, when she thought of Phillip Charming, her heart wouldn't shatter in a million pieces.

Chapter 25

Phillip Charming never said he'd sleep on a problem.

He frogged on it.

While he thought that terminology sounded incredibly stupid, it was what he'd been left with. He didn't sleep, really. He was a man, he was a frog. He figured that he slept as a frog. Sometimes he had vague memories of napping on a fat lily pad in the sun, and those memories were foggy and strange. Albeit, nice.

After he'd left Zuri's, he realized he wanted her to tell him no. He wanted her to tell him not to marry Ravenna.

As if she would ever do such a thing.

Zuri was the most selfless person he knew. She'd never ask him to give up his humanity just for one more night with her.

Except that's what he'd wanted her to do.

He didn't understand why.

So he'd frogged on it.

When the sun set and he crawled, wet and sad from the fountain, he knew why. It was because he was scared. He was scared to lose himself.

But he was smacked in the face, or perhaps it was a lily pad, with the realization that marrying Ravenna just to hold on to his human form was also losing himself. He was trading everything he knew to be good and right to hold on to something that was no longer meant for him.

He didn't want the rest of eternity without Zuri.

And it wasn't that he longed for oblivion or anything of that nature. It was completely the opposite. Phillip hadn't really known what it was like to live the life he'd been given until Zuri. If she left him of her own accord, that was a different matter entirely.

But *he* wasn't leaving him.

He'd chosen to leave her because he was scared.

He could have one more night with the woman he loved beyond all reason, or forever without her.

When he took into account that forever without her also meant that she'd think she wasn't enough, that his beautiful, powerful, vibrant, and absolutely vital Zuri would think any less of herself, he just couldn't do it.

He knew what he had to do.

Phillip was afraid of what was to come, he was honest with himself about that. But he was more afraid of forever without her.

Especially since there was no guarantee that marrying Ravenna was going to work. He was operating under the assumption that it would, but even then, this wasn't right.

It wasn't what a man in love would do.

It definitely wasn't what Prince Charming would do.

A voice startled him. "Figured it out, have you?"

He looked up to see Hunter standing there picking his teeth with a chicken bone. Wait, was it a chicken bone? He hadn't seen Bronx in some time.

"Uh . . . so I know you and Esmerelda have gotten to be friends. That's not someone we know, is it?" he asked.

Hunter stopped what he was doing and looked at the tiny bone, and then laughed a deep, belly-shaking laugh. "No, but I have been terrorizing him just a little bit."

"Hasn't he been terrorized enough?"

"Not yet. Did you know, a few weeks ago, he would show up outside her den and sing at the top of his lungs in the middle of the day while she was trying to sleep?"

"What a little shit. What is his problem?"

Hunter shrugged. "I think he likes her, but he has to learn that we do not express affection by hurting creatures."

Phillip realized that held true for himself as well. "You got me there."

"Uh-huh," Hunter said. "So, like I asked. You figure it out? Frog on it long enough?"

"Yeah, I'm a dumbass."

"No argument from me there," Hunter said.

"You should know, it was Ravenna who proposed to me. Sort of. You scared the shit out of her."

"*I* scared *her*? You have to be kidding me. She could smite me into a dung beetle. She has nothing to fear."

"Now who's being a dumbass?"

Hunter looked around and then pointed at himself. "Me? What are you talking about?"

"Never mind. Anyway, I need to go talk to her. Call off the madness."

"Good plan."

"Can I tell you something?"

"I'd hope so. I'm supposed to be your best friend. But after you befouled the mineral baths, I haven't heard much from you."

"Shut your muzzle. We've both been busy. I hear you went out drinking with my true love."

"I hear you're going to marry mine."

They looked at each other and laughed.

"Zuri thinks you're pretty great. She told me Gwen suggested you guys go out."

"The matchmaking in this town is ridiculous. I thought maybe when everyone had other people to worry about they'd leave us locals alone. I was so wrong. It's even worse."

"Meddling godmothers." Phillip shook his head.

"So you were going to bare your soul?" Hunter teased.

"Yeah, kinda."

"Oh, shit. Okay. Sorry. Go on." Hunter motioned with his hand for him to continue.

"I'm scared, Hunter."

"I think that's a completely reasonable reaction to the choice you have to make."

"I don't want to be a frog. I'm not going to know who I am. I'm not going to remember you. Or the last time I get to spend with Zuri."

"Can I ask you something?"

"You just did."

"Okay, smarty breeches. Why do you think that Happily Ever After isn't for you? I mean, I know why Ravenna thinks it's not. I know why I thought it wasn't, but why can't this work out?"

Phillip gestured to the space around them. "Have you been paying attention?"

"I have. Have you?"

"This is not helping."

Hunter snuffled. "The Enchanted Forest for the trees, my friend."

"After I go talk to Ravenna, you want to hang out? Watch some stupid comedies from the eighties and eat popcorn?"

"*Police Academy*, bro." Hunter nodded. "I'll be waiting."

"Oh, and Hunter?"

"Yeah?"

"I haven't said this as often as I should've. Thanks for being here when I need you."

"That's why they give me the best-friend cape." He wrapped the red cape around himself and bowed with a flourish.

"I thought that was your adventuring-through-the-forest cape?"

"It does double duty," he said. "See you back at the castle, my friend. This'll all work out, you'll see."

"When did you get to be such an optimist?"

"I don't know. Since I realized we're all magic and this

is completely ridiculous, so anything has to be possible?" He shrugged and meandered back through the underbrush toward the castle.

And Phillip, he began the trek through the woods toward Ravenna's.

Esmerelda met him halfway. "Hey, is Hunter coming later?"

"I don't think so. We've got a guys' night planned."

"Your bachelor party? Can I come? I promise I won't be a party pooper," Esmerelda asked.

"No, it's not like that. We're just going to eat popcorn, drink mead, and watch some old movies."

"That's rather boring, but I should've expected it. Goody Two-Hessians. So boring."

"I haven't worn my Hessians in a century. What are you talking about?"

Esmerelda tittered. "I need to do something nice for Hunter. Did he tell you about that Bronx?

"He did. I don't know what Bronx's problem is, but apparently, he's been in his nest for some time. He won't come out. He's binge-watching all those fashion and makeover shows."

Esmerelda seemed pleased with herself. "Good. Maybe he'll leave me alone, now."

"One would hope."

"So, Hunter. What's nice that I could do for him?"

"He just likes to help. He's that kind of guy." Phillip walked along. "Maybe a bottle of mead? After the cherry incident at the godmothers', the brothers are trying a batch of cherry mead. That would be a nice gift."

"Good plan. Thanks, Charming."

"Anytime, love."

"You're awfully cheerful for having just broken your own heart. This doesn't bode well," Esmerelda noticed.

"You are correct."

"Oh," Esmerelda said. "She's going to be disappointed,

but this isn't unexpected. She told me to hold off on talking to Grammy to officiate."

"Don't tell your mistress I said so, but she's a better person than she knows."

Esmerelda tittered. "Oh, she'd be so mad to hear you say so. But if we're being honest, I've known it for years. She takes too good care of me to be a bad person. She never asks me to do anything I disagree with on moral grounds, and she buys me toys and gives me all the fresh fruit I want. And ear scratches. She lets me sit in her lap as long as I want, even when she has to work on a new potion or on the accounting at the bank."

"She loves you."

"She told me she loved me once. In 1982. She was stoned. But I knew she meant it just the same."

They arrived at the door, and Esmerelda let him inside.

"Wait here. I'll tell her you've arrived."

He waited for Ravenna and tried to plan out what he was going to say. He'd meant to do that on the walk up there, but he'd been so engaged with Esmerelda, he hadn't had a moment.

Phillip knew this wouldn't hurt her feelings in a romantic way, but he wanted to preserve the new level of friendship they'd found. It was honest and good. He liked Ravenna. He didn't want her to think he'd chosen being a frog over marrying her.

He'd chosen being a frog over losing Zuri.

Ravenna glided into the room wearing a dress of black velvet and lace and looking every inch an Evil Queen. He thought that about her frequently, and he admired the effort she expended keeping up appearances.

Not that Ravenna wouldn't be evil as shit if crossed, but there was more to her than that.

It took her one second to ascertain the situation, and she gave him a sad sort of half smile.

"I see," she said, and her tone wasn't unkind.

He wouldn't go so far to say it was kind, but there was no rancor, no anger. No bitterness or even sadness. Yet, it was still gentle.

"I promised I'd tell you. So here I am. I can't marry you, Ravenna."

"I figured as much."

"I need you to know that I value your friendship. I like you more than I expected to."

She snorted. "Oh, please."

"No, really. If things weren't about to go the way I suspect, I'd suggest a group game night. Cocktails and Dungeons and Inquisitions."

"Really?" She arched a brow. "And not just because you know your best friend has it bad for me?"

"Nope. I like who you are. Even when you're evil."

"For fuck's sake. Of course you do. Prince Charming likes everyone."

"No, I don't. Really. But I do like you."

"You're so rude." She sniffed and looked away. "Why do you have to tell me you want to be friends and then go be a frog forever?"

"Shit happens, darlin'. That's all I've got for that."

"If you turn into a forever frog, you can come live in my fountain. No one will eat you. I'll feed you strawberries every day. I promise."

"Hey, what the hell, right? Might as well take good care of future frog me. Thanks, Ravenna."

"Was it Zuri who made you see the light?" she asked.

"In a way. She didn't ask me to, of course. But I realized that I love her."

"You already knew that you loved her, dumb-dumb."

It was his turn to snort. "Yeah, okay. But it's because I love her that I can't let her think for one second she's not enough.

One last day with her is worth whatever time I'd buy if you and I got married."

She took his hands. "I understand. I expected it sooner, honestly."

"Why didn't you say something?"

"Would you have listened? No. But you're actually Prince Charming. You've earned the title. This is who you are. There's no other choice you could make. And I have a confession."

He arched a brow. "Oh, really?"

She looked sheepish but only for a moment. "I never thought this was the right path, but I was scared. I don't know who the bride in the vision was, but I know it wasn't me. I promise I'll come get you. You know, after."

"How do you know Zuri wasn't going to keep me with her?"

"She's a fairy-tale princess, Phillip. Not a saint. But you tell her I'm going to take care of you, so she doesn't worry."

"Aren't you worried people will start to think you have a heart?"

"Nah, I figure it took the godmothers three hundred years to forgive you. I've got nothing to worry about." She smiled at him, and it was an honest, open, and genuine smile.

It transformed her face.

Ravenna was coldly beautiful, like a piece of art in a museum. A carved figure in marble. But her real smile brought that cold marble flesh to life like Pygmalion.

"Thank you, Ravenna. For everything."

"Phillip, before you go, don't you think Zuri would look gorgeous in lavender?"

"She'd look gorgeous in anything."

"Obviously." Ravenna rolled her eyes. "But a lavender wedding dress?"

"I'm not that lucky."

"Why not? We live in Ever After. Anything is possible."

"Don't give me hope. It's just cruel at this point."

"Don't you know, Phillip? That's what I do."

He studied her. "We're still friends. Be as mean as you want."

"Jerk," she said. "Why do you say such mean things?"

"I guess because I'm Prince Charming. It's what I do."

Chapter 26

The day of the Markhoff wedding rehearsal dawned dreary and cool. The rain would be gone by breakfast, because that's just how things in Ever After worked, but Zuri thought it was a fitting start to the kind of day she knew lay ahead.

She had so much to do, she'd be lucky if her head didn't fall off and roll away.

She'd considered asking Petty if they could clone her just so she could get everything finished.

Hansel had worked his fingers to the bone and, with a little boost of magic had managed to somehow rebuild the stage and even finish the chandelier moon.

He needed a bonus.

And probably a vacation, just like all the rest of them.

Wedding season had only just swung into full gear. She was terrified and excited to see what summer would bring.

Then she reminded herself that she wouldn't be in Ever After to see it.

That morning, when she'd awakened, she'd found a note scrawled on her shower mirror. It read, "Don't go."

As quickly as she'd read it, it had been erased and replaced with "Who will do your hair?"

Zuri didn't want to leave the castle, and really, who *would* do her hair? She'd gotten so used to it always being perfect without having to put in all the long hours with a hot comb, or worrying about not getting it wet, or all the other things that came along with maintaining her current style.

Anna found Zuri in the ballroom before the rehearsal.

"You've been through so much planning our wedding. I want you to know how much it means to us that you've still persevered. We are going to recommend you far and wide. I mean, from that crazy allergic reaction to our best man being your ex-boyfriend and breaking up with the new boyfriend, and pulling this together so beautifully for us, you've just had so much to deal with."

"Breaking up with my current boyfriend? What do you mean?"

"Weren't you dating the handsome B and B owner?" Anna asked.

"I . . ."

"Oh, I understand that you want to keep your personal life out of work after Alec and Chicago. He's the one who told me that you and Phillip broke up. Is it true that he's going to marry someone else, too?"

She coughed. "We weren't dating. We were just friends. Yes, he's marrying Ravenna."

"Honey, you've been through so much."

"I'm fine. I promise. Is everyone here? Are we ready to start the rehearsal?" Zuri peered around Anna's shoulder to both check for all participants and to disengage herself from that conversation.

"It's all going to work out," Anna promised.

"It is! You're going to have a beautiful wedding. Where's Jordan?"

"He's on his way. He wanted to try out the pumpkin carriage. He's bringing Grammy."

"Oh, good."

"We also wanted to say that while we loved Jenn, after meeting you, we see why she wasn't right for Alec."

Oh God, not more of this. "Funny. After meeting Jenn, I saw why I wasn't right for Alec."

Anna nodded. "Fair enough. Oh, look. They're here."

Zuri looked to where Grammy had entered with Red in tow behind her, and Jordan had a bluebell flower in hand for his bride.

Zuri still thought they were a lovely couple. As long as they stayed out of her romantic life.

Grammy looked sharp as ever wearing a gray velvet tux with a blue silk vest, and matching bow tie and suspenders. Zuri gave her a nod of approval. Grammy grinned, showing all of her sharp teeth.

Grammy took her place on the stage and waited for everyone else to take their places. Zuri watched as the bridesmaids went to their marks, as did the groomsmen, and finally, the best man.

Alec flashed her a thumbs-up, and she returned the gesture. She would be happy to see Anna and Jordan finally say their vows both for the culmination of all their hard work and to finally be rid of Alec's presence. Somehow, he'd even gotten the mostly reasonable Anna and Jordan in on his antics. The sooner she could put more distance between them, the happier she'd be.

The lights in the ballroom dimmed, and the chandelier moon flickered to life. As Anna and Jordan began to play their parts, Zuri was carried away in the story of their love. This might've been the best idea she'd ever had.

She watched as the other participants were caught up as well, and her heart soared.

Jordan swept Anna into his arms and carried her up the stairs to stand before Grammy, where he sank to his knees to replace her lost slipper, and Rosebud had managed to re-create a beautiful pair of actual glass slippers. Obviously, magic.

Grammy began speaking, and a sudden sense of dread washed over her as Zuri realized everyone had stopped to look at her.

Alec had stepped out of place.

Oh no.

"Boy, what are you doing?" Grammy asked.

"I'm waiting for you to get to the part where you ask if anyone has any reason why these two shouldn't be married."

"What, did you sleep with Anna, too?" Zuri asked.

Everyone gasped collectively.

Grammy turned to look at him and smacked him with the holy book she held in her hands. "Stop it. Get back to your place, son. Read the room."

"No, I need to speak. I can't hold my peace."

Then she realized he'd planned this with Anna and Jordan. They looked at her expectantly, as if some kind of miracle were about to unfold. The crowd collectively followed their lead.

"I warned you, Alec."

The crowd turned back as a unit to Alec.

"And the wedding has been planned. Your part is finished."

"You're right about that," Zuri said, as fury rose in her chest.

"Make the next wedding you plan ours. Marry me, Zuri!" He sank down on one knee.

The crowd gasped.

"I already planned one wedding for you, Alec. You don't get two."

They gasped again and turned their heads back to Zuri. It was almost as if they were watching a tennis match from hell.

Zuri, however, was done.

She'd had enough.

She removed the Bluetooth headset from her ear, put down her planner, and turned on her heel and strode toward the door.

Alec rushed after her.

"Castle, I would enjoy never being in the same room with Alec Marsh again."

Stairs appeared before her, and with a sigh of gratitude, she realized they led directly to her room.

Alec gave chase, but when he approached the first stair, the doorway closed, leaving him with no way to follow her.

"Thank you."

She fled to her room and decided that it was time to pack. She'd told Alec her terms. He'd blown past her boundaries again and again, and it was time to enforce them.

Zuri was finished.

This had been her last wedding.

At least, for some time.

All she had left to do was pack and say farewell to Ever After.

And Phillip.

Zuri decided, for once, that she was going to be selfish. She was going to worry about her own needs instead of everyone else's. She didn't have it in her to say goodbye to him again.

The other night when he'd come to her rooms and they'd had drinking chocolate, she'd said everything she needed to say to him.

Zuri knew he'd said all he could say, too.

So what was left except more angst and sorrow?

She didn't want it. She'd had enough.

Zuri tried to put her clothes into her suitcase, but as soon as she'd folded something, it was back where she'd found it.

"Castle. Come on."

If she hadn't been used to magic, she would've screamed her head off when the dress form that held the lavender dress Rosebud had given her bounced down the stairs from her bedroom.

"I'm not wearing that to travel."

The dress form rattled, as if the castle was shaking it at her.

"I hear you. I don't want to leave you, either. But I have to." She sighed. "You could help me pack."

Her suitcase slid across the room and out the balcony doors.

She dashed after it and saw it flap its two pieces like wings until it was in the middle of the lake and then drop like a stone.

Zuri didn't feel much like laughing, but the sight of the angry swan darting out of the way of her flying suitcase was too funny.

"Listen, Castle. I have to go. I'm going even if you don't give me my clothes. I can come back and visit. After my heart isn't broken."

Her suitcase was suddenly back and miraculously dry. It flipped open on the couch.

"You could pack for me?"

No help was forthcoming.

"Okay, fair enough." She got up and began putting things back into the case.

A glittery purple comb appeared on the table, and she picked it up to inspect it. It was embossed with print that read, "Castle Styler."

Oh! The castle had given her a gift.

It would keep doing her hair.

"Well, shit." She sat down and held the comb close to her chest as fat tears slipped down her face.

A blanket wrapped itself around her shoulders, and a hot cup of drinking chocolate appeared within reach.

She sniffed but allowed herself only a moment to be comforted. It would be easy to stay here in this place that had become her home.

Her shelter.

Her vision of Happily Ever After.

She had to get a new vision.

With a puff of green fairy dust, Zeva appeared, looking confused. "What's going on? How did you do that?"

Zuri looked up at her sister's confused face.

"Wombmate, why are you crying? Do I need to stuff someone's head up their own ass, because I'll do it."

"No." Zuri sniffed.

"How did I get here, though?"

Zuri wiped at her tears with the back of her hand. "I guess the castle thought I needed you."

"What's happened?"

"Nothing new. Just that I'm leaving."

"Are you sure that's what you want to do?" Zeva narrowed her eyes. "I thought you loved it here."

"I do. I can't watch Phillip marry someone else. I can't live here with all this wonderful magic and know it's not for me."

"It is for you! You just have to have faith."

"You keep telling me that, but here we are, and do you know what faith got me?"

"Tell me," Zeva encouraged, and sat down next to her.

"It got me a proposal from Alec. That definitely wasn't my heart's desire. The wish coin was broken. Magic is broken." She slumped. "Or maybe it's me. *I'm* broken."

"Zuri, honey, you're not broken. Why would you think that?"

"I'm the common denominator, here. When it seems like the world is against you, it's time to stop and look at what everything has in common. Me."

"No, no. That can't be true. Don't lose your hope now. It's too beautiful. It's too important."

"I just can't hope anymore. Not right now." Zuri slouched, dejected.

"After all that you've seen, after you've been the guiding hand in so many people's Happily Ever Afters, how can you not believe?"

"I believe. I do."

"Then why are you running away?"

"Because it's too much to see everyone else get what I want. I know it's selfish and awful, but . . ."

"It's okay to rest and give yourself space. That's not selfish or awful. Not in the least." Zeva hugged her close. "But if you've ever trusted me, believe me when I say this is not the time to rest. It's the time to fight."

"How, Zeva? How do I fight against magic? How do I fight a curse? I'm not anything special. I'm just Zuri Davis, wedding planner." She slumped further. "Groom stealer."

"You're going to have shaken wedding planner syndrome if you try to come at me with that mess again. No. That's not what we're doing."

"Then what are we doing?"

"Fighting."

"You keep saying that. How?"

"Tell Phillip that you love him and you're not letting him go. Tell him that you're staying together no matter what. Tell him that you *believe*." Zeva rattled Zuri's shoulders.

"I can't do that."

"Why not?" Zeva fairly shrieked. "This job is so hard. It's like being a social worker but I can't make anyone listen to even half of what I say."

"Because I can't ask him to sacrifice his humanity for me."

Zeva palmed her forehead with a loud thwap and then leaned back. "Ow. I have to stop doing that. Anyway, you're not asking him to do anything of the sort. You're asking him to believe."

"Did you miss the part where I believed we shared True Love's Kiss? And nothing happened."

"Believe now, more than you ever have before."

"Alec did that earlier. He believed. He asked me to marry him during the wedding rehearsal. The whole crowd seemed to expect me to say yes."

"You are not Alec."

"No, I'm not. And I'm not going to ask Phillip to make that choice. I'm leaving now."

"Aren't you going to at least say goodbye?"

"We already said our goodbyes," Zuri said.

"But?" Zeva prompted.

"But nothing."

"There's something. I know you too well. I can feel it on the tip of your tongue. Tell me."

"Fine." Zuri knew she'd never leave it alone if she didn't tell her. She'd be ninety years old, on her deathbed, and Zeva would ask her if she remembered that time in Ever After when she'd asked her what she'd been about to say and Zuri refused to tell her. "I promised him I'd say goodbye again when I left. But I just can't."

"What if saying goodbye to him again would change everything. Would you do it?"

"Are you speaking to me as an FG in training, or as my sister?"

"Neither. I'm asking you a question as your best friend."

"What could it possibly change?" She was tired of fey things like what-ifs and hope. Zuri needed something solid and real.

"I don't know, but Mama didn't raise us to break our promises."

"Oh, you played the Mama card. That's low." Zuri shook her head in disbelief.

"You know what's low is breaking your promise to someone you claim to love."

"Ugh. Fine. I'll wait until dusk, and I'll tell him, okay?"

"Okay."

She'd agreed too easily. "That's it? You're not going to try to get me to stay longer?"

"Do you want me to?" Zeva flashed a smug grin.

"No." Zuri crossed her arms. "Maybe. I'm going to miss you, Zeva."

"I can come visit you anywhere that you are. Well, at least after I'm done with FGA. I'd love for you to stay in Ever After, but you said that's not what you need. Since I love you, what can I do but let you go?"

"You're really too wise for your own good."

"Not really. Being an FG in T is teaching me that I really don't know anything. No one should give me the wheel for anything. Ever. I know nothing."

"I'm sure there's some kind of philosophical point in there somewhere," Zuri said.

"Uh-huh, but I'm too tired to chew on it."

"Me too."

"Wanna build a blanket fort?"

This was the medicine she needed more than any exotic location, or anything else she could think of. A blanket fort with her sister, and the castle helping.

This was home.

How would she ever leave it?

How could she not?

Chapter 27

He didn't have to knock on Zuri's door.

The castle knew exactly where he wanted to be, and even though he'd instructed the castle not to take him places without his verbal request, he found that he couldn't be upset.

He admired the blanket and pillow fort that had been constructed in the middle of the room. Phillip was impressed it had a makeshift drawbridge. He was sure only magic held it together, but he liked it nonetheless.

"Permission to enter?" he said.

"Phillip, what are you doing here?" Zuri poked her head up out of the top of the pillow fort.

"What do you think I'm doing here?"

"I don't know, that's why I'm asking." She dropped back down into the depths of the pillows and blankets. "I was just coming to find you to say goodbye, as I promised."

"Will you stay one more night?"

"Phillip, we can't."

He wanted to blurt out that they could, it was his last night as a man, but he knew it wasn't fair to put the weight of his choice on her.

"We can. Just talking. I wouldn't insult you like that." He supposed maybe it was asking too much of her anyway.

"Okay," she relented.

"I thought you were going to wait until after the Markhoff wedding was over before you left," he said.

"I was, but Alec proposed to me during the rehearsal."

"That bastard."

"I know. It was so embarrassing. Everyone was looking at me expectantly. As if he'd somehow convinced them all that this was a good idea. What in the actual hell?"

"We can still fry his memory."

"No. I handled it. I quit the wedding. I told him what I'd do. And I did. I'm sure that everything will still go off perfectly, because I do know what I'm doing after all, but I won't be there. I instructed the castle to please make sure I was never in a room with him again."

"That's fairly devious. I like it." He sank down toward the makeshift door. "Are you going to let me in, or is the castle not supposed to let us be in the same room, either?"

The pillow drawbridge opened, and he crawled inside.

The inside was much bigger than the outside had led him to believe, but he should've expected it because it was magic.

The interior was spacious and filled with brightly colored carpets, filmy curtains, and mountains and mountains of silk embroidered pillows.

And of course, cups of drinking chocolate.

At first, his brain tried to remind him constantly that this was the last cup of drinking chocolate he'd have. The last things he'd ever talk about. The last sights he'd see.

He had friends he wanted to tell goodbye, but all of it paled in comparison to spending this time with Zuri.

Phillip finally managed to turn that part of his brain off. He didn't want to think of this as the last of anything.

He was just an average Prince Charming, and this was his princess.

In their pillow fort castle.

Phillip wouldn't tell her that this was his Happily Ever After. She'd find out soon enough.

He didn't feel like he was cheating her of anything, she was the one who'd decided this was goodbye. So he was confident she'd say anything she'd wanted to tell him.

"This is pretty amazing."

"Yeah, it's a lovely little retreat. I'm going to miss your castle."

"I think she's going to miss you."

"Yeah, she flung my suitcase out the window at a swan earlier, so I got the point."

He was overwhelmed with the need to touch her. Just to hold her so that he could anchor himself in the real.

She scooted closer to him, and he reached out a hand to touch her but then dropped it. "Zuri?"

She seemed to know what he was asking, and she laid her head on his chest.

It felt so good to hold her close. To smell her hair. To feel her solid presence in his arms.

Then, he realized he was fucking this all up. He didn't want to put the weight of his choices on her shoulders, but how would she ever know he picked her if he didn't tell her? He hadn't thought any of this through.

She thought she was saying goodbye to a man who had agreed to marry someone else.

He was, in essence, taking her choice away from her.

Phillip wasn't going to screw this up. It was the last thing he could do for her. It wasn't selfish of him to let her know how much he loved her.

That he loved her more than himself.

It was a gift that he could give her.

The thing that she would take with her when he was gone.

Hunter was right. He was kind of dumb when it came to these things. But it wasn't like he'd had a lot of experience.

"Zuri, I have to tell you something."

"God, what else can there be? I don't think I can take anything else."

"Just this. I broke off the engagement."

She shot up. "Why? Why would you do that?"

He watched as the answer dawned on her, and she shook her head.

"No, Phillip. You can't do this."

"It's done," he said. "Come here and let me hold you."

She bit her lip and was choked by a sob. "No. You just go undo it. I won't let you do this."

"You are it for me, Zuri Davis. I got to choose between a thousand forevers and one more night with you. How many of us get that choice? I'm so damn lucky that I get to pick you."

Her lips quivered. "This is the dumbest thing you've ever done. By far and away. I mean, it's dumber than courting two Blossom sisters at the same time."

"No, baby. It's the best. None of all my long years were actually spent living until I met you. This is my Happily Ever After." Then he remembered Bluebonnet's words. "It may not be the way I envisioned it, but it's mine."

"Phillip . . ." She let him pull her back down to him. "You don't have to let this curse win just to prove you love me. I know you love me."

"But you don't know what you're worth. You're everything."

"I've been crying for the last week, and it's all your fault."

"Be mad at me after I'm a frog. Go see Ravenna and feed me dragonflies as revenge. You know I hate getting their wings in my teeth."

"Ravenna?"

"Yeah, she wanted me to tell you that she's going to make sure nothing eats me. She's going to keep my froggy self to save me from the mermaid fountain. Not that I'll know the difference." He managed a dry laugh.

"You won't have any teeth." She sniffed.

"There's my girl."

She slapped at his shoulders. "I can't believe you weren't going to tell me. What were you going to do? Sit here with me until you had to hop to Ravenna's and just never come back?"

He pulled her tighter. "I hadn't really thought it through, actually. I didn't get any further than not being able to let you go thinking you weren't my everything."

"And how would I have known that if you didn't tell me? Oh, I'm so mad at you."

"Yeah, I know. It was a tough balance between not wanting to burden you with my choices and wanting you to know. But you're smart. You'd have figured it out." He kissed her forehead. "Be mad at me later."

"I will!" she assured him. "So what do you want to do for your Happily Ever After?"

"Just this."

"Really? You're not going to leverage your last night on earth to get me to do some kinky sex game?"

"Nope. I had a lot of that before I met you. A lot. I mean, the last century or so I was celibate because who can be bothered without some kind of deeper connection? I couldn't be, anyway."

"You don't have any wild fantasies about us?"

"Are you disappointed to know that this, right here, is my wildest fantasy come to life? Just you and me, together. For the rest of the time I have left. However long that happens to be. This was my fantasy before I knew my curse was going to become permanent."

"You're ridiculous." She curled more closely into him.

"I know. That's why you love me, though."

"It is."

"What about your fantasies? Is there anything you want to do with me?"

"Besides everything? I suppose just this."

"Screw all that angst, and the unnecessary goodbye. These are the moments that make a life."

She clung to him more tightly.

For his part, he was simply content to hold her.

It wasn't long before the roof of the makeshift fort disappeared, giving them an unfettered view of a black velvet sky that glittered with diamond stars and bursts of comets.

"I wonder how many people are looking up at these same stars," Zuri said. "When I was in high school, I had a boyfriend once tell me that wishing on stars was stupid, because they were all dead. Their light was the last burst of energy they had to give, and to ask for more was selfish."

"I never thought of it that way."

"Me either. I still don't know if I think it's bitter, deep, or, somehow, kind of beautiful. He works for the space program now."

"That's fitting. It seems like he's still asking more from the stars, isn't he? He still wants to know their secrets."

"Don't we all?"

Her fingers intertwined with his, and he found himself drifting toward sleep. He fought to stay awake.

"If you want to sleep, sleep."

"My body wants to sleep, but I want to be awake."

"If this were any other night, what would you do?" she asked.

"Hold you until dawn. I don't usually sleep when I'm a man."

"What would you do without this stupid curse?"

"I'd fall asleep with you in my arms because I'd know I'd have tomorrow."

"Then let's pretend you have tomorrow."

Zuri shifted and changed their positions. She was the big spoon, and he let her. He got to bury his face in the comforting softness of her cleavage and feel the sweet warmth of her body wrapped around him.

This time it was Zuri who kissed his forehead and stroked his hair. Zuri who hummed a soft lullaby while the edges of his consciousness shifted to a dream world where forever with her was real.

This was it, he realized. And it was okay.

He didn't want to go with a sad goodbye. With tears. With regrets.

He'd slip away while she held him in her arms, and he couldn't ask for more.

"Love you," he murmured as the darkness pulled him away into a soft cocoon where there was no pain, no loss, and Zuri's sweet embrace was forever.

Chapter 28

Zuri came awake slowly, in shades of no and more no. She knew that when she awoke, she'd be alone and her Prince Charming would be gone.

She wasn't ready to face that world.

She'd put off telling him goodbye; she could put this off, too. Not forever, just for a little bit longer.

A loud cackle, however, jerked her into wakefulness.

"What's up, fuckers?" Petty asked.

"What the hell are you doing here?" Zuri shrieked.

"Securing your Happily Ever After, that's what." Petty replied in a smug tone.

"Oh my God, shut up," Phillip mumbled.

Phillip!

Mumbled!

He was there! It was dawn! He was him. He wasn't a frog!

"Ah, I see it's finally taking root. Okay." Petty clapped her hands. "Chop-chop. We have things to do. We need to start planning this wedding because Zeva has to go to FGA and can't visit for some time. That is, unless you don't care if your sister is at your wedding."

"Petty, it's the middle of the night, and you're ruining my Happily Ever After. Get. Out," Phillip grumbled.

"No, no. It's dawn. It's past dawn. It's time for breakfast. We're all starving, and we're all waiting for you to ring the castle bells so we can celebrate the engagement of Ever

After's king . . . er, mayor, whatever we want to call it for the normies. Move. Your. Green. Butt."

"It's not green anymore!" Zuri cried.

"It's going to be if you don't get moving," Jonquil advised knowingly.

Phillip sat up and looked around. He checked himself with his hands. First, checking all of the angles of his face. His shoulders. He hugged himself and checked his arms. Then his legs, before looking to Zuri.

His eyes were still that intense, surreal green.

"Zuri, is this real?"

"If it's just your froggy fantasy, do you really want to wake up?" Petty asked kindly.

"No. Never," he said. "Wait, yes. It's not really Happily Ever After if I'm not with Zuri."

"Right answer, Prince Charming."

"I don't understand why True Love's Kiss didn't break the curse," Zuri asked.

"It did. It was his love for you that had to be true. He had to love you more than himself. That's all." Petty shrugged her shoulders.

"You could've told me and saved us all that angst," Zuri groused.

"I tried."

Zuri remembered Zeva telling her that she had to have faith. She remembered Zeva's words when she asked what Zuri would do if one more night would change everything. How she was so close and it was too important to give up now.

If she would've left, she'd have lost it all.

Phillip would have, too.

She looked up at the castle. "Thanks for not letting me leave. I guess you knew what you were doing."

"You were trying to leave? Oh, my dear. You would've ruined everything," Petty said.

"The castle helped. So did Zeva. She told me I couldn't give up."

"She was right. And much too close to breaking the spirit of the rule if not the letter. She's a sneaky one, isn't she?" Petty asked. "But I suppose I knew that."

"Zeva reminds me of you, Petty. When you were younger," Bluebonnet said.

"Dearie me. That means we're really in for it." Petty shook her head. "So, hey, Zuri, why don't you show him that dress Rosebud gave you. It's beautiful. I think it would be the perfect wedding dress."

"Petty. No one said we're getting married," Zuri said.

"No?" Phillip asked her. "I suppose we can wait if that's what you want."

"Why are you two the most stubborn charges I've ever had?" Petty asked.

"I bet you say that about all of them," Zuri teased.

"I do. Right now, you're the worst. Listen, after all this work, you're getting married. I've decided. You have to help us plan all these other weddings, and we need you happy and fulfilled. Both of you. So get with the program."

Phillip grinned. "I don't know. It's all up to Zuri. Wait, is that dress that Petty is talking about by any chance lavender?"

Zuri looked up to see Petty's eyes twinkle with mischief, and pink fairy dust exploded around her in a bright display of mini fireworks.

"It is," Zuri replied with a smile.

"The bride in Ravenna's vision was wearing a lavender dress," Phillip said.

Warmth and joy welled up inside her as she realized this fairy tale really did belong to her.

"Well, if you've seen the dress," Zuri began, unable to resist giving Petty a hard time. "Then I couldn't possibly use it for my wedding dress."

"What have I told you two about fate?" Petty huffed.

"Don't fuck with it," they repeated together in monotone.

"Well, at least you're listening part of the time. Come on, ring the castle bells so we can all celebrate the breaking of the curse and another Happily Ever After. I've been dying for this one," Petty said.

"You?" Phillip arched a brow and scoffed.

"Yes, me. Every day of your curse . . ." She trailed off and looked away to the left. Then she coughed. "Every day of your curse after the first hundred years has been agonizing for me. I felt so awful. I'm so happy for you, Phillip. FGI wishes you the happiest of Happily Ever Afters."

"Do you really?" He arched a brow.

"Yes!" Petty cried.

"Then get out so I can start enjoying it properly."

Petty cocked her head to the side. "I really don't see . . . Oh. *Oh!*"

"Yes, oh! Go. Shoo." Phillip waved her out.

"You did not just shoo me. I swear, I'll . . ."

"Go ring the castle bells for us?" Zuri asked hopefully.

"Okay, but after shenanigans will you promise me we can start planning the wedding? Please?" Petty begged.

"I will not. Phillip hasn't asked. Let our love story finish unfolding," Zuri pleaded.

"I think we should get started. If she's still here when I get naked, that's on her."

"I thought you said you didn't have any kinky fantasies?" Zuri teased.

Petty fluttered her wings anxiously. "Oh, okay. But I'm ringing the bells."

"Yes, please go ring the bells," Phillip implored.

Once the godmothers had gone, Phillip pounced on Zuri, pinning her to the ground, and she giggled when he dived for that place on her neck that they both liked so much when he kissed it.

"So this is really real, right?" he murmured against her skin.

"Would imaginary me tell you it was real even if it wasn't? I think I would."

"Is this really ours?" he asked her. "Do we really get Happily Ever After?"

Zuri considered. "I think doubting it after all this time and insulting it to its face, we should just take the win, honestly." She looked up into his green, green eyes. "This belongs to us. Let's take it and make it everything we want."

"Would it be anticlimactic if I begged you to marry me now? Petty sort of stole my thunder."

"No. This is perfect. When we look back on this moment, we're going to tell our children that even after their godmother burst in on us and demanded we fulfill her HEA expectations, we still took our future by the horns and made it everything we wanted."

"Is that what we're doing? It would serve her right if we went on a long vacation to a Tibetan monastery where she couldn't find us."

"But would it serve us right?" Zuri asked. "I'm ready to plan this wedding with you, and our life. I want to wear that lavender dress and meet you in front of Grammy and my sister and vow to make you my family, and my forever."

"That sounds like a proposal. Did you just propose to me? Because I like it."

"I did. Marry me," Zuri said. "Be my Prince Charming forever."

"When you put it like that, what's a guy going to say besides hell yes?"

"I could think of a few things, but they involve doing other things with your mouth besides talking."

She arched a brow and flashed him a naughty grin.

"Good God, yes."

He had her naked before she realized what was happening, but Zuri was more than happy to surrender.

He worshipped at the altar of her womanhood, bringing her body to life in the way only he could, and it occurred to her that she'd gotten everything she ever wanted.

Zuri Davis, who'd thought she'd failed at everything, had built a solid business, a new home, and a new self.

No, not a new self. She'd found her true self. Her true strength. Her true passion.

After persevering through the darkest night, after believing when it seemed all was lost, she won her heart's desire.

She got to spend her days and her nights with Prince Charming himself.

This was her Happily Ever After.

Just as her husband-to-be's ever-talented tongue pushed her beyond the limits of desire and bliss, the castle bells rang, resonating throughout the kingdom with all the echoes of her joy.

Maybe there was something to be said for those wish coins after all.

THE FAIRY GODMOTHER ROUNDUP

Petty, Jonquil, and Bluebonnet were on their way to the office when Jonquil stopped and handed a tiny jar of cherry jelly to a chipmunk. "Don't eat that all at once, and do not, under any circumstances, give it to the squirrels."

"You're just breeding more rivalry, Jonquil." Bluebonnet crossed her arms.

"I think after this rather elegant heist that I deserve more credit," Jonquil said. "Do you know how many different threads I had to pull, tug, tighten, and even trip over to get here? But I did it. We always look to Petty to be the master matchmaker, but I did this mostly on my own." She looked between her sisters. "Well, getting all of the players into place anyway. I was the one who recommended closure. I was the one who got the Markhoff wedding. I was the one who suggested we hire Zuri."

"All true," Bluebonnet agreed.

Petty considered. "You're correct, Jonquil. We don't give you enough credit. I think mostly because you've always been the grumpy one. I'm sorry. I'm more than happy to let either one of you take the reins whenever you're feeling motivated. I guess I always do it because I've always done it. But we don't have to do it that way."

"Thank you," Jonquil said, and stuffed her hands in the pockets of her smock. "I do see now why you drink so many more ice cream sodas than Bluebonnet or me. This is stressful."

"Why thank you, sister." Petty sighed. "I think this all turned out perfectly. It was a bumpy ride, but we got there. And thank you both so much for helping me right that wrong."

"We just have to keep remembering that we don't teach lessons. We hand out the keys to Happily Ever After," Bluebonnet said.

"And we try to get the clods to use them," Jonquil added.

"Hey. *Hey.* FGI?" a voice yelled at them.

"I've never been addressed so," Petty said.

"I'm going to pretend I didn't hear it." Jonquil shrugged.

"He's not going to stop. It's that Alec guy," Bluebonnet said.

"Oh no. This isn't going to end well for any of us, is it?" Petty asked.

"FGs! Hey, FGs!"

"Lord help me not to turn that man into a frog," Petty grumbled.

"He's already a frog. A slug, really." Jonquil sniffed with disdain.

"What?" Bluebonnet snapped. "Couldn't you come into the office like a normal person instead of yelling at us from across the square?"

"I wanted to ask you if you provide matchmaking services along with wedding planning," he asked, as he approached them out of breath and wheezing from running across the square.

It had obviously taken him more effort than he was used to expending, but Petty rather thought anything he tried to do in Ever After would yield him that sort of result because he was anathema to Happily Ever After.

The town itself didn't like him.

Petty was fine with that.

"No, we hadn't thought of it."

"I'd like to be your first client. I can pay," he said.

"It's not about money, dear." Petty took a step toward their offices.

"Look, I know you might be miffed with me but, I'll do anything," Alec said.

"Anything?" Bluebonnet cocked her head to the side.

"Whyever would you make that kind of offer?" Jonquil asked.

"I want what Phillip has," he said.

And just like that, without any of the godmothers so much as lifting a pinkie, Alec Marsh was a frog.

"Petty!" Bluebonnet gasped. "What did you do?"

"I did absolutely nothing," Petty swore. Then looked at their other sister. "Jonquil?"

"It wasn't me!" Jonquil looked around. "Is Zeva here?"

"Not that I know of." Petty did a quick scan. "It looks like Ever After gave him his wish. He wanted what Phillip had. That's what Phillip had." She shrugged.

"Mm-hm. Pays to be specific," Bluebonnet said, and scooped him up to put the blorping frog in her pocket.

"Put that down. You don't know where it's been," Petty said.

"I have my own plans. You just wait and see," Bluebonnet replied.

"Now, let's see. We still have to plan three more weddings. We have to finalize the spring carnival, and figure out where Lucky and Ransom are going stay. Maybe the castle, they'll definitely be here for the carnival."

"Oh, I'm so excited to see them!" Bluebonnet squealed.

"Guess who else? Juniper said she can definitely make it for Samhain!" Jonquil added.

"Really? I can't wait to see her. I've missed our little boo so much," Petty said.

"Me too," Bluebonnet said. "Everything is coming up roses."

Petty would've agreed with her until they rounded the corner and saw that everything was not, in fact, coming up roses.

It was coming up frogs.

There was a line of frogs that started outside the door to Fairy Godmothers, Inc., and wrapped around the block.

They were single file, as if they were waiting to come inside.

As soon as one of them saw the trio, they all turned and began to ribbit incessantly.

"Well, it looks like the frog-kissing booth is back on for the carnival," Jonquil said.

"A fairy godmother's work is never done," Petty said. "We might as well get started."

"Who knew there were so many cursed frogs?" Bluebonnet asked. "I was sure we only did the one."

"Me too," Petty replied.

"Looks like it's another adventure." Jonquil shrugged.

Indeed, another adventure.

Petty cast one last look over her shoulder, and she saw Gwen and what she so loving referred to her as her little monsters walking toward the grassy center of the park in the town square. She winked at the boy child, and he nodded and promptly tripped his mom so she fell right into Roderick's arms.

Petty cackled as bits of pink fairy dust filled the air.

Unfortunately for her, she didn't see the new FG in town who took particular offense to Petty's particular form of meddling with her charge.

New adventures, indeed.

Keep reading for more
wild adventures in matchmaking with
Petunia, Jonquil, and Bluebonnet
in
IT HAPPENED ONE MIDNIGHT.
Coming soon from
Saranna DeWylde
and
Zebra Books.

Petunia Blossom had almost reached peak fairy godmother. She and her sisters, Bluebonnet and Jonquil, were so close to the pinnacle of greatness.

In the last year, they'd recruited a new fairy godmother in training for the academy, they'd helped break a curse (Petty chose to ignore the fact the curse was her fault to start with; she was counting it as a win), and they were working their magic right under the noses of mortals.

Further, they'd managed to not only save their sweet little town of Ever After, filling up all the stores of magic with love, but they were exporting it to the fairy realm and to the rest of the world.

Petunia was quite pleased.

The only thing missing was their granddaughter Juniper's Happily Ever After.

She sighed over her morning tea and toast in their cottage kitchen.

Jonquil stopped what she was doing with the black lace and bloodred hydrangeas she'd been fiddling with, attempting to create a bouquet that would suit the Dracula-themed wedding. Nothing seemed to be quite right.

"I recognize that sigh, dearest. Tell us what kind of plot you're hatching?" Jonquil encouraged.

"Me?" Petty feigned innocence.

Bluebonnet snorted. "Obviously, you. Shall I start some ice cream sodas?"

Petunia grinned. "Yes. I think you should."

"As long as it's not Gwen and Roderick again. You know they asked us to leave them alone," Jonquil warned.

Petty waved her off. "No. Fie on them at the moment, anyway. How dare they resist our good intentions?" She laughed. "I do understand, and I'm giving them their space. I'd be upset if someone continued to try to push me to someone I wasn't ready for."

Bluebonnet dropped the glasses she held, and they shattered on the ground. "Did you just say you were wrong?"

"Let's not get hysterical," Petty said. "Of course not. I wasn't wrong. We planted the seeds. They just have to take root and are slumbering through the long winter. Just wait. They will work out on their own."

Bluebonnet used her wand to clean up the mess and reconstitute the glasses. "Mm-hm." She fixed Petty with a sharp glance. "Your stance wouldn't have anything to do with the fact that Ransom and Lucky are taking them along to Brazil, does it?"

Petty looked around, her eyes wide. "Whatever would I do in Brazil?"

"Aha! Caught you. I didn't accuse you of going to Brazil." Bluebonnet crossed her arms over her chest.

Jonquil nodded sagely. "She's got you there."

Petty rolled her eyes. "No, she doesn't. I would assume that to meddle with them in Brazil, I would need to be *present in Brazil*."

"Oh, please. You're a fairy godmother. You can meddle from anywhere."

Petunia shrugged. "Whatcha gonna do?"

"Not bother those kids. Until it's time," Jonquil said. "That's what you're going to do."

"I'm not. But sometimes things happen. Call it fate," Petunia said.

"I'll call it Petunia," Jonquil said with a snort.

"I swear, I'm not going to do anything. I promised. But if, say, their accommodations might have *accidentally* overbooked, and they have to share a room . . . a very small room on a very hot night . . ."

"We all know that's your favorite trope." Bluebonnet began making the ice cream sodas to fortify them with the sugar they needed to plot Happily Ever Afters.

"It works! But actually, I really promise I haven't done anything. But a godmother can hope." She grinned. "No, it's time to switch hats."

"But, I've not gotten a new hat in so long." Jonquil patted her hair.

"Not like that, dear. We need to work on a project closer to home. Not a godmother hat but a grandmother hat," Petunia explained.

"I'm still not following. What's wrong with godmother hats? I mean, we could get some pointy cones of wisdom to wear for the Dracula wedding, but I think they wanted to go with the obsidian and ruby tiaras for the bridesmaids. Plus, we don't want to offend any witch guests in attendance," Jonquil said.

"Sister. Darling. Light of my Happily Ever After," Bluebonnet began. "She means Juniper."

"Oh!" Jonquil pressed her palm to her forehead. "I swear, it's like the sprites have run off with the last two brain cells I had to rub together."

"You need sugar. You'll feel better in a moment," Bluebonnet promised.

"Speaking of that, we should definitely take a vacation in November. We deserve it. I was just thinking this morning that we have accomplished so much. We haven't ventured out of

Ever After for anything but work in a long time. Now that we have magic to spare, we should go to Jamaica or something."

"Oh, I agree. We can use our portal passes, so we'll still have time for the Christmas weddings," Bluebonnet said.

"I need you to know, sisters, that I absolutely cannot be asked to put on my youthful body. I am quite comfortable in this one, and I will be on the beach as I am," Jonquil stated.

"Thank the powers, me too." Bluebonnet brought them their ice cream sodas. Today, they were butterscotch with chocolate chips.

"As if. I want to rest, not be bothered by some man in a Speedo."

They all paused, obviously considering.

"I mean, maybe. It's been a long time. My clock tower has bats in it," Petunia confessed. "Bats. I mean, they're very nice but . . ."

"Girl, you and me both," Bluebonnet said.

"Spiders and webs, I say." Jonquil nodded. "I was torn, for a moment, between thinking I needed to get out there, so I know what our charges are dealing with, and deciding that this is not going to be a working vacation."

"Too right. How about this. We should go to Miami, spend a weekend in our younger bodies, then go to Key West with other old folks. Maybe do some diving, swim with the turtles. Read some Dee J. Holmes and Jasmine Silvera. Drink things out of coconuts," Petunia offered.

"I like this plan. Can we stop on the gulf side of Florida, too? I want to go to Captiva," Bluebonnet said.

Jonquil snorted long and deep. She sounded like a truffling pig. "You just want to go to Captiva to get some of that ghost pirate booty. That's what you're about."

The three of them stopped, sighed, and were all obviously considering the merits of ghost pirate "booty."

"Oh, hell yes I do." Bluebonnet leaned her cheek into the bowl of her hand. "I don't know about you two, but Captain

Drake Gregorian in those breeches is just the cure for what ails me."

Petunia thought about calling her one-time friend Jack Frost, but then dismissed it entirely. What would he do in Florida besides be miserable? Anyway, this wasn't about them. It was about Juniper.

Petty cleared her throat. "Sisters. Back to the task at hand."

"Which is?" Jonquil prompted.

"Um . . . where was I?" Petty asked.

"Hats," Bluebonnet said.

"Oh! Right. Hats. Not godmother hats but grandmother hats. Juniper, of course!"

"She's coming to visit, isn't she?" Bluebonnet asked.

"Yes, I was going to suggest we call her, because I have a plan," Petty said.

"You always have a plan," Jonquil replied.

"Well, yes. Do you remember when we used to go visit April and Juniper? The little boy next door who would come over and play?" Petty asked.

"Little Tomas! He was adorable." Bluebonnet waved her wand, and an image of Tomas shimmered in the air. "He's not so little anymore. Why, he's a man." Bluebonnet sounded as if the fact were a scandal instead of a natural progression. Little boys grew into men. It was just how things worked.

"Neither is our Juniper. She's a woman grown, and it's time to give her a story like the ones she writes about. Tomas has always been her one. I can see the threads. Only, they've been running parallel for so long, they need a . . . shall we call it, inciting event to knock them together. Then, when they untangle, they'll discover their threads entwined not in a tangle but a forever plait."

"That's very poetic, Petunia. Juniper must get her writing skills from you," Jonquil said.

"She gets your pragmatism," Petty said. "And Bluebonnet's sweetness."

"Wait, how is she our granddaughter again?" Jonquil asked. "I'm sorry, I forget these things."

"There are three of us, so I understand why you're confused," Bluebonnet said. "And it was so very long ago. Do you remember that time in the Cotswolds when we foiled Rumpled Butt Skin?"

"That guy! I hate that guy," Jonquil moaned. "I'd blocked it all out."

"I remember it fondly. Because I hate that guy. And I'll never say his actual name out loud. Ever." Petty crossed her arms over her chest. "Anyway, that baby he tried to take, we protected her when we gave her some of our essences, essentially claiming her for fairy. So anyway, Juniper is a descendent of that baby."

"Don't tell her I forgot," Jonquil whispered. "I feel terrible."

"Circumstances being what they are, it's totally acceptable. It's not like you said you didn't love her, or wouldn't help her. You'd just managed the impossible and scrubbed Rumpled Foreskin from your mind. I wish I could. I admire your resourcefulness," Petty commended.

"I shall forever call him Rumpled Foreskin. That's my favorite yet," Bluebonnet mused.

"So. Juniper?" Petty prompted.

"Yes, yes." Bluebonnet waved her wand, and the hologram of Tomas disappeared. "Your plan?"

"Well, you know how she hates it when we matchmake . . . Do you remember when she and Tomas were little, they decided if they weren't married by thirty, or some ridiculous number—thirty-four, yes, that's it. If they weren't married, they were going to marry each other?"

"You're not going to expect her to keep that promise, are you?" Jonquil asked.

"Not exactly, but I think we can use it to our benefit. We'll get her to bring him with her, and then we'll work our magic!" Petty grinned and took a gulp of her ice cream soda. "And nature will work hers."

Jonquil gasped. "I can't believe I forgot this!"

"What now?" Bluebonnet asked.

"The Dracula bride! Betina! She told me she was reading Juniper's Dark Underworld series when she met Jackson. When I told Betina that Juniper was our granddaughter, she asked if she could get signed copies of *Phoenix* for her bridesmaids' gifts."

Petunia grinned. The fates had clearly spoken. "This gives us the excuse we need to call her."

"Quite, quite," Bluebonnet said, and downed the rest of the butterscotch soda.

Petty pulled out her cell phone and dialed Juniper's number. When Juniper answered, Petty put the phone on speaker so that Jonquil and Bluebonnet could hear her.

"Sweet pea! You're on speaker!" Petty said.

"Hello, Grandmothers." Juniper's voice was cheery. "Hold on a minute, will you?" In the background, she whispered, "No, no. Not that one. Oh my God, what is that? *No.* Why is it yellow? Stop playing. I'm about to get hangry." Back into the phone, she said, "Sorry, I'm helping Tomas pick out a suit for his firm's fundraiser, and he promised me lunch. What are you troublemakers doing today?"

"We won't keep you long, dear. We just wanted to double-check you're still going to be able to make it for the Samhain celebration and the fireflies?" Petunia asked.

"And to ask a tiny favor," Jonquil interjected.

"A favor? Of course! Anything!"

"Anything?" Bluebonnet questioned.

"Anything except let you fix me up. That's not the favor, is it?" Juniper grumbled.

"No, no. The bride in one of the weddings we're planning has asked if she could get signed copies of *Phoenix* for her bridesmaids' gifts," Jonquil said.

"Oh my God. Seriously? This is the best thing that's ever happened to me. Of course. This just made my year," Juniper cried.

"Betina's wedding will be on Samhain, so if you're here . . . ," Petty prompted.

"Of course I'll be there and bring books. I wonder if she'll let me post this on social media? This is too cool," Juniper said.

"So, how is Tomas?" Petty ventured.

"He's doing very well. And no, before you ask, he's not seeing anyone. Nor does he want to see anyone," Juniper said.

"Of course he's not seeing anyone. Otherwise, how is he going to marry you?" Petty said.

"Oh stop, Gramma Petty."

"Do you two still have that deal? About getting married?" Bluebonnet asked, being helpful, since Juniper told Petty to stop.

"Of course," Juniper said, obviously teasing. "But that's just when we get old."

"Thirty-four isn't old. I think that's a good age," Jonquil offered.

"You should bring him to Ever After. We need to start planning. You're going to be thirty-four next year, and we want to make sure you have the kind of wedding you want."

"Gramma Bon-Bon—"

"You are taken, right? I mean, if you weren't," Jonquil looked around the room at her sisters before continuing, "we'd just have to try to set you up with someone wonderful. You need inspiration to write your books."

"I have plenty of inspiration. And if you could never say that again, that would be wonderful."

"Inspiration?" Jonquil said, confused.

"Do you know how many men have tried that line on me?" she groaned. "They find out what I do and then get all smarmy and actually the opposite of every romance novel hero ever and say, 'I, uh, could offer you some inspiration for those dirty scenes.' As if the whole point of the book is just the sex and not the part where love conquers all. Fucking savages."

Petunia nodded in understanding even though Juniper couldn't see the action of support. "And they are obviously undeserving of you, your talents, your heart, or your bed."

"Gramma Petty! Don't talk about my bed," Juniper cried.

"Well, why not? It's a normal, natural, beautiful thing, and—"

"Oh God, that's worse. Just stop. Please. I'll do anything."

"Even bring your fi—Tomas?"

"He is not my fiancé," she said.

"Oh, definitely bring your fiancé, we'd love to see him," Bluebonnet chirped.

"Tomas and Juniper, finally sitting in a tree . . ." Jonquil singsonged obnoxiously.

"Tomas is my best friend," Juniper tried to argue.

"Of course he is, lovie. It's really the thing when you marry your best friend. It's the sleepover that never stops!" Bluebonnet said.

"We haven't seen him since you were both little. Oh, Juniper. I'm so happy for you," Petunia said, trying her best not to giggle.

"Grandmothers. I—" she began in a stern voice. "Wait, you absolutely can't try to set me up with anyone if I bring a fiancé."

"We would never do that," Bluebonnet said. "It goes against the fai—" Jonquil slapped a hand over Bluebonnet's mouth. "Against the code."

"What code?" Juniper asked.

"Never you mind that," Petunia said. "You go ahead and get back to picking out your clothes for the benefit. A fiancée's work is never done. But be sure to bring something for the masque. It's going to be amazing."

"You'll both love it," Bluebonnet said.

"I need to make sure Tomas can get the time off," Juniper said weakly.

She needs to talk him into it, Petunia mouthed silently.

I'm texting with Estella right now. She'll guilt him into it, if she has to, Jonquil mouthed back.

Bluebonnet cackled loudly. "I'm sure he will."

"Okay, gotta go. We have a lot to do for this wedding. Did we tell you it's going to be at Blackheart Castle, along with the masque?" Petunia said.

"Blackheart Castle? Where's that?" Juniper asked.

"Lots of changes since you've been to Ever After. You'll see," Bluebonnet promised her.

"Hanging up now. Love you, love to Tomas. See you soon," Petty said.

"Byeeeeee," Jonquil said, and dragged the word out to the last possible second.

"Love you both!" Bluebonnet added.

Petunia clicked the button to end the call and looked around at her sisters with a very satisfied look on her face.

"I think it's wise we get April and Estella in on this scheme. Never underestimate the power of a mother who wants to see her children happy," Petty said.

"Yes, good one, Jonquil," Bluebonnet agreed.

Jonquil studied them. "Do you ever think maybe we shouldn't push so hard? Juniper seems very happy with her life the way it is."

"Here we go," Bluebonnet said. "I know this is your role in the group, but it's tiresome."

"You need more sugar," Petty suggested.

"You always think I need more sugar," Jonquil drawled.

"You always do," Petunia said.

"That's a fair point, I suppose." Jonquil nodded.

"Listen," Bluebonnet began. "She is happy, and that's

wonderful, but the right person complements that happiness. And she wants someone. I know she does. She's told me she'd like to fall in love, and we're going to make it happen."

"I suppose." Jonquil cocked her head. "I just want to make sure we're doing what's best."

"I know," Petunia said. "We have this talk before every mission. Did you know that?"

"It's my job to keep us grounded. To make sure we're on the right path," Jonquil replied.

"Yes, and we appreciate you," Bluebonnet said. "But we're jumping right in the thick of it with Juniper. It's time."

"I can't wait to watch her realize she loves him," Petunia said with a sigh.

"I can't wait to watch him realize that love is for him, too." Bluebonnet's sigh joined her sister's.

"I can't wait for that vacation." Jonquil went back to fiddling with the bloodred hydrangeas and the black lace for the bouquet. "This thing is giving me fits."

"Remember: pirate booty," Bluebonnet encouraged.

"*You* remember pirate booty. *I* want no such thing," Petunia said.

Jonquil arched a brow. "The maid doth protest too much."

"Mind your business. We have Happily Ever Afters to engineer before we can even think about vacation."

"We should get new business cards. *Happily Ever After Engineer*," Bluebonnet said.

"Oh, I like it," Jonquil agreed.

"We are so late. Zuri is going to kill us. We're supposed to talk scheduling with her this morning," Bluebonnet said.

"Already on it. I texted her and told her to take the day off. With our compliments. I think she and Phillip are going to take a long weekend." Petty winked.

"Did you see the fireworks from the castle last night? Their love lit up the sky with actual rockets," Bluebonnet said.

"I know." Jonquil grinned widely. "We do good work."

Petty knew in her heart and in her bones that what Jonquil said was true.

Though, she couldn't shake the feeling that they were on the verge of something more than simply peak fairy god-mother. Petty wasn't sure what it was, but she didn't like it.

Not in the least.

Connect with Us

Visit us online at
KensingtonBooks.com
to read more from your favorite authors, see books
by series, view reading group guides, and more.

for sneak peeks, chances to win books and prize packs,
and to share your thoughts with other readers.

facebook.com/kensingtonpublishing
twitter.com/kensingtonbooks

Tell us what you think!

To share your thoughts, submit a review,
or sign up for our eNewsletters, please visit:
KensingtonBooks.com/TellUs.